"What is

"Neeca," she said, swallowing.

His brows crunched. "Why did you write that?"

A lump lodged in her throat and she shook her head, neither able nor willing to speak.

He put his hand on her chin and forced her eyes to his. "Why, Neeca?"

Unable to add lying to her list of sins, she told him. "Because you called me that."

"It was so important?"

She pursed her lips and nodded, braving his eyes.

He looked at the parchment again, following the words with his finger, hovering over the last few. "And what did you write of last night, Neeca?"

She bit her lip. He was too close, too close to knowing how important he had become.

He cupped her head in his hand and tilted up her chin to force her to meet his eyes. Even her lips quivered, wanting to feel his again....

* * *

The Knave and the Maiden
Harlequin Historical #688—January 2004

Harlequin Historicals is proud to introduce debut author BLYTHE GIFFORD

THE KNAVE AND THE MAIDEN

BLYTHE GIFFORD

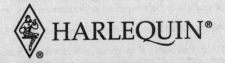

HARLEQUIN®

TORONTO • NEW YORK • LONDON
AMSTERDAM • PARIS • SYDNEY • HAMBURG
STOCKHOLM • ATHENS • TOKYO • MILAN • MADRID
PRAGUE • WARSAW • BUDAPEST • AUCKLAND

ISBN 0-373-29288-0

THE KNAVE AND THE MAIDEN

This edition published by arrangement with Harlequin Books S.A.

® and TM are trademarks of the publisher. Trademarks indicated with ® are registered in the United States Patent and Trademark Office, the Canadian Trade Marks Office and in other countries.

Visit us at www.eHarlequin.com

Printed in U.S.A.

Available from Harlequin Historicals and
BLYTHE GIFFORD

The Knave and the Maiden #688

Please address questions and book requests to:
Harlequin Reader Service
U.S.: 3010 Walden Ave., P.O. Box 1325, Buffalo, NY 14269
Canadian: P.O. Box 609, Fort Erie, Ont. L2A 5X3

To Don and to Daddy
I wish you were here to enjoy it.

Thanks to Julie Beard, Michelle Hoppe,
Lindsay Longford, Margaret Watson, Pat White
and all the members of Chicago-North RWA.
Without you, I would not be here.

Chapter One

Readington Castle, England, June 1357

"God brought me back from the dead, Garren," William said. "You were His instrument."

Garren looked at his friend, lying in his bed with the hollow cheeks of a corpse, and suppressed a snort. When William, Earl of Readington, sprawled among the scattered bodies on the battlefield at Poitiers, God had not lifted a finger.

Now, watching the candlelight waver in benediction over William's pale face, Garren wondered whether he should have, either. Death in the French dirt might have been kinder.

But Garren would fight God for William's life as long as he could.

"You were the only one," William said. "The others left me for dead."

Or left him for live French prisoners they could ransom.

But William was not dead, although there had been days Garren was not certain the Earl lived. As the victorious troops traipsed across France and finally sailed back to En-

gland, William existed in an earthly purgatory, alive because
Garren forced water and gruel and prechewed meat between
his teeth. ''I was just too stubborn to leave you.''

''More than that.'' Between each word, William gasped
for a breath. ''You carried me. On your back.''

''You and your armor.'' Garren smiled, tight-lipped,
swinging a mock blow to William's shoulder. ''Don't forget
the armor.''

Readington's family had rejoiced more over the return of
the armor than its wearer. While the rest of the English
knights carried home booty, Garren carried only William.
Carried William and left behind the wealth that had been
the promise of the French campaign.

It had all seemed worthwhile as William gained strength.
But in the weeks since his homecoming, the retching had
started. Some days were better, some worse. Now he lay on
a deathbed curtained in red velvet, high in a tower overlooking a countryside of damp, fertile earth he would never
ride again. His hands curled into useless claws. He ran red
or brown all day from one end or the other. Servants
changed the bed linens, a futile task, but a sign of respect.
There was little else they could do.

At least, Garren thought, William could die in his own
bed.

''One…more…thing I must ask.'' His cold fingers
clutched Garren's with the strength of death.

I gave you life, what more can I do? Garren thought, but
as he looked at William, just past thirty and unable to rise
from his bed, he was uncertain whether life had been such
a valuable gift.

''Go on the pilgrimage for me.''

Pilgrimage. A prepayment to a God who never delivered
as promised. A journey to a tomb that sheltered the bones

of a woman and the feathers of an angel. "William, if God has not yet cured you, I doubt the Blessed Larina will."

"I will pay you."

Garren snatched his hand away. He had given up virtually everything for William, gladly. All he had left was his pride. "You can find fools aplenty to be your palmer on the journey."

Pain wrinkled William's face. His left arm cradled his stomach, trying to hold back the next bout of retching. "Not…trust."

Garren mumbled something meant to be soothing, neither yes nor no. He cradled William's bony hand in his large, square ones. How far they had come together since William had taken him on, a seventeen-year-old no one else wanted, much too old to start training as a squire. Everything he was he owed to this man.

William clung to Garren's arm, pulling himself up, half sitting. Only five years older than Garren, he looked as if he had lived four score years. After a glance around the chamber as if to reassure himself they were alone, William reached beneath his pillow and pulled out a folded parchment, no bigger than his hand. Red wax, indented with the Readington crest, doubly sealed the thin thread that pierced the layers. "For the monk. At the shrine."

Taking the message from William's shaking fingers, Garren wondered how he had managed to hold a quill to write.

William's voice quavered, too. "The seal must be unbroken."

Garren smiled, silent. Even in the monastery, he had been a poor reader.

William shook his arm, forcing his attention. Forcing an answer. "Please. There is no one else."

Garren looked into his friend's eyes, eyes that had seen

so much by his side, and knew that for as many weeks as William drew breath, he would say yes.

He nodded, clearing his throat. "But I don't want your money." This journey should be a gift.

William rolled his head *no,* leaving a new chunk of blond hair on the linen under his head. William knew his funds would take him no farther than the next battle. A weak smile curved his pale lips. "Take it. Buy me a lead feather."

A leaden pilgrim's badge. Proof of the journey. A token to flaunt his faith. Garren gripped William's fingers. "I'll bring something better. Since you can't travel to the shrine, I'll bring the shrine to you. I'll bring you a real feather." Somehow it seemed appropriate, to violate a shrine to comfort a man with faith. At least you could see a feather. Hold it. Touch it. Not like the false promises of the Church.

Skin already pale, blanched. "Sacrilege."

A chill skittered up Garren's back. Stealing a relic. Violating a shrine. God would punish him. He nearly laughed at the thought, a residue of training over experience. Garren had seen the puny extent of God's mercy. God's punishment could scarcely be harsher. "Don't worry. No one will miss a small one."

Still shaking his head, William closed his eyes and slipped into the near-death sleep that was his life.

The door opened without a knock and the lilting voice of William's younger brother Richard grated on Garren's ears. Richard, who would not go on pilgrimage for his brother for love nor money. "Does he still breathe?"

"You seem eager to hear me say 'no.'"

"It is just that this state can scarcely be called living, don't you agree?"

Garren did, but not for Richard's reasons. "Perhaps. But as long as he breathes, he is the Earl of Readington." Richard, however, need only wait. He would be Earl soon enough.

"What is that?" Richard reached for the folded parchment as if he had the right.

Garren shrugged and slipped it into his tunic. It nestled stiffly below his ribs. "It must be a petition to the saint." Now that he had said yes, he dreaded the journey. Not the days of walking, but the company of all those trusting pilgrims who believed an invisible God would answer their prayers if they only paid His price. Garren knew better. "He asked me to go to the shrine and pray for his recovery."

Richard snickered. "By the time you arrive, you will be praying for his soul."

And by the time I return, Garren thought, I'll be praying for my own.

Kneeling before her private crucifix, the Prioress turned from contemplating the chipped paint on Christ's left hand as the girl strode into her office, barely bending her knee in greeting.

The Prioress rose with creaking knees, wondering why she had granted this audience, and settled into her own chair. Dominica was a slip of a girl who knew no better than to be grateful that the Priory had taken her in and raised her and given her useful work to do, the cleaning and the laundry and the cooking for the few who remained.

The Death had taken its toll. There were too few serfs to plant the crops or to harvest what grew. Christian charity followed a full stomach. Of course, Lord Richard could have made it easier.

Without asking permission to speak, the girl interrupted her thoughts. "Mother Julian, I want to accompany Sister Marian to the shrine of the Blessed Larina."

The Prioress shook her head to clear her ears. The request

was so outrageous she thought she had misheard. No please. No begging. Just those piercing blue eyes, demanding. "What did you say, Dominica?"

"I want to go on the pilgrimage. And when I return, I will take my vows as a novice."

"You want to join the order?" This was what came of raising the girl above the state in life that God had intended for her. She should have given the foundling to the collier's wife when she had the chance. "You have no dowry."

"A dowry is not required," the girl said, as if reciting the text on preaching. "Faith is required."

The Prioress bit her tongue. She was not going to argue theology with an orphan. It took more than faith to feed and clothe twenty women. "You cannot take the veil."

"Why not?" The girl lifted her chin as if she had the right to disagree. "I can copy the Latin manuscripts as well as Sister Marian."

Our Lord preached forgiveness, she reminded herself, trying to soften her tone of voice. "What makes you think you have a calling, Dominica?"

The girl's blue eyes burned with the fervor of a saint— or a madwoman. "God told me."

"God does not speak to abandoned foundlings." The Prioress clenched her fingers in prayer until her knuckles turned white and her fingertips red. This was all her fault. She had let the girl sit with them at meals and listen to the Scripture readings. Likely the chit flattered herself that she understood God's will because she had heard God's words. "God speaks through His servants in the church. God has said nothing to *me* about your joining the order."

"But Mother Julian, I know I am meant to spread His word." She stepped closer and lowered her voice. "I want to copy the texts into the common tongue, so the people can truly understand them."

The Prioress beat prayerful fingers against her lips. *Heresy. I have a heretic living under my roof. If the Readingtons find out, I will never see another farthing from them. I should never have let her learn her letters.*

The girl was still speaking. "I belong here. I know it. And after I reach the shrine, you will know too because God will give me a sign." Dominica's face beamed with the kind of faith the Prioress had neither seen nor felt in many years. "Sister Marian will be my witness."

Sister Marian had always spoiled the girl. "Who will pay for this journey? For your cloak, your food? Who will do your work while you are gone?"

"Sisters Catherine and Barbara and Margaret have said they will bear my load. And Sister Marian said she will pay for my food from her dowry." She looked defiant. "I won't eat much."

"Sister Marian's dowry belongs to the Priory now." The Prioress cradled her throbbing head in her hands. What had become of obedience? This was what came of allowing the Sisters to keep lapdogs.

"Please, Mother Julian." The girl fell to her knees, finally humbled. She tugged at the Prioress's black habit with ink-stained fingers, nails bitten so close that the garden dirt had nowhere to cling. "I must make this journey."

Shocked, the Prioress looked into her eyes again. They burned with faith. Or fear.

Suddenly, she could see where this could lead. The girl would never return once she discovered life beyond the walls. She had a shape most would envy, those who were not looking for a cloistered life. If only she'd tumble for the first man who flattered her. She'd come back with a swollen belly and there would be no question of her taking the veil.

Mother Julian sighed. Maybe not. The searing intensity in those blue eyes would be more than most lads would fancy. Well, let it be God's will. Better she go and take her dangerous ideas with her before the Abbot or the Earl found out, although that would leave the problem of who would do the laundry and the weeding. They could hardly afford to pay a village lass.

"All right. Go. But speak no more of your heresy. If there is a hint of trouble on the journey, you will have no home here when you return, with or without a veil."

Dominica raised her hands and her eyes to heaven. "Thank you, Heavenly Father." She ducked her head and scampered out without asking permission to leave.

The Prioress shook her head. No thanks to me for my many kindnesses, she thought. Only to God. Well, God would have the care of her now.

Dominica's breath burst from her body. Relief lifted her on her toes, almost floating her down the hall. The soft, sure feeling settled over her. God always answered her prayers, even if she had to help Him a little. What the Prioress and Sister Marian did not know about this journey would keep.

Sister Marian sat in the sunny cloister courtyard, teaching Innocent to sit up. Or trying to. Like Dominica, the shaggy black dog was a stray no one else wanted. Hard to love and hard to train.

"She said 'yes,' she said 'yes.'" Dominica swirled Sister around until her black robes billowed. Innocent barked. "I'm going, I'm going."

"Shhh, hush." Sister tried to quiet both Dominica and the barking dog, who was running in a circle to catch his too-short tail. That was a trick Dominica had taught him.

"Good boy," Dominica scratched him behind his one remaining ear. The other was missing. "Don't worry, Sister." Dominica hugged her. "Everything will work out. God has told me."

Sister's eyes widened and she glanced toward the corridor. "Don't let Mother Julian hear you say God talks to you."

Dominica shrugged. No use telling Sister that Mother Julian already knew. "It's like the scripture says: *Knock and it shall be open to you,*" she said in Latin.

"And if she hears you spouting Latin, she will change her mind."

"But if God is trying to speak to us, why shouldn't we open our ears to hear?"

"Just be sure you aren't putting your words on God's lips."

Dominica sighed. God had given her ears, eyes, and a brain. Surely He expected her to use them. "Anyway, we're going and when we come back, I shall take my vows."

Sister sat and gathered Dominica's fingers in hers. Dominica loved the feel of Sister's hands. Soft, for they did not have to wash or weed, the fingers of her right hand were set stiffly, permanently, in position to hold the quill. As a child, Dominica had envied Sister the writer's bump on her middle finger, rubbing her own each day, hoping it would grow.

"Just remember, my child, when God answers our prayers, He may not give us the answer we want."

"How could there be another answer? My whole life is here." She loved the ordered, predictable days, the quiet of the chapel, where she could hear the hushed voice of God, the brilliant red, blue and gold ink that illuminated His words. All she ever wanted was to finally, fully belong. To be embraced as a Sister. "I can read better than Sister Margaret and copy better than anyone but you."

Sister sighed. "You are pushing again, Dominica. There is no guarantee that God will grant you what you seek."

"Oh, God I am sure of. It is the Prioress who worries me."

Sister raised her hands in submission. "When you have lived longer, you will be less sure of God. Come, let us gather our things." She rose, slowly. Her hips were as accustomed to the writing bench as her hands. "We must be ready to leave tomorrow."

And when they returned, Dominica thought, the message would be safe in the right hands and she would never need to leave her home again.

All that was required was faith. And action.

"We need money, your Lordship." The Prioress forced her neck to bend in supplication. Humility before Lord Richard did not come easily.

She had trapped him into hearing her petition, approaching after the midday meal, when the Great Hall was still crowded with watching knights, squires and servants so he could not refuse. But the hall was empty now of everything but the smell of boiled mutton. Her stomach growled.

"Why do you want money, Prioress?" Richard asked. Narrow of shoulder and of nose, he slouched in his chair and picked at his ear, then flipped the wax from under his nail. "I thought nuns had no need of worldly things."

She wondered if he showed such disrespect for all his petitioners. The donation she requested would be no hardship. "Food, ink and funds for the annual pilgrimage, your Lordship."

"Times are difficult." Legs crossed, he swung his foot back and forth, studying it intently.

"Your father was a great patron of our work at the Priory," she reminded him. The old Earl's tapestries still cloaked Readington's Great Hall, though since his death, the place seemed colder. She never felt his loss more than when she looked at this dark-haired, sallow-skinned second son. "He promised to support our work of copying the word of God."

"My father is dead."

"Which is why I come to you."

"As you know, it is my brother you must petition. And it is impossible for me to allow that now."

"We pray for him daily. Does his health improve, your lordship?"

Lord Richard tried to smother his smile with a grave expression. "Well, Prioress, perhaps you had better hurry to finish his Death Book. But, there is always hope." He snickered. "The mercenary plays palmer for him on the pilgrimage."

She crossed herself. "The knight who brought your brother back from the dead?" The entire village knew the tale. She had even heard blasphemous talk of him as The Savior.

Lord Richard flopped back in his chair with a pout. "If you believe his account. A man who fights for coin instead of for fealty can scarcely be trusted."

A curious criticism, she thought, since Lord Richard had managed to avoid fighting in France at all. "A landless knight must do what he can. God works in mysterious ways."

His lips curved. "Doesn't He? Well, perhaps your prayers and the mercenary's visit will soften Saint Larina's heart to cure the lingering effects of my brother's wounds." Boredom saturated his voice. "Who goes to fulfill the perpetual vow this year?"

"Sister Marian." She hesitated for a moment. "And Dominica."

Lord Richard uncurled himself, spine straight, feet flat on

the floor, and met her eyes for the first time. "The little scribe? Is she old enough to travel?"

Did everyone know the girl could write? Pray God she had said nothing to him about her heretical ideas. "In her seventeenth year, my lord."

His nose twitched as a weasel's might. "And still a virgin?"

The Prioress drew herself to her full height. "Do you have so low an opinion of my stewardship?"

"I'll take that for a 'yes.' What does she seek on this pilgrimage?"

Clasping her hands, she considered his curiosity. Perhaps she could use it. "She wants to join the order and she seeks a sign that God approves."

"Because you do not?"

She assessed him for a moment. There might be a reason to tell him the truth. "No. I do not."

"Then we have something in common. I have another interest. In the mercenary," he said. His dark eyes glowed. "My brother's gratitude seems to extend to perpetual support, as if this Garren were a saint. I would have him see what kind of knave the man really is."

She already knew what kind of a knave Lord Richard was. No doubt his brother did, as well. The Prioress waited for his proposition. She did not think it would be a pleasant one.

"Offer this Garren money if he will seduce the little virgin. He seems to do anything for a bit of coin. And when she accuses him, we shall each have something we want."

"Milord, I cannot—"

"You don't want her to be a nun. Neither do I. And once Garren is disgraced, William will have to throw him out." He paused, smiling. "If he lives that long. If not, then I'll be the righteous one. And then I'll have a few personal tasks for the girl.'' His smirk left no doubt that those tasks would take place in the bedchamber. ''Don't worry. She may still do laundry for you, Prioress, in her idle hours.''

''Milord, how can you ask such a thing?'' And how could she consider it? Because she was responsible for twenty lives besides Dominica's. Lives already pledged to God. And when the Earl died, the fate of those lives would rest in Lord Richard's hands.

''If you do, I might be able to give you the support you need. And a generous incentive to the mercenary for his sin.''

No hint of trouble, she had told the girl. This scheme would assure she never took the vows. Of course, hadn't she herself wondered, nay, hoped for just such a thing? Perhaps God was answering her unspoken prayers. ''And I'm sure your remembrance of the Priory will be generous.''

He laughed, a chittering sound that rattled on the roof of his mouth. ''Well, that all depends on how successful you and the Blessed Larina, are, doesn't it?''

The girl had the Devil's own eyes. Maybe this was the fate God had meant for her. And the mercenary? He and God could wrestle for his soul.

''I promise nothing,'' she said, cautiously. ''I can but prepare the table.'' And pray for forgiveness.

''I promise nothing, either.'' He squinted at her. ''Prepare it well.''

Garren, though he had given up God as a lost cause, was still shocked when a nun asked him to violate a virgin.

''Dominica is her name,'' the Prioress said, settled in her shabby chamber as if it were a throne room. ''Do you know her?''

Speechless, he shook his head.

"Come." The Prioress beckoned him to the window overlooking the garden. "See for yourself."

The girl knelt in the dirt, facing away from him. Her hair lay like poured honey in a thick braid down her back. She hummed over her plants, a soothing sound, like the drone of a drowsy bee.

Of its own accord, his heart thumped a little harder. Even from behind she had a pleasing shape. It would not be difficult to take her, but the idea rekindled a sense of outrage he thought long dead.

"I'll not force her." He had seen too much force in France. Knights who took vows of chivalry and then took women like rutting boars. The remembrance churned in his stomach. He would starve first.

"Use whatever methods you like." The Prioress shrugged. "She must not return from this trip a virgin."

He looked back at the girl, digging up the weeds. He was no knight from a romance, but he had a way with women. Camp followers across France could attest to that. Every woman had a sweet spot if you took time to look. Where would this one's be? Her shell-like ears? The curve of her neck?

She stood and turned, smiling at him briefly and the purest blue eyes he had ever seen looked into his wretched soul. He felt as transparent as stained glass.

And for a moment, he shook with fear he had never felt before a battle with the French.

He shrugged off the feeling. There was no reason for it. She was not that remarkable. Tall. Rounded breasts. Freckles. A broad brow. Her mouth, the top lip serious, the bottom one with a sensual curve. And an overall air as if she were not quite of this earth.

She turned away and kneeled to weed the next row.

"Why?" He had asked God that question regularly without reply. He didn't know why he expected a country Prioress to answer.

The Prioress, broad of chest and hip, did not take the question theologically. Her dangling crucifix clanked like a sword as she strode away from the window, out of hearing of the happy hum. "You think me cruel."

"I have seen war, Mother Julian. Man's inhumanity is no worse than God's." He had a sudden thought. The usual resolution to a tumble with a maid would find him married in a fortnight. "If it is a husband you need, I'm not the one. I cannot support a wife."

I can barely support myself.

"You will not be asked to marry the girl."

He eyed a neatly stitched patch on her faded black habit and wondered whether she had the money she promised. "Nor fined."

"If you had any money you would not be considering my offer. No, not fined, either. God has a different plan."

God again. The excuse for most of the ill done in the world. Hypocrites like this one had driven him from the Church. "If you do not care for my immortal soul, aren't you concerned about hers? What will happen to her? Afterward?"

Her eyes flickered over him, as if trying to decide whether he was worthy of an answer. "Her life will go on much as before."

He doubted that. But the money she offered would be enough for him to give William the gift of the pilgrimage. Enough and more. William would be dead soon. Garren would have no welcome under Richard's reign. All he owned was his horse and his armor. With England and France at peace, he had no place to go.

With what she offered, and the few coins he had left from

France, he might find a corner of England no one else wanted, where he and God could ignore each other.

"Can you pay me now?"

"I'm a Prioress, not a fool. You'll get your money when you return. If you succeed. Now, will you do it?"

The girl's happy hum still buzzed in his ear. What was one more sin to a God who punished only the righteous? Besides, the Church didn't need this one. The Church had already taken enough.

He nodded.

"Sister Marian also goes to the shrine. She knows nothing of this. She wants the girl to fulfill her vow and return to the order."

"And you do not."

The Prioress crossed herself. A faint shudder ruffled the edge of her robe. "She is a foundling with the Devil's own eyes. He can have her back." Her smile was anything but holy. "And you will be His instrument."

Chapter Two

"Look. There he is. The Savior." Sister Marian's words tickled Dominica's ear. She whispered so no one would overhear the blasphemous nickname for the man who, like the true Savior, had raised a man from the dead.

"Where? Which one?" Dominica did not bother to whisper. The entire household had gathered in the Readington Castle courtyard to witness the blessing of God's simple pilgrims before they left on their journey. The sounds of braying asses, snorting horses and barking dogs assaulted her ears, accustomed to convent quiet. At Sister's feet, Innocent barked fiercely at every one of God's four-legged creatures.

"Over there. By the big bay horse."

She gasped. He was the man she had seen through the Prioress's window.

He certainly did not look holy. His broad shoulders looked made to stand against the real world, not the spirit one. Dark brown curls, the color of well-worn leather, fought their way around his head and onto his cheeks, where he had begun to grow a pilgrim's beard. His skin had lived with sun and wind.

Then he met her eyes again. Just like the first time, something called to her, as strongly as if he had spoken. Surely this must be holiness.

With an unholy bark, Innocent dashed across the courtyard, chasing a large, orange cat.

"I'll get him," Dominica called, too late for Sister to object. It was going to be difficult to keep Innocent safe among the temptations of the world.

Her first running steps tangled in her skirts, so she swooped them out of the way. Fresh air swirled between her legs. Laughing, she scampered around two asses, finally scooping Innocent up at the feet of a horse.

A large bay horse. With a broad-shouldered man beside it.

The Savior was taller than he looked from a distance. A soldier's sword hung next to his pilgrim's bowl and bag. Something hung around his neck hid beneath his tunic, not for the world to see. A private penance, perhaps.

"Good morning," she said, bending back her neck to meet his brown, no, green eyes. "I am Dominica."

He looked at her squarely, eyes wary and sad, as if God had given him many trials to make him worthy. "I know who you are."

At his glance, her blood bubbled through her fingers and around her stomach in an oddly pleasant way. "Did God tell you?" If God spoke to her, He must certainly have lengthy conversations with one so holy.

He scowled. Or repressed a smile. "The Prioress told me."

She wondered what else the Prioress had told him. The dog wriggled in her arms. She scratched his head. "This is Innocent."

The smile broke through. "Named in honor of our Holy Father in Avignon, no doubt."

That, she was sure, the Prioress had not told him. Dominica raced on, not giving him time to wonder whether the name honored the Pope or mocked him. "We are all grateful to you for bringing the Earl back from the dead," she said. "Did he stinketh like Lazarus?"

"Pardon?"

"The Bible says 'Lazarus did stinketh because he hath been dead four days.'

The corner of his mouth twitched. "You did not hear about Lazarus's stench in one of the Abbot's homilies."

Best not to tell him she had read it herself. "At the noon meal, the Sisters read the Scriptures and let me listen." She waited for a sign of anger. Could one so touched by God discern her small deception?

"The story of Lazarus hardly sounds appetizing," he said. "But, yes, we both did stinketh by the time we got home."

"Of course, the Earl had not been dead for four days when you brought him back to life."

The amusement leaked away and his green eyes darkened to brown. "I did not bring him back from the dead. I simply would not let him die."

Dominica thought this a very fine theological distinction. "But you had faith in God's power. 'He that believeth in me though he were dead, yet shall he live.'"

"Be careful who you believe in. Faith can be dangerous."

His words, bleak as his eyes, seemed as simple and as complex as scripture. She remembered the end of the Lazarus story. It was after the Pharisees learned what Jesus had done that they decided he must die.

"You know my name, but I do not know yours, Sir...?"

"Garren."

"Sir Garren of what?"

"Sir Garren of nowhere. Sir Garren with nothing." He bowed. "As befits a simple pilgrim."

"Have you no home?"

He stroked the horse's neck. "I have Roucoud de Readington."

"Readington?"

"A gift from the Earl." He frowned.

Why would he frown at such a wonderful gift? Readington must value him highly to give him such a magnificent animal. "And you are at home on a horse?"

"I have been a mercenary, paid to fight."

"And now?"

"And now a palmer," he muttered, "paid for this pilgrimage."

Dominica was not surprised to have a palmer on the journey. She was surprised that it was The Savior. "What poor dead soul left twenty sous in his will for a pilgrimage for his soul?"

"Not a dead one—yet."

He must mean the Earl of Readington himself, she thought, relieved. The secret was in good hands, if she would only stop asking questions. "Forgive me," she said. "Keep the secret of your holy journey in your heart."

"I am no holy man."

Her question seemed to irritate him. How could he deny he was touched by God? They all knew the story. Today he journeyed to the Blessed Larina's shrine. By Michaelmas, Dominica thought, he was likely to have a shrine of his own. "God selected you as His instrument to save the Earl's life."

He searched her eyes for a long, silent moment. "An instrument can serve many hands. God and the Devil both make use of fire."

She shivered.

The bell tolled and like a flock of geese, the gray cloaked pilgrims fluttered toward the chapel door. She put Innocent down and he trotted back to Sister Marian, tail straight up. Dominica tried to follow, but her legs refused to walk away.

"Please," she whispered, "give me your blessing."

He shrugged into his gray scleverin as if the cloak were chain mail. "Get your blessing from the Abbot with the rest of the pilgrims."

"But you are The Sav—" She bit her tongue. "You are special."

His eyes blazed, their mood as changeable as their color, and she felt a hint of the danger faith might bring.

"I told you," he said, "I am nothing holy. I can give you none of God's blessing."

"Please." She grabbed his large, square hands with trembling fingers. Kneeling in the dirt before him, she touched her lips to the fine dark hairs on his knuckles.

He snatched his hands away.

She grabbed them back, put his hands on her bowed head and pressed her palms over them, desperate to hold them there.

His palm stiffened. Then, slowly, his hand cupped the curve of her head and slid down to the bare skin at the back of her neck. His fingers seared her like a brand. Her chest tightened and she tried to breathe. The smell of the courtyard dust mingled with a new scent, rich and rounded. One that came from him.

The braying church bell faded, but the sense of peace she had expected did not come. Her heart beat in her ears, as if all four humours in her body were wildly out of balance.

He jerked away, waving his hand in a gesture that could have been benediction, dismissal or disgust.

"Thank you, Sir Garren of the Here and Now," she whispered, running back to the safety of Sister and Innocent, afraid to look at him again, afraid she had already put too much of herself in his hands.

* * *

Garren's palms burned as if he had touched fire.

God's holy blood. She thinks I'm a saint.

He laughed at the blasphemy of it.

His body's stiff response was a man's, but the fall of the pilgrim's cloak disguised that along with all his other sins.

This job would be too easy. Too pleasant. His hands ached to touch her soft curves, but he winced at taking advantage of the burning faith in her eyes. She thought him touched by God somehow. What a disappointment it would be to discover how much of a man he was.

He shook off the guilt. She had to learn eventually, just as he had. Faith was a trap for fools.

Garren turned to see the Prioress, standing before the chapel door, smiling as if she had seen the entire scene. As if she wanted to see him take the girl here in the dust of the courtyard.

The girl, with her wide-eyed faith, was no match for the Prioress. The thought angered him. Maybe he could even the odds. Maybe he would cheat the Church. Tell the Prioress he had taken the girl and take the Church's money for a sin he did not commit. Naturally, the girl would say she remained pure, but she would be damaged just as if he had taken her. But free. She would be free from the clutches of the Church.

Smiling, Garren patted Roucoud, handed the horse's reins to a waiting page, then joined the other pilgrims. Maids, knights, squires, cooks, pages, even the Prioress and Richard stood respectfully aside as they walked across the courtyard to the chapel. He hoped William could not see from his window as Richard usurped the rightful place of the Earl of Readington.

Aware of his fellow travelers for the first time, Garren counted the group as they walked through the church door.

There were less than a dozen. A young couple holding hands. A scar-faced man with an off-center nose. A plump woman, a merchant's wife by the weave of her cloak. Two men, brothers by the cut of their chins. A few others.

Each was adorned with a cross, either sewn into the long, gray cloak or, for the merchant's wife, hung around her neck.

Dominica, a head taller than the little nun beside her, walked with those sea-blue eyes focused on God, ignoring the wiggling dog in her arms. The dog's left ear flopped in time to his wagging tail, but the right one was missing, bitten off, no doubt, by a cornered fox. At the church door, she put him down and turned back three times to make him stay. Garren grinned. The dog, as least, was not reverent.

As Dominica passed into the shadow of the chapel, Richard laid his hand on her shoulder and whispered in her ear. She pulled away, hurrying ahead without even glancing at him.

Garren clenched his fist, then deliberately stretched his fingers. He needed no more reasons to hate Richard.

Richard and the Prioress turned to Garren, the only pilgrim still in the courtyard. A breathless household stood aside, lining a path for him to enter the Readington chapel.

The wooden doors seemed miles away.

He trudged past them on leaden feet, eyes on the stone peak above the door, trying to ignore their stares and whispers. His cape with its cross, stitched on at William's insistence, the relic case around his neck, all seemed a costume borrowed from a miracle player. William's mysterious message lay coiled against his chest.

Only his sword and the shell around his neck felt familiar. The lead shell clanking against the reliquary was a souvenir of the family snatched away by a God who had not saved them, even though they had paid His price.

"Come, Garren." Richard never honored him with *Sir.* "God and the Abbot await."

Dust motes chased themselves in the stream of late morning sun that stopped short of the altar. Garren knelt next to Dominica at the altar rail. Her eyes on the Abbot, she spared him no more of a glance than she had Richard.

The Abbot, who had traveled all the way from White Wood to give the blessing, intoned in Latin, designed to make him sound closer to God's deaf ears than the rest of us, Garren thought.

The girl moved her lips with his words, almost as if she understood them. Her hair shimmered around her head like a halo. She was young and vulnerable and untouched by the world and he had the strangest sensation that despite it all, she was stronger than he. He suddenly wondered whether he could touch her and remain the same person.

The Abbot switched to the common tongue. "Those who have gathered to go on pilgrimage, are you ready for this journey? Have you set aside worldly goods to travel simply, as did Our Lord?"

Garren watched Dominica nod, wondering what worldly goods she owned. He had few enough. In nine years, he had amassed no more than he could carry.

"When you reach the shrine, you must make sincere confession or your journey will not find favor in the sight of God and the saints. Will you all make your confessions?"

Murmured *yes*es rustled like dry leaves. Garren held his tongue. He would confess to God when God returned the favor.

"And particularly Lord Richard asks that each of you pray for his beloved brother, the Earl of Readington, who was saved from death only to live in a state too near to heaven and too far from earth."

A faint, forceful voice, William's own, interrupted. "I thank my brother, but I shall ask for my own salvation."

"What the—?" Richard sputtered.

Garren half rose, wanting to believe in miracles, wanting to see William standing tall and strong again. Shielding his eyes against the sun, Garren turned toward the church door. A reclining figure, almost too tall for the litter, lay silhouetted against the sunlight. William, pale and thin as a wraith, was carried on his pallet by two footmen, one holding a pewter pan in case of need.

The crowd inhaled with a single breath. Then, hands fluttered from foreheads to shoulders, making the sign of the cross against a spirit raised from the dead.

William waved his two servants forward. The crowd parted as he was carried to the altar rail, where the Prioress bent over him. Richard, with petulant lips and pitiless eyes, stood erect.

The Abbot, flustered, rolled his eyes to Heaven for guidance. There was no ceremony for this occasion. "Already God has given the Earl strength from your pure intentions." His voice swelled. "You who take this journey, pray for a miracle!"

William lifted a hand. "Thank you for...prayers."

Garren's heart twisted at the sound of William's voice. Once so strong in battle, it quavered as one twice his age.

"I have ordered," he continued, "first day's food for all."

"A magnificent gesture, my Lord Readington," the Abbot said.

Richard scowled.

William waved his hand as if brushing away a wisp of smoke. "And let it be known," he stopped for a breath. "Garren walks for me and carries my petition to the Blessed Larina."

William grabbed his stomach and turned, retching, just in time to hit the pewter pan. Garren closed his eyes, as if William's pain would not exist if he did not see it. As if he could close his eyes and bring back the past.

"Let us end with a prayer for Sir Garren's success and Lord Readington's recovery before I bless the staffs and distribute the *testimoniales*," the Abbot said, quickly.

Garren walks for me, William had said. What would they think of him now?

Dominica smiled at him, but the rest looked awestruck, as if they really saw a man of God.

Everyone except the Prioress. And Richard.

Chapter Three

Dominica pressed her forehead against the altar rail, trying to concentrate on God instead of the Earl's sudden appearance. Completing the ceremony, the Abbot kissed her staff and placed it, solid and balanced, in her outstretched hands. She pressed her lips against the raw wood, stripped of bark, then set it in front of her.

Next, the Abbot handed her the *testimoniales,* the scroll with the Bishop's magic words that made her truly a pilgrim. Her fingers tingled as she slipped it into her bag, next to her own parchment and quill. Later, when no one could see, she would compare the copyist's letters with her own.

Bowing her head into her hands, she searched for the voice of God inside her, trying to ignore The Savior on her left. She wondered if he was watching her. He was as solid as the staff in her hands. The kind of man you could lean on. She studied him through her fingers. Clutching his staff like a weapon, he looked like a man used to standing alone, not leaning on a staff. Nor a friend. Nor even God.

Squeezing her eyes shut, she brought her mind back to the reason for her journey.

Please God, give me a sign at the shrine that I am to keep my home in your service and help spread your word.

She wanted to add "in the common tongue," but decided not to force that point with God just yet.

She opened her eyes and peeked through her fingers past Sister Marian on her right. A servant daubed sweat from the Earl's forehead. God had spared him nearly ten years ago at the height of the Death and taken his father instead. She still remembered weeks of mourning when the old Earl died. Sister Marian's eyes had been red for days. But God had spared the son. Surely God had sent The Savior to protect him again.

She added a prayer for the Earl who surely deserved God's help. And hers.

The Abbot spoke his last amen and her fellow pilgrims rose, leaning on their staffs, and filed past the Earl on their way out of the chapel, giving thanks for his gift of food.

When Sister Marian stopped before him, he thanked her for her work on the Readington psalter, clutched in his white-spotted hand.

Sister brushed the thin, blond hair from his damp brow as if he were a child. Many were afraid to touch him now. They whispered "leprosy" when they saw the mottled black-and-pink-and-white spots on his skin.

Dominica quaked a little, too, when it was her turn to bend her knees before him. But he had been so nice to her as a child. Not like Richard.

He lifted a finger to his lips. "Remember. A secret."

She pursed her lips, nodding, and looked for Lord Richard, still talking with Mother Julian and Abbot. Make sincere confession, the Abbot had said. Did keeping a secret require the same penance as a lie? She thought not. A lie had words. Words made it real.

As she moved on, The Savior knelt beside the Earl, clasping the dying man's shoulder in a gesture that might have been called tender. Sir Garren will hurry, she thought, relieved. We'll be there in time for The Blessed Larina to save him.

With Sister, Dominica circled back to the altar rail, kneeling for a final blessing from the Prioress. She wanted words that would keep her company until she was safe at home again. But instead of a kiss of peace, the Prioress hissed at her, too softly for anyone else to hear. "Remember, any hint of trouble and you will have no home with us." Then, she turned her back, murmuring to Sister Marian in Latin.

Dominica gripped her staff. A knot in the wood scraped her palm. No home at the Priory meant she had no home at all.

Her own blessing complete, Sister Marian leaned on her staff and straightened her reluctant knees. She was not more than two score years, but copying had made her body old and chanting had kept her voice young.

Dominica, still shaking from Mother Julian's words, offered her arm. Together, she and Sister shared slow steps toward the chapel door. Cool tears blurred her fellow pilgrims into a lumpy, gray cloud in the middle of the sunny courtyard. Surely God would not let the Prioress stand in the way of His plan for her life.

As they paused in the doorway, she swiped the one tear that escaped.

"What is the matter, child?" Sister patted Dominica's arm with stiff fingers. "Why do you cry? Have you changed your mind? Do you want to stay here?"

More than anything, she thought, forcing a smile. No reason to disturb Sister Marian with words not meant for her. She shook her head and wiped the back of her hand against the scratchy wool. "Of course I want to stay here. That's why I am going away, so I need never leave again."

"Outside the Priory, the world is large. Many things can happen."

"And I plan to write about them so I can remember when I return." She patted the sack where her precious parchment and quill lay.

"You say that now." Weary sadness shadowed Sister's eyes. "Perhaps you will not want to come back."

"Of course I will." Even the thought of being abandoned to the world made her long for the comfort of the Priory. "I know every brick in the chapel, every branch on the tree in the garden. It is where I belong."

Sister Marian blinked as they stepped into the sunshine. She reached up, squaring the scleverin on Dominica's shoulders. Sister Barbara had stitched the rough gray wool cloak in loving haste, since Dominica's fingers were better at copying than stitching and Sister Marian said the cloak she wore on pilgrimage five years ago was still perfectly fine and she did not need another.

"Have you ever missed having a mother, Neeca?"

She smiled to hear Sister use her baby name. "Dominica" had been too big for a little girl's tongue. "I've had lots of mothers. You, Sister Barbara, Sister Catherine, Sister Margaret." She laid her hand atop Sister's, covering it easily.

Sister shook her head and flashed her dimple. "And none of us has been able to make you stop biting your nails." The smile faded. "Have you missed having a father?"

"How can I miss something I have never had? Besides, I have our Heavenly Father. And I have promised my hands to Him to spread His holy word." She raised her face to the sky, eyes closed, letting the sun's warmth fade the Prioress's words. "I know what God intends for me. Faith allows no doubts."

Sister shook her head. "I could not teach you everything. Even the most faithful doubt. Faith is moving ahead in spite of doubt."

Faith can be dangerous, The Savior had said. She looked

back into the chapel where he still knelt, clutching the Earl's hand. His broad shoulders cast a protective shadow over the pale, fading body.

Fides facit fidem, she answered, silently. "Faith makes faith."

Garren squeezed William's clammy palm, as if his own strength could force his friend back to health. William's very skin was flaking away, his body dissolving to free his soul.

"I will deliver your message without asking why and bring back a feather even though it be a sin," Garren said, looking over his shoulder. Richard still spoke to the Abbot and the Prioress whispered to the girl and the Sister, too far away to hear him. "But don't pretend to these people I am some kind of prophet."

. A smile whispered on William's lips. He seemed in less pain this morning. "Perhaps you are closer to God than you think, my friend."

"You know better," Garren said, shaking his head. "If God listened to *my* prayers, *you* would be going on this pilgrimage." Bracing his elbow against William's, he pushed as if to arm wrestle. The weight of his arm pressed William's down without effort. "When I get back, we'll arm wrestle for the palmer's fee. Winner pays."

"I thought dice was your game."

"I won't leave this win to chance."

"The palmer's fee is little enough compared to what you gave up for me."

"And a pilgrimage is little enough compared to what you did for me." Anything he had to do to repay him would be worth it. Anything. He blocked out the thought of Dominica humming.

Whatever strength had raised William from his bed had

drained away. Pale skin stretched across his broad forehead, tight as on a skull. "Besides, unless you hurry, I shall not be here for you to argue with."

"You had better be," Garren said, through clenched teeth. "You'll want to see the saint's feather I'm going to bring you."

William shook his head, muttering against a blasphemous act, but Garren did not listen. He owed William more than he owed God. *I'll do whatever I have to do to get there and back in time to see him again. In time to give back some of what I owe.*

He could feel God laughing at his vow.

A soft rustle behind him announced the black robed Prioress. "How good to see you outside your room, Lord Readington. It is an answer to our constant prayers."

Garren had no doubt that was true. Beneficences from the Readingtons meant their livelihood and Richard was not known as a generous patron.

"Thank you for your prayers, Prioress." William nodded toward Dominica, lending her arm to the Sister as they walked to the door. "Dominica goes, too?"

Curious. Garren was not even aware William knew her.

"She begged me to let her go, my lord." The Prioress raised her eyebrows. "We shall see where God leads her as she sees the world for the first time."

Garren looked at the Prioress in disgust, but she refused his glance. It was not God who would lead the girl astray. "Who is she, William?"

This time, the Prioress threw him a sharp look.

Though William's eyes had faded like an overwashed tunic, there was still a flash of humor left. "You've savored your share of ladies, Garren. Don't tell me you haven't noticed this one. Yellow hair. Twilight eyes."

"It sounds as if you have noticed her yourself," Garren

countered. Framed in the open door, the Sister straightened her cloak. Sunlight stroked her hair. William was wrong. It wasn't yellow. It was more the color of sweet ale, when the light from the fire shone through it.

"My family is responsible for the Priory and all who dwell there."

A chill settled on his back. What if William had an interest in the girl? He shrugged off the thought. More likely William would be dead by the time they returned and never know her fate. The thought did not comfort him. "William—" he began.

"Well, my Lord," the Prioress interrupted, "since you are well enough to leave your room, I have been seeking an audience to ask…"

"Brother, how foolish of you." Richard rushed over, leaving the Abbot alone, and nearly knocking the Prioress aside with his elbow. "The effort has obviously been too much. Niccolo, come!"

Garren started as the Italian materialized out of the shadows. He wondered how long the man had lurked there.

All nose and lips, Niccolo had been left behind by one of the Lombardy moneylenders. It was their money the King had borrowed to pay mercenaries like himself who fought in France. Richard had given the man a room. No one was quite certain what he did there. Practiced alchemy, Garren suspected. Lead into gold. A fool's errand.

Richard claimed Niccolo was searching for the right golden elixir to cure William's wasting illness. Strange how many ills gold could cure.

Niccolo kept his head bowed and his eyes hidden. "Yes, Lord Richard."

"He should never have been allowed to leave his room in this condition," Richard said. "I think he needs another of your healing remedies."

Niccolo clapped and the two attendants stepped forward. William's fingers slid from Garren's as they lifted the litter.

"Hurry back, Garren."

"Farewell, brother," Garren whispered, wondering whether he would ever see William alive again.

He turned to the Prioress as Richard trailed after the litter. "You did not tell me the Earl had a care for Dominica." It was the first time he had said her name aloud. It filled his mouth.

A red flush bloomed next to the white edge of the woman's wimple. "The girl was not made for the veil. That should be evident. We had an agreement. Honor it."

"Honor? A strange word, Prioress, for what you've asked."

Her glance slid toward Richard. "God works in mysterious ways."

"You seem eager to blame God for all the sins of man. I must take responsibility for my own."

"Then do so. I trust the sum is persuasive enough."

"It is." He felt tainted at the words, but the sin could hardly be worse than what he had done for the King's wages. He wondered again where she would get the money. And why it was worth so much to her. Another of God's mysteries, no doubt.

Suddenly, he was anxious to leave, to get on with the journey, to breathe the wind, to do even this futile thing for William. He bowed to the Prioress and, without a word, strode out of the chapel into the sunny courtyard.

Dominica pointed to him. "There he is."

His fellow travelers stared.

"Is he the one?"

"This is the man?"

One voice sounded like another. The faces looked at him expectantly, indistinguishable as a flock of dirty sheep.

Dominica nodded.

"We need a leader," one curly haired young man said. Next to him, a woman, as like him as a Gemini twin, held his hand. "It should be The Savior."

They paused, waiting for him to do something. He groaned. There would, of course, be piety required on a pilgrimage. "Yes," he said, "I'm sure Our Lord Jesus will lead us every step of the way." There. He had said the proper words in response.

"No," the young man said. "The Savior. You."

Chapter Four

The Savior. You.

Garren stifled a laugh. The world even played jokes on God.

Morning sunlight polished ten expectant faces awaiting his answer. He could pick them out now, one by one. The little nun. The Gemini couple, holding hands. The merchant's wife, a well-rounded woman with a well-used look. The brothers. The scar-faced man, scowling. A squire too young to earn his spurs. A tall, thin man the wind would blow over.

Dominica, lips parted, face glowing with faith.

In him.

Not one of them could wield a sword against thieves or find food in the forest. Not one knew how to survive.

He knew. France had taught him.

"I will lead you," he said, "because I can get you there safely." And bring you back quickly enough to see William one more time, he thought. "Not because I'm anyone's Savior."

"Savior? Who've ye saved?" the scar-faced man growled. There, at least, was one man who did not hold him in awe. White hair, coarse as straw, framed his battered face.

He could have lived one score of years or three, but whatever the number, they had been hard ones. "No man can save me. Not even God can save me." He stomped away.

Unease rippled through the pilgrims like wind through hay grass ready for cutting.

"What's that?" The plump woman turned one ear toward him. "Say again? This is my deaf ear," she said, loud enough to hear herself, patting her right ear. "And this one works," she said, pointing to her left. "Speak up. Has anyone traveled this way before? When I went to the shrine of Saint James in Compostela, we had a new guide and we were lost in the Pyrenees for a week before we could get to Spain and nearly…"

As she rambled on, his shell pressed more heavily against his chest. He wondered whether God and Saint James had answered her prayers.

Dominica touched the woman's arm to get her attention without shouting. "Sister Marian has been to the shrine of the Blessed Larina. More than once."

The little nun plucked Dominica's sleeve. "Neeca, please…"

Neeca. They called her Neeca. Garren said it silently, his tongue tickling the roof of his mouth.

The merchant's wife, broad as two of the Sister, looked the little nun up and down. "More than once, has she? Then maybe the Sister should lead us instead of this Savior fellow."

Garren let himself join the laughter that washed away the scar-faced man's anger.

The merchant's wife, still laughing, strolled over to him, the Compostela shell around her neck clanking against the gold cross and the pewter badge of St. Thomas Becket sitting sideways on a horse. She kneaded his arm muscles, as if she were sizing up a horse.

Dominica's gasp at the disrespect amused him.

"You look like a trustworthy sort," the woman said. "Broad shoulders. Strong arms. Fought at Poitiers?"

The word smelled like French dirt. He clenched his fist. "Yes."

"A great victory. And you brought the Earl of Reading-ton back to life." She nodded her approval. "If God is watching so carefully over you, He will take care of us."

God, he thought, shaking off her fingers, had nothing to do with it. "I'm a soldier, not a saint. Your souls are your own affair." The muscle between his shoulder blades ached, as if he had hoisted a heavy sword along with the respon-sibility for their safety. "Pick up your food. Say your fare-wells. We leave within the hour."

Except for Dominica and the Sister, they scattered like cooing pigeons. This Savior business was all the girl's do-ing, he thought, and he was going to end it now. "Dom-inica," he began.

She backed away from his frown. "I'll get your food, Sister," she called over her shoulder, running toward the kitchen, the shaggy black dog waddling at her heels.

The little nun spoke. "Her faith is an unwelcome burden to you, I think."

He studied her for a moment. Her handed-down habit was long and full, giving the tiny woman the look of a child wearing her mother's gown. Weariness tugged at her pale blue eyes. *Sister Marian wants the girl to fulfill her vow,* the Prioress said. He wondered if it were true.

"Thank you," she continued, "for agreeing to lead us. This is not easy for you."

He shuddered as if a spirit had spoken. He did not want her to think he sought the mantle. He was here for William, not for God or aggrandizement. "I am not what they think I am, Sister."

"None of us is, my child." No one had called him child in a long time. "Only God truly knows us."

"Then God knows I am an impostor," he said, with bravado he did not feel. "A fake. A fraud. I am a palmer, Sister," he said, loudly, as if he were proud of it. "I'll be paid for this journey."

And for other things he did not want to share.

"Many pilgrims walk with secrets," she said, as if she had heard all he had not said. Her melodic voice demanded no confession. "God loves us anyway, no matter what our secrets."

He searched her face for a hidden meaning. No, this woman did not know what the Prioress had planned for her precious Neeca. "You have spent your life far from worldly temptations. What secrets can you have, Sister?"

"The ones God has helped me keep."

He wondered why she told him this and he felt a twinge of envy for the certainty of her faith, a faith that had been forged not through reading the ritual, but in a pact between her heart and God's. God had kept his promises to Sister Marian. So far.

If the Churchmen he had known had been so holy, he would still be in the cloister. And he would be content to leave Dominica there.

"You called her Neeca," he said, beating back the guilt for what he would do.

Her pale skin turned paler, as if he had startled, or scared her. "What did you say?"

"I was speaking of something new. You called the girl Neeca. Why?"

A smile soothed the lines around her eyes. "I have known her since she was born. She called herself that when she was learning to talk."

"Since she was born? I thought…" He stopped. No need to tell her he had spoken with the Prioress.

"Did I say born? I meant since God left her in our care." Too short to reach his shoulder, she tapped his arm with gentle fingers. "And now she will be in yours."

He wanted no more reminders of his betrayal. "So you have made this journey before, Sister."

"Three times. I went the year of the Death to pray for all the souls in the Earl's care. Only the Sister who traveled with me and the Earl himself died." Her eyes still carried the shadow of that Death. "The Saint protected the rest of us. Now, we send someone every year to thank her. I went again the first year of Pope Innocent's reign."

"And the third time?"

She looked away from him and across the courtyard toward the kitchen. "Years before." Picking up her staff, she leaned stiffly, into her first step. "Now, if you will excuse me, I must gather my things."

He watched her, feeling the pain of each footfall. She might have made the journey before, but she had been younger then. "Sister, I would ask a favor."

"Of me? What is it, my child?"

"I know you would prefer to walk the journey with the rest of us, but…" But what? What excuse could he find to spare her the aching steps? "…but my horse Roucoud is accustomed to a weight on his back. It will be hard for him to walk empty." No need to tell her she was so small the warhorse would barely know she was there. "Besides, you have traveled the route before. If you rode, you could watch the road and help guide us."

"Bless you, sir, for your kindness." A dimple creased her cheek. "It is troublesome, is it not, to have a horse that needs weight on his back when you are weary of riding? I was just praying for God's help on this journey and there you are.''

"Do not confuse my help and God's, Sister. They are two entirely different things." She would discover that later, he thought, to her regret.

"Sometimes God's help comes from where you least expect it."

And so does God's punishment, he thought.

With Innocent at her heels, Dominica fled to the dark, smoky kitchen. Rabbits, wood pigeons and a fat goose, more meat than Dominica had ever seen, swung from the rafters. The smell of drying blood mixed with fresh-baked bread. Scullions scampered in and out, jumping at the cook's shouts as quickly as she had jumped to escape The Savior's anger.

He had frowned like Moses, as if he knew she had told the nice young man and his wife that he raised Lord William from death. Well, what if she had? If I had done something so wonderful, she thought, I would want everyone to know. Of course, as the Prioress always told her, Pride goeth before destruction. It was one of Mother Julian's favorite Proverbs.

"Stand in line! Give me a minute!" the cook yelled. A young scullion boy ran in and added a loaf of yesterday's bread to the odd collection of cheese and dirt-covered vegetables strewn atop the wooden table. The cook, muttering, was trying to divide them into eleven equal pouches. "I wish the Earl's piety came with a day's notice."

Standing patiently at the end of the line next to the deaf woman, Dominica stifled covetous envy of her finely woven cloak. The woman ducked her head and smiled up through her eyelashes at the tall, thin man on her other side.

He smiled back, bending from his hips with a bounce.

Dropping her gaze, afraid to be caught staring, Dominica blinked at the sight of red hose hugging the woman's ample ankles. Despite her bosom full of badges, this worldly woman looked nothing like a pilgrim. Could she be a repentant prostitute?

"The food is important," the tall man said. "Good for balancing the humors."

The woman cupped her hand around her good left ear. "Oh, you are a physician, good sir?"

"I am James Arderne," the tall man said, folding his entire body into a bow. "I am a physician from near St. John's."

"Ah, well, we shall be glad of your company on the road."

"Where is your home, Goodwife?" the Physician said.

"Bath," she answered. "And it is Good Widow. Agnes Cropton." The red-hosed widow wiggled her fingers in a wave as the physician bowed a farewell.

Widow. Judge not, Dominica reminded herself, repenting her wicked thoughts of the pious widow, that ye be not judged. "I am sorry for your loss."

"Which one?"

"Your husband who died. Oh, pardon, and for the loss of your hearing, as well." Dominica sighed, longing for the silence of the convent. It was easier to talk to God than to strangers.

"I meant which husband." The woman popped a piece of cheese in her mouth when the cook's back was turned. "As for my hearing, it was my worthless second husband who made me deaf. Beat me about the head and shoulders one too many times. God struck him dead," she said nodding emphatically. "But that was many years ago."

"Next! Come along!" the cook yelled.

Dominica jumped.

The Widow's words flowed on. "I'm glad we have a physician with us. Some terrible illness can strike on the road. When I was in…"

Cook jerked the Widow's sleeve. "I said 'come.' Are you deaf?"

"Yes, I am," the woman answered, raising her head and her eyebrows. "God keep you for your concern."

Cook threw the packet of food at her, snarling. "And keep that dog away from the table!" he yelled at Dominica. "Look, he already ate a piece of cheese! I'm not feeding animals, too."

The Widow winked.

Even stretched on his stubby legs, Innocent couldn't reach the table, but she scooped him up with her left arm and took the last three parcels of food with her right. "For Sister Marian and The Savior," she called back to the scowling cook as she walked out of the kitchen beside Widow Cropton. "Today, I wouldn't mind having one deaf ear," Dominica moaned.

"Well, it can be handy when I don't want to be bored. What's your name, dearie? Where are you from?"

"Dominica." Squinting in the sunlight, she scanned the courtyard for Sister and The Savior as she set Innocent down. "I live at the Priory."

"You don't look like a nun."

"I'm not yet. But I will be." The very words made her smile.

The Widow harrumphed. "Not looking like you do."

Dominica's hand flew to her face, pressed her cheeks, touched her forehead, slid down her nose, tugged her ears. The Prioress said her eyes were frightening. Was there more? Was she deformed? "What's wrong? We have no mirrors at the Priory."

"Nothing when you smile." She pinched Dominica's

cheek. "Smile more, girl. Show that dimple. Don't worry. You'll catch a husband."

"But I don't want a husband. I want to be a nun."

Widow Cropton shook her head, as if she neither believed nor approved. "That's a last resort, dearie. Pretty girl like you won't need to waste away in a nunnery."

It is not a waste to spread God's word, she thought, but decided it was not her place to explain God's plan to Widow Cropton. "Do you go on pilgrimage to ask the Blessed Larina to let you hear again?" she said instead.

The Widow snorted. "Well, I suppose." She patted the badges on her ample bosom. "Although Saint James and Saint Thomas did no good. Perhaps a good woman saint can help."

"So you've been on pilgrimage before?" She spotted The Savior and Sister, standing next to his big bay horse.

"Five times." She laughed, heartily. "Once after each husband."

"Five?" She turned back to the Widow in shock. "What happened to them?"

"Oh, they all died. They were much older than I, then." She stroked her chin and neck, where the skin was losing its grip before disappearing into the folds of her wimple. "Men are such weak creatures, my dear. If they don't get killed in battle they get smallpox or fall off a horse or drown in the river." She shook her head.

Dominica was trying to listen, but she kept turning to watch Sir Garren. The Savior, she thought, did not look weak. Sleeves turned back to bare his sun-warmed arms, he hoisted a sack behind his horse's saddle. The effort flexed muscles beneath his skin. In fact, he looked nothing like the thin, pale portraits of the saints on the Church walls. More like a strong, sheltering oak tree.

But the Widow obviously knew much more of men than she did. "So you are not married now?"

"No, or I wouldn't be here. Or need to be. There's more than one reason to visit the saints, dearie." She winked. "Nothing ever happens in Bath, you know."

"Nothing ever happens at the Priory either, but I wish I could stay there." Safe with God and silence. "I've never been away before."

"Oh, you have a treat ahead. You never know what each day on the road will bring, although if I had known this was such a backwater, I might have changed my mind. Everyone required to walk! Everyone still in gray cloaks! When I went to Saint James's shrine in Compostela, Spain, I was carried by an ass every step of the way for nearly a year there and back and no one complained that I was not showing proper piety."

Dominica nodded, watching Sister again, worried. They would be back before Saint Swithin's Day, with luck, but Sister's steps between the scriptorium and the chapel were slower than they once were and she had refused Dominica's suggestion that she ride on the Priory's extra ass.

"So," the Widow said, loud enough to draw her back from her worries. "Well, this Savior fellow, what's his name?"

"Sir Garren."

"He reminds me of my fourth husband." She patted Dominica's arm. "He was my favorite. There's much to be said for husbands, dearie, even the bad ones. Sometimes it is good to have a man to warm your bed and to whisper in your good ear."

"But he's The Savior!" The Widow's words seemed blasphemous, but no more so than the feelings that stirred thinking about Sir Garren warming her bed. Dominica wanted to remind the Widow that she was going to be a nun and would have no need of men, but the Widow had noticed James Ardene across the courtyard and she lifted her hand to wave.

"Excuse me. I think I'll ask the Physician if he brought any marjoram. I can tell you I'll need a poultice for my swelling feet before we reach Exeter."

Dominica turned to see Garren lifting Sister Marian onto the horse and tucking her into the high-backed saddle with a tenderness that reminded her of his care of Lord William.

She sighed, relieved that Sister would ride and wondering how he had persuaded her. But he was The Savior. Sister would listen to him.

She would thank him, even if she had to brave his frown. And her fears.

Chapter Five

Standing next to the huge warhorse, Dominica stretched up to hand Sister her portion of food. Then, ducking her head to avoid meeting his eyes, she thrust the other bag at The Savior, who was tying supplies behind the saddle. She was not ready to say her speech of thanks. She needed to plan the words so she would not say the wrong thing.

As the sun reached its height, she and the rest of the chattering pilgrims followed The Savior across the Readington castle drawbridge and toward the west. Beside him, Sister swayed atop Roucoud, both her legs dangling to one side. Dominica walked on the other side of the huge warhorse, close to Sister, but hidden from The Savior. Innocent trotted at her feet, a safe distance from the horse's hooves.

Between the castle and the Priory, the fields rolled yellow and green and familiar in every direction. West, beyond the Priory, each step carried her farther from all she had known. Widow Cropton's drone tickled her ear, drowning out the lark's song, as she described every detail of her past pilgrimages. By midafternoon, she had described the journey across the Channel to Calais. Dominica felt as if she, too, had traveled as far as France, for she no longer recognized the land around them.

Her thighs already ached and she envied Roucoud's muscles, bunching and flexing beneath his reddish coat with every powerful step. She peeked around him. The Savior moved as powerfully as his horse, one step following another.

She silently mouthed several words of thanks she might say to him, wishing she could write them instead, but she had brought barely enough parchment to record the journey. Finally satisfied, she repeated them in rhythm with each step. She would not say them aloud until she could be alone with him and Sister could not hear. Sister never liked being fussed over.

Beneath her gray wool cloak, Dominica steamed like Cook's baked bread by the time The Savior called a stop. When he lifted Sister Marian off Roucoud, Dominica saw damp stains under his arms. *He's hot,* she thought, surprised. She had not expected a near saint to have a sinful body that sweated just as hers did.

She watched, surreptitiously, as he disappeared into the woods. *He must have bodily needs, too.* The shocking picture of The Savior relieving himself popped unbidden into her mind. More than the sun heated her cheeks and she held the wicked image a moment longer than she should have before begging God's forgiveness.

After he returned and Sister went into the woods, Dominica walked over to him, ready to speak. She tilted her head back. She could meet many a man's eye, but he was taller than the Abbot. Almost as tall as Lord William.

Taking a deep breath, she said the words she memorized. "Thank you for persuading Sister Marian to ride. In even this small way, you are a savior."

"I am no one's savior!" he said, through clenched teeth, glancing toward the other pilgrims. Only strong will, she thought, held back his shout. "Stop telling people I am."

"But you saved Lord William!" She had practiced no more words, so the ones she had been told tumbled out. "At Poitiers, where our glorious Black Prince triumphed with God's help."

"Only if God created all Frenchmen cowards." A scowl clung to his face like morning fog. She always seemed to make him angry.

"But it was a miracle!" She was sure that's what she had been told about the glorious victory. "We were outnumbered, surrounded, and yet the French forces were scattered as if by an unseen hand."

"I believe only in hands I can see." He thrust his hands before her face. Large, square hands. Callused. And, she knew, oddly gentle. "These hands carried Readington home, not God's."

Dominica had pictured a white-gowned wraith, floating a few inches above the ground, stretching thin fingers toward Lord William, who simply rose and walked. This man hoisted Lord William over his shoulder like a sack of the Miller brothers' flour.

"Carried him with God's help." Her hands made the sign of the cross. "Everyone knows that!"

He dropped his hands to his side, sighing with exasperation. "Everyone knows nothing. I did no more for him than he did for me."

She blinked. "Lord William brought you back from the dead?" The Earl was strong and kind and God had certainly protected his people from the Death when many others were taken, but she had never heard rumors Lord William might bring them back to life. "I thought he gave you a horse."

The man was silent, then, as if he had slipped into the past. "He gave me a new life."

Wondering whether she should risk asking what he meant, she ignored Innocent's bark until he ran in front of her, short legs churning, chasing a scampering rabbit across the road and into a field. The waving green wheat swallowed the rabbit, as well as Innocent's plump, shaggy black haunches.

"Come back," Dominica cried, lifting her skirts to run after him.

The Savior grabbed her arm. "He's a terrier. You can't run after him every time every time he runs after a rabbit." A smile tugged at The Savior's lips.

"He'll get lost! He's never been outside the convent before." She did not even know where she was. How would Innocent find his way back? Less than a day away from home and the world suddenly seemed a frightening place.

Innocent's bark faded.

The Widow called from behind her, laughing. "Tell him to bring back our dinner."

"But he likes turnips," she cried, thinking how many times she had pulled his dirt-covered nose out of her garden. She bit her lip. What if he didn't come back? "Where will he find turnips if he runs away?"

The Savior's fingers still curled around her wrist, warm on her skin. "Let him enjoy the chase."

"What if he never comes back? How will he take care of himself?" She wished Sister would come back. Sister would understand.

"Any dog missing one ear has seen something of life," he answered, not letting go of her arm. Her skin pulsed beneath his fingers.

His other ear made up for it, she thought. It stood up like a perky little unicorn's horn and then flopped over at the top, bouncing when he chased his tail as she had taught him. Using turnips. And if he never came back she didn't know how she would bear it.

She poured out the story to Sister, as The Savior lifted

her back on the horse. "God will guide him back to us, if it is meant to be. Have you prayed?"

Dominica shook her head, ashamed she had not, but not at all certain that God had time to look for lost dogs.

Sneering at Dominica as he strode past her, the squire faced The Savior, chest to chest, close enough to prove he was a fighting man, too. Perhaps he feels he has something to prove, she thought, for he was beautiful as a blond, painted angel. "Sir Garren, let's go. We're not going to stay here waiting for a dog, are we?"

Sir Garren, though it was hard to think of him that way, smiled with the patience he seemed to show everyone but her. "We are going to stay here until I say it's time to leave." There was steel in his voice. Enough to remind Simon, to remind all of them, that he was the leader and accustomed to command. "Why don't you check the woods to make sure we are all here, young Simon?"

The young squire's ears turned red, but he stalked off into the woods.

Before Simon returned, Innocent, pink tongue panting between shaggy black whiskers, poked his nose out from the young wheat. Trotting back to her, he started to chase his tail, as if to cajole her forgiveness. Dominica snatched him up, squeezing him tight, comforted by the heaving bellows of his warm little chest against hers. "Bad dog."

Sister scratched behind his good ear.

"Don't reward him for running away! Next time he might not come back."

"You see, Dominica. You must have faith in God."

Or in The Savior, she thought to herself, who had delayed their departure long enough for Innocent to come back.

Dominica thrust the limp black bundle up to Sister. "Here. Carry him on the horse so he won't run away again."

Sister looked at The Savior for approval. "The horse may not like dogs, my child."

"Roucoud is remarkably tolerant," he said. A smile seemed to be hovering around his lips.

"He can't ride horseback all the way to Cornwall," Sister said, but she settled the dog in front of her. Exhausted, Innocent flopped over the saddle as the group resumed its walk.

Threats lurked everywhere, Dominica thought, striding ahead as if she might out-walk her worries. She knew the journey would have dangers, wild boars or even dragons but she never expected to lose Innocent.

The Savior caught up with her, shortening his stride to walk beside her. "Don't worry about the dog." Amusement gilded his voice. "Judging by that missing ear, he wasn't raised in a convent. He had quite a life before he came to you."

She watched him out of the corner of her eye. The more she saw him, the harder it was to picture him with wings. "So did you."

He didn't frown, exactly, but his face changed as if he had dropped a cloak over it. "Any soldier has."

He was much more than a simple fighting man, but talk of his special relationship with God seemed to annoy him. "Have you see much of the world?"

"Enough." He used words as sparingly as a monk.

"Tell me of God's world."

"You've never left the convent?"

"Only to go to the castle." Trips she wanted to forget. At least the encounters with Sir Richard. "Is it true there are dragons at the edge of the sea?"

"I have only been as far as France. And the Widow Cropton has described the countryside in more detail than I ever could." Amusement softened the lines etched in his face.

Unlike the stern saints in the portraits, he seemed to tolerate human frailties. Except hers. "But let us enjoy today. War is no subject for a summer's day stroll with a lovely lady."

She studied his eyes to see if he made fun of her, but they were warm and no longer angry. She was no lady, but the word made her stand a little straighter and she lifted the hair that hung down in front of her and flipped it over her shoulder, wondering if that was the sin of vanity.

"What is a subject for a stroll with a lady?" she asked. "Talking is not allowed in the Priory." And when she did talk, the Prioress always scolded her. When she wrote, she could ponder every word.

"The beauty of the day." His voice turned husky. "The beauty of her eyes."

Startled, she turned. His eyes, gazing into hers, were deep green, the dark lashes were straight and thick. And she felt as if he had reached inside of her and touched something around her heart. Or her stomach.

Some instinct kept her feet moving as she looked down at the footworn path. "The Prioress calls them Devil's eyes."

He muttered something she could not hear. "No chivalrous knight would do so. He would compare them to the brilliant blue of a predawn sky."

"Yours are more like green leaves with the brown tree bark showing through."

His laughter stung like a slap. She had said something wrong again.

"That is not the expected response," he said, smiling.

Well, at least she had not made him angry again. "Why not? You said something about my eyes. Shouldn't I say something about yours?"

"No. You should sigh and blush."

She did both. "I've never talked to a man for very long." "I don't know all the rules. It seems very confusing."

He squinted toward the sun. "The world is a confusing place."

"Which is why I belong at the Priory. Perhaps talk of the Lord would please you," she said, hopeful.

"Nothing would please me less."

At least the Priory's rule of silence prevented awkward situations such as this one. Perhaps he would want to talk about his home and family. "Where did you grow up?"

His look was sharp. "It doesn't matter."

Heat flushed her cheeks again, but instead of the sun or a blush, she felt the sin of anger. "Did I say something wrong again? You wanted to talk. Sighing and blushing do not lead to lengthy discourse."

His glance, hot and brief, burned her cheeks. "Discourse is not why we talk."

His meaning was as unfamiliar as Latin used to be. She did not belong here. She longed for the familiar routine, where she knew what to do every minute of the day. There was never any doubt about what words to chant to God. "My presence displeases you. I shall withdraw. Again, I thank you for your kindness to Sister Marian."

She turned her back on him and walked the late afternoon hours beside the Widow Cropton, who did not expect her to talk. By supper, she had heard the widow recount her journey from Calais to Paris on her way to Compostela.

And Dominica had picked out a few words she would write about The Savior.

He had made a mess of it, Garren thought, trudging alone toward the west-moving sun. She would never talk to him again.

Habit kept his eyes flickering from one side of the road

to the other; kept his ears open for the clop of unfamiliar hooves. Even here, on Readington lands, thieves might prey on pilgrims. But today, he saw only yellow buttercups bobbing atop tall, thin green stems; heard only sparrows cheeping cheerily.

No one approached him. Behind him, the pilgrims clustered around the Widow, listening to her prattle. Was it Dominica who chuckled? He should have been the one to coax her laughter.

Instead, he had growled like an irascible wild boar and she fled. The charm that had captivated the women of France deserted him.

Well, it wasn't entirely his fault. How was he to seduce a woman who knew nothing of the game? How could he bed one who kept her eyes on God instead of on the wonders of life before her?

He filled his lungs with sweet English air, savoring the moment of peace. Today was all he had. The past was too painful. And the future? He knew the futility of trying to earn your place in heaven. God snatched away the good as quickly as the wicked.

And she was definitely one of the good. Or perhaps she had never faced temptation. He would tempt her. When he looked at those fathomless deep blue eyes, he knew someone would. It might as well be him.

He let his mind drift. Neeca in his arms, her hair flowing over him like honey, her breasts, round and full and responding to his lips… He was grateful that he walked ahead of the crowd, where no one could see his member respond to the thought.

It was nice that he was attracted to her. Nice, but not necessary. He was doing this for money, just as if he plied his trade with the strumpets on Rose Street.

The thought made him feel unclean.

No, not for money. Everyone wanted to make him either saint or sinner. An instrument of God or a money-grubbing mercenary. He was neither. Despite what they thought, it was not money he wanted.

I belong at the Priory, she said. Where did he belong? Not at the monastery. Where did you grow up? Garren of nowhere. Garren who had no home.

Home. He could hardly remember the look of it. Gray stone under gray skies. Brooding green trees, never changing with the seasons. One tower, or was it two? Always on the lookout. Waiting for an attack from either side of an ever shifting border. The English soldiers screaming as loudly as the Scots. He had left at age six, as each child must, never returning until those awful weeks eleven years later when Death soaked the walls like a black, winter rain.

Sometimes, a whiff of heather would take him back. His mother had loved that smell. She had stuffed some in a little pillow for him to sit on while he listened to her tell him how Christ turned water into wine and made many loaves from few.

Fairy stories. He found that out just in time, just before he would have promised his life to poverty, chastity and obedience.

He shrugged off the unwelcome memories. Past is past. Look at today. He looked out on William's land again. Green fields hugged gently rolling hills, each field stitched neatly to its neighbor with greener trees. Blue and copper butterflies clustered as thickly as the yellow and white flowers they sat on. What would it be like to have a home in a lush, sweet land like this? No invaders had ripped the land apart for nine generations. No stink of blood soaked the soil. No savage soldiers' cries, living or dead, drowned out the twitter of sparrows.

He envied William the land he walked on. He wanted his

own earth beneath his feet. Maybe, after he had repaid William. Maybe, after William died and Richard forced him to leave. Maybe, he could find some land, abandoned or unattended. Some land that with a strong arm he could make his own.

But first, that meant taking the girl to bed. Next time, he would be gallant and charming and eventually she would tumble like a tavern maid. He would not have to face her eyes when she rolled beneath him.

Stand straight and speak kindly.

He shook his head. It was as if his mother spoke in his ear. He was six again and she was saying goodbye as he sat atop the horse that would carry him away.

The thought distracted him as he called a halt for the day beneath a grove of trees beside a cold spring and assigned guard duties for the night. No sense tiring them all at once, especially Sister. They had many days of walking ahead.

He splashed cold spring water on his face and down the back of his neck. He would talk to the girl again.

Stand straight and speak kindly. God will watch over you.

God had some things to answer for. But he might try his mother's advice on the young Dominica.

Chapter Six

Standing just beyond the reach of the fire's warmth, Dominica scanned the group, looking for The Savior, or Sir Garren, if that's what he insisted she call him. Not that she wanted to call him anything at all. She was looking for him so she could avoid him. And if she saw him, she would refuse to speak to him. Why should she? Everything she said made him scowl.

She tossed back her hair and bit her lip. It was probably sinful to hold a grudge against one with a special relationship with God, but he was so rude today, she felt justified in ignoring him.

He had settled the group early for the night. After the evening meal, Sister Marian gathered the pilgrims into a mismatched choir. It was strange to hear singing that did not echo on stone. But Sister Marian, her clear voice praising God with each note, led them with enthusiasm, even for the Widow, whose deaf ear let her sing happily in her own rhythm. At least when she was singing, she wasn't talking.

"Your faith gives you wings to fly like Larina
To fly like Larina, to fly like Larina;

Your faith gives you wings to fly like Larina
Into the arms of the Lord.''

Dominica hummed along, tapping one foot, happily reminded why she was here and what she would find at the
end of her journey: a sign from God that she could go home.

She counted the singers. Sir Garren was not among them,
nor were Simon and Ralf. Perhaps he was standing guard
with them.

She felt a shield at her back, blocking the wind, and
turned. Sir Garren loomed behind her, tall and straight as a
tree. ''You do not join the singing?''

Her throat clutched the hum. She was not going to speak
to him. She was not certain she *could* speak to him. But he
had asked her a direct question. She had to say something.
''Singing is not my talent. Mother Julian has always been
clear about that.''

A frown creased his brow. Everything she said brought a
frown. He smiled at Sister. He even smiled at Innocent.
What was it about her that made him frown? ''You dislike
singing?'' she ventured.

''I dislike announcing our presence to thieves.''

A gust of wind rustled the ragged oak leaves behind her.
Hand-shaped shadows waved along the ground. Dominica
swallowed. Thieves. Something new to fear. Bravery had
been easy when, sheltered by cloistered walls, all she had
to fear was Mother Julian. ''God protects pilgrims.'' And it
is your task to protect us, she thought.

He opened his mouth and then shut it with a deliberate
smile. ''Don't worry.'' He brushed a lock of hair back from
her forehead. She shivered at the touch of his fingers, yet
she felt reassured. ''We are still close to William's land.''

At least he had not frowned.

This time, however, she would not speak. Ignoring him,

she looked back at the singers and hummed through closed lips waiting for him to go away.

He stayed. Back straight as a soldier, he stood so close to her she could sense the rise and fall of his chest. She wondered whether it were covered by the same dark brown hair as his fingers, scolding herself for the thought. Even if he were no saint, she should not think of him as a man. Nuns never thought of men that way.

She jumped when he spoke again, his voice soft somewhere above her left ear. "I must ask your forgiveness. I spoke like the rudest peasant instead of a chivalrous knight."

Refusing to look at him, she kept her gaze on the fire, hoping he could not see her satisfied smile. "I know little of chivalry."

Large, warm hands cupped her shoulders. He turned her, gently, but firmly, to face him. Firelight flickered over his face, softening the rough edge of his chin and the harsh lines around his eyes. "I am sorry. I have no excuse for ill treatment of another."

She chose her words carefully, trying to resist the pleading look in his eyes. "It is not my place to judge a man who is one of God's messengers."

His chest rose with an inheld breath, as if he were ready to berate her again, but sighed instead. "At least you are no longer calling me The Savior." He shook his head. "Life treats us ill enough. We should be kind to each other."

Sorrow lurked in his voice. Chagrined, she regretted her petty game. He preached kindness, just as the Savior did. And practiced it, too. She had seen it in his care of Sister and all of them. He had asked for forgiveness. Surely she could forgive ill manners. "I forgive you."

Some of the pain behind his eyes dissolved. "Thank you."

She couldn't look away. Her chest rose and fell with his, and she had a strange, dizzy sensation that they breathed as one person.

Behind her, the singing dissolved in laughter. She stepped away from him and looked back at the fire.

He cleared his throat. "Why don't you talk now?"

She did not want to talk to him. She did not want to stand near him. She did not want to feel so shaky and uncertain. She filled her chest with air, relieved that her breath was her own again. "I am not experienced with talking. At the Priory, we speak only with permission." No need to tell him she didn't always wait for permission.

"I give you permission." It sounded more like a command.

What did he want of her? She turned and let her words fly without planning. "What should I say? I am not to speak of your eyes or your home and family or the war or God. I cannot speak of my travels, because I have none."

Now he was the one who kept his eyes on the fire, refusing to face her. The singers started a round, and completed the three parts. Still, he did not answer. For a man who wanted to talk, it seemed to come no more easily to him than to her. "Tell me of your life at the Priory," he said, finally.

She smiled, happy to talk of home. "I tend the garden, do the wash, clean." No scowls this time. A determined smile carved his face. Should she tell him about her writing?

A cold, wet nose nudged her ankle. She picked up Innocent, burying her nose in his fur, smelling the unfamiliar earth he had explored. "And I feed the dog." He washed her face with a scratchy tongue. "Find any turnips, boy?"

Sir Garren scratched behind the shaggy black ear and Innocent busied his tongue with the broad palm instead of

Dominica's face. Laughing, she turned back to The Savior, or whoever he was. "Did you have a dog as a child?"

"I don't remember."

At first she thought that he didn't want to speak of his childhood. Then, the puzzlement in his voice hit her ear.

He could not remember. This was a man who had not been a child for a long, long time.

She watched in wonder as he patiently let Innocent's pink tongue clean every one of his fingers. "How came you to know Lord William?" she asked, finally.

"He took me as his squire when I was seventeen."

"Seventeen? A knight's training begins as a child."

"I had much to learn. My training was…interrupted." The words came through lips narrowed by a harsh life.

"Interrupted by what?"

"I had just left the monastery."

A shudder chilled her spine. Had he broken his vows? Was he an outcast monk? "Were you defrocked?"

"I was just completing my novice year. I had not taken my vows." A haunted look lurked about his eyes. "All I could offer was a rusty sword arm, not even a sword."

He gave me a new life, he said of the Earl of Readington, with the fierce loyalty men normally reserve for God. Even she knew how generous the Earl had been to take on a penniless, ill-trained squire. "Why did you leave the monastery?"

He was silent while the crackling fire shot a shower of sparks into the twilight sky, blue as if it had been ground from azurite. The first star blinked. "This was after the Death," he said, finally.

She crossed herself. He had not answered, but she understood. Many strange events had come upon the land seized by that terror almost ten years ago. God had nearly destroyed the world. She still did not understand how the comforting God who spoke to her could let such a plague loose upon his people. "God punished us so harshly. We must strive to do his will each day so tomorrow will not bring such a punishment again."

He shook his head. "We must strive to enjoy today because God may snatch us away before tomorrow comes."

"But if He does, there's a reason. There is always a reason for God's plan."

"Can you explain it?"

She searched his eyes, wondering whether God had sent him to test her faith. There must be words she could say to convince him of the rightness of God's plan. *"Sola fide."*

"What?"

He did not understand her Latin. She must have mispronounced the words. "By faith alone."

Light from the fire flickered over his face. Shadows from his strong brows concealed his eyes. "You really believe that, don't you?"

"Don't you?"

The Miller brothers, one with a low voice and one higher, filled the silence with their harmonies. Faith is a trap for fools, he had said, this man who saved people but walked away from God.

"I believe," he whispered, staring at the fire, "that we owe each other more than we owe God."

She realized she had not breathed, waiting for his answer.

Day One: Faire weather. Walked until vespers. Pleasant land.

Lip out, Dominica watched the morning sun spill pink over the horizon. One sheet of paper lay atop a rock. Her letters, small and tight, filled the precious page edge to edge, as she'd been taught.

But were they the right words?

Just one day away from the Priory, she was farther away from home than she had ever been. She could not even name the place they had slept. Everything was fresh and unseen and untried and she was exhausted with the newness of it all.

The cheeping sparrows hopped close enough to touch. She must enjoy this time. These days. Write them down so she could remember later. When she would never be able even to speak of them without permission.

She wanted to write about how funny Innocent had looked chasing the rabbit and the way the young married couple walked holding hands and that she was worried about how tired Sister had seemed last night.

She wanted to write about him.

She dipped the quill into the ink and tapped out the excess.

Smooth straight path. Slept under stars.

Stars. How inadequate. Thousands and thousands of tiny candle flames lit by God. She could hardly bear to shut her eyes for the wonder of sleeping under such a ceiling.

She added a word. *Many.*

She frowned at her stingy parchment, a rescraped and reused scrap no one wanted any more, not good enough to copy God's words. She had room for only a word or two to help her remember later.

What word would she choose for him?

The Savior was too blasphemous. Garren too personal.

The Man, she wrote.

She stared in horror, then struck through the words, blunting the point of her quill, hiding them with an ugly black blot, wishing she could blot them out of her mind.

He must be more than a man. For if he were only a man, she might be only reacting to him as a woman.

* * *

Alone in the shelter of the small grove before the day's journey began, Garren thought about his plan. He did not know whether it was a good one.

He took the tarnished, dented silver reliquary from around his neck. Unwrapping the scrap of leather tied around it, he pulled apart the slender, silver tube. Inside, he had hidden three goose down feathers he would exchange for feathers from the shrine. Somehow. When no one was looking.

He thought again of just giving William the goose down. After all, there must be enough true feathers of the Blessed Larina to fly to heaven. Most relics were frauds. William would never know.

But a promise made to William bound him more tightly than an oath made to God.

A branch snapped and he pulled his dagger.

Dominica stood transfixed, staring at the feathers nestled in their white linen shroud. The skin behind her freckles paled. Then, she looked at him, blue eyes so piercing he feared she could see him plucking the goose down from the aviary dust.

"It is a blessed feather from Saint Larina's wings," she whispered. "The wings God gave her."

Well, what harm would it do to a girl who already believed *sola fide*. She must not know his real plans. "Yes, yes it is." He lifted a finger to his lips. "But you must tell no one." He rocked the feather as if it were a precious child. "I'm to deliver it to the shrine, but the fewer who know, the better. You understand."

Her blue eyes, already wide and round, grew larger. Both eyebrows lifted. One, he noticed, arched like a bird's wing. The other ended as if the wing had been broken. "Where did you find it?" Her whisper's echo turned the grove into a chapel.

"I am not free to tell you." he intoned, mimicking a priestly monotone. "You understand."

She smiled with a sigh that sounded like relief. "I knew you were special the minute I saw you in the Prioress's office. I had a warm feeling, like when I pray in front of the stained glass window."

I had a warm feeling too, he thought, but it had nothing to do with prayer.

She uttered some Latin words, solemnly.

He blinked and nodded, trying to look as if he were striving to remember the exact chapter and verse she recited. Even at the monastery, he had been a poor student.

"That's 'Give all honor to God's messenger,'" she said, with a self-satisfied grin. "I wrote that one."

"You what?"

"Well, sometimes, I put the words together into sayings of my own." She ducked her head. "Please correct me if I get it wrong."

He nodded, sagely. No reason for her to know the limitations of his Latin.

He nodded to the cloth. "You must tell no one about the feathers," he said. No need to spread another fable about his special link with God.

She peered at them, but kept her hands behind her back. "A relic carries all the power of the saint. It can work a miracle."

Miracles. The girl believed in miracles. "Have you ever witnessed a miracle like that?"

"I know all the stories."

"What if they are only stories?"

"How can you ask that?"

"There are more pilgrims than miracles."

"God helps those who believe."

"So if you aren't cured it's your fault because you didn't believe, not God's because He doesn't care?"

The fierce blue eyes flashed. "There are many miracles. There's the miller's son who drowned but was revived by Thomas of Cantilupe and the monk who wrapped his swollen arm in Becket's stole and was cured and…"

"And the miraculous resurrection of The Earl of Readington at Poitiers," he said.

"Yes. It was a miracle, what you did." She reached for the feather, her finger hovering above it, as if it were giving off heat. "May I…may I touch it?"

You may pick it up and throw it on the ground and stomp it in the dirt from which I plucked it, for all the holiness it carries, he thought, jealous for a moment that she looked at the feather with the kind of desire a man would like to see directed at him.

"Touch it gently," he said.

"I have a very important request of God." She impaled him with her eyes. "Will the Blessed Larina help me?"

He knew how God answered prayers. He had begged God for his parents' lives. God answered no.

"God listens to our prayers," he said, bitterly. "He just may not give us the answers we desire."

She nodded, sighing. "That's what Sister Marian says. That's why I want Larina's help. Sometimes, God needs a little push."

She believed God would listen to her personal prayers. Just as he had once. He didn't know whether to pity or envy her.

She stroked the feather gently. Her grin blossomed and with it, a dimple. "My finger tingles," she whispered.

His body tingled, too, for reasons that were less than holy.

Her next words were Latin again, so he put on his thoughtful face.

"'You must have all faith so as to remove mountains.'" She grinned. "Paul's letter to the Corinthians. I changed that one a little."

He stifled a laugh along with a twinge of sympathy for the Prioress. "Remember, no one must know I carry the feathers."

She twisted her fingers before her lips as if locking them with a key, a childish gesture that made him smile. "You have given me a gift beyond measure," she said. "How could I refuse?"

And he nearly blurted out that it was only a goose feather, don't believe, but he couldn't bear to shatter the shimmering glow of faith that surrounded her. Yet.

"Will she mind if I tell you what I pray for?"

He wanted to say don't tell me. He wanted to know nothing more of her that might grab his heart. Instead, he shrugged. "Tell me or don't. It will make no difference to God."

"That's an odd sentiment for a man who carries relics to a shrine." She licked her lips and bit her lower one, not quite sure whether to release the words. "I've told no one outside the Priory." A shy smile, wistful, broke over her face. "Of course, I've known no one outside the Priory."

Her lips parted slightly. Her blue eyes opened wide with wonder and faith. In repose, her face was plain. Ordinary. Round. The lips unbalanced. But her eyes blasted a window to her soul.

And to his.

Suddenly he wanted very much to know what she thought about in the dark lonely hours between matins and lauds when the convent was hushed and there was only God to keep you company.

"Tell me," he said, clasping both her hands in his and,

for the first time, not fearing to lose himself in her eyes. "Tell me what you want."

She moved closer, close enough that he caught the womanly scent of her and he was glad he was sitting because the smell made his knees weak. Her breasts rose and fell beneath the gray pilgrim's cloak until he could feel his body prickling with most unholy urges.

"I want to join the order," she said.

Even though he knew what she would say, her words twisted his stomach. She wanted to waste her life praying to a God who would never answer. His fingers started to curl into fists at her foolishness and crushed her fingers instead. She believed in a God who never answered prayers the way you wanted. For God's answer to her prayer was staring her in the face, though she did not know it. God's answer to her prayer was Garren.

And he had the oddest feeling of satisfaction that he would liberate her from the trap of God. Free her as he had been freed. By sad disappointments. "You're sure?" he said finally.

She tugged her fingers away and he opened his hands, suddenly aware of how tightly he held her. "Oh, yes," she said. "It's what God intends."

He stood abruptly and turned his back on those eyes. The morning sparrows chirped brightly. "How do you know what God intends?"

"You sound just like the Prioress. I just know. I feel it. I belong there. It's the only place where I..." Her voice trailed off. "It's where I belong."

Whirling back, he waved a finger in her face. "How do you know where you belong? You've never known anything else." If he took away her convent life, what would he give her in its place? He fought the wave of guilt. There must be other things a woman could do. "Maybe you would rather marry."

She sat back as if he had struck her. "I've had no thoughts of marriage."

"Most people marry."

"You haven't."

"I have nothing to offer a wife." The words tasted like sour wine.

"What about your home?"

Home. The very word hit like a fist. "My home is in the hands of the Church."

"You gave your home to the Church? When you joined the monastery?" She stood, crossing herself, and bent her knee a little in deference.

He snorted. He had given his home, his hopes, his very life to the Church. And been rewarded with betrayal.

She kept watching him, the broken-winged eyebrow raised, as if expecting him to tell the story.

He sighed. Yet another proof of saintliness he didn't need, but neither did she need the truth. He reached for her hand. "Stand up. Don't make me into something I am not."

Her blue eyes were troubled. "You are not what I thought at first."

When she first looked at him, he thought she could see right through him. But her faith blinded her. She saw a saint instead of the sinner he was. What would she do when she discovered the truth?

Garren shrugged off the thought and stuffed the feathers back into the silver case. This was all for William. William was worth anything. Garren's fingers slipped as he tried to retie the leather cord.

"Here, let me help. Tie the first knot and I'll hold my finger on it while you tie the bow." She pressed her finger on the first knot. A callused, black smudged bump decorated the middle finger of her right hand. He recognized it. The brothers who copied all day had well-developed writer's bumps. He rubbed it with his thumb. "What is this?"

She snatched her hand away and switched hands, holding the knot awkwardly with her left hand. "Nothing."

She ducked her head to hide behind her hair and it curled atop his knee, nearly covering their hands. He gathered the golden strands gently in his hand and lifted them behind her shoulder. "It looks like the hand of a copyist."

She didn't answer, but the realization chilled his bones. Where else but in a Priory's scriptorium would a copyist find a home?

Her breath trembled as he tied the knot and she slipped her finger away. "I must go now." She did not meet his gaze again. "May I have your blessing first?"

He started to say no, but she was already on her knees before him with her hands on his knees and his hands ached to touch her again. Trembling, he let them rest on her head, then leaned to press his lips against her hair.

She looked up, startled, and scampered into the trees like a wild deer.

And he sat, twirling the reliquary with the goose feathers between his fingers for a long time.

Chapter Seven

Walking back through the trees to the camp, Dominica rubbed her fingers against her scalp searching for the spot the Savior's lips had touched. He must have left a mark, seared the skin.

This was no mere man, she thought, relieved. Her reactions were not a woman's. This was a messenger of God, chosen to carry Larina's feathers.

She shook her head. It was not her place to question God's plan, but he seemed a strange choice, this man who put people before God.

She traveled beside Larina's feathers. Her shoulder blades itched, as if ready to sprout her own wings. Surely this was a sign God blessed her journey. She couldn't wait to tell Sister.

Keep God's secret, he had said. She slowed her feet, rubbing her thumb across the ink-stained writer's bump on her middle finger. She was not used to keeping secrets from Sister, except, of course, the strange feelings she had for him.

Well, there would be no more secrets to keep. She would not think of him as a man any more.

No one noticed as she returned to the clearing, where the

fire's smoke had dwindled to a black smudge as the pilgrims gathered for the day's journey. Sister held a bit of travel biscuit above Innocent's nose. He jumped on short stubby legs, begging for it.

"You should be eating that yourself," Dominica said.

Beneath the black robes, Sister was thin as a spirit, but this morning, the lines around her eyes had faded. It was as if she had become younger with each step away from the Priory.

"It's just the last bite," Sister said, waving it as Innocent jumped again and snatched it. Sister scratched behind his ear as he licked invisible crumbs from the fingers of her other hand. "Did you do your devotions, Neeca?"

She left camp to find a quiet place to listen for God's voice. Instead, she had found God's messenger. Surely asking for his help constituted a devotion to God.

Dominica nodded, not trusting words to be a secret without becoming a lie.

Sister squeezed her hand as she rose from the ground. "I feel like walking this morning."

"Just don't tire yourself."

"Good morrow, Sister." The young squire bowed before them, shoving back the blond hair that fell across his forehead. His body still carried the delicacy of childhood, Dominica thought, although his large hands and feet, like a dog's, had outgrown the rest of him. Not like The Savior, whose hands perfectly matched his strong arms and broad shoulders.

"Good morrow, young man," Sister said. "Forgive me for forgetting your name. I cannot keep so many new people in my old head."

"I am Simon, Sister," he said, looking at Dominica, his smile sweeter than his glance. "Squire to a noble knight who graciously gave me leave to make this pilgrimage."

"I am Sister Marian and this is Dominica."

He did not bow over her hand, and she had not expected that, but he seemed to speak to her chest, instead of her eyes. "And you, Dominica, where are you from?"

"I live at the Priory, too."

"Well, when danger comes, don't worry. I can protect you." He patted the hilt of his sword, then bowed. Swaggering to the head of the group, he slapped The Savior on the shoulder, as if they were longtime comrades in arms.

Dominica looked at Sister, rolling her eyes and stifling a smile.

Sister shook her head. "I guess I don't need to warn you to watch yourself with that one."

"I feel no temptation there," Dominica said. The young squire seemed no more than a boy next to The Savior, who, of course, she could never think of as a man.

Bright sun and blue sky blessed their second morning on the road. Behind her, the Widow Cropton told a long, loud tale of being set upon by robbers in the Pyrenees who were struck in the middle of their crime like Paul on the road to Damascus and knelt in the dirt to beg forgiveness and ask to join the pilgrims. Only Sister and the Physician listened intentionally, but the Widow spoke loudly enough for all to hear.

In front of her, the young married couple, Jackin and Gillian, blocked her view of The Savior and Simon. Holding hands, they walked so close no daylight glimmered between their cloaks. Once, when he thought Dominica's head was turned, the man kissed his wife on the lips.

Dominica looked away, to watch the copper, orange, brown and blue butterflies, like flying flowers, lure Innocent to the chase. How could pilgrims focus on things of the flesh when they were on a spiritual quest?

As the morning wore on, however, Dominica, too, became preoccupied with her flesh. Rocks pricked her feet through the thin leather soles with every step. The ache stretched up her calves and thighs to rest in the small of her back, making her glad Sister had remounted Roucoud. Only The Savior seemed to walk without faltering.

By the time they stopped for the midday meal, Dominica felt a martyr's pain, but instead of feeling pious, she wondered whether the Widow was right and they all should have had horses.

As the rest of the group sat to eat, she slipped away into the trees to spend a few quiet moments praying for strength, forgiveness, and protection from temptation. Kneeling beside a white-flowered hawthorn bush, she closed her eyes, inhaled the sweet scent, and listened for God's voice.

Instead, she heard a woman's giggle.

Her eyes flew open. She peered through the fragrant, thorny branches into a small clearing.

Jackin knelt astride Gillian. Beneath him, Gillian lay with her skirts up and her legs bare.

As bare as Jackin's backside.

Dominica crouched behind the thorny bush, afraid to stay, too shocked to leave, and thinking that God had a very strange way of answering prayers.

Jackin kissed his wife's lips, her eyelids, her ears and her neck. He kissed her as if he were hungry and she were food. And she kissed him back, her giggle turning to a moan.

On his knees, rocking as if in the ecstasy of prayer, he moved faster and faster, his head flung to the sky.

Gripping the branch, Dominica squeaked as a thorn poked her finger. Her hand slipped and the branches clattered. Jackin and Gillian didn't hear. Their world was no larger than the two of them.

Finally, he cried out and collapsed over her.

In the quiet that followed, Dominica held her breath, sure

now he would turn and see her watching. Instead, he covered Gillian's face with kisses again, nuzzling her neck, whispering to her until she chuckled.

Dominica's heart thumped in her ears.

"Hold!"

A peasant waving a rusty sickle stepped out from behind a tree on the other side of the clearing. Tall, with scraggly black hair and watery eyes, he looked as if he hadn't eaten in a long time. He poked Jackin's back with the sickle. "Give me your money."

Jackin's face went slack and his buttocks tight.

Dominica's blood pounded in her head. *Oh God, send Garren. Quickly.*

"We are poor pilgrims," Jackin said, in a voice tight as his buttocks. "We have nothing to steal."

Gillian, skirts bunched at her waist, clutched her husband's elbow. The thief glanced at her, tongue twitching at the corner of his mouth. Then he shook his head. In two steps, he reached Jackin, pulling his head back and holding the rusty sickle under his chin like a drunken barber.

Dominica swallowed in sympathy. The blade would not cut cleanly.

Hurry, God.

"You've something to spare. I know the saint expects an offering," he said, rubbing the curved blade over the bobbing apple at Jackin's throat. Knobby bones stuck out on either side of the serf's wrist. "Come on. Off her now."

Stumbling, Jackin stood, his breeches hobbling his ankles. Between his legs hung what looked like a small, damp sausage.

Gillian rolled away, frantically pulling her skirts to her ankles. "Please, don't hurt him."

Her cry grabbed Dominica's chest. If God had not sent Garren, he must mean for her to do something.

She stood, the earth soft beneath her feet, and walked around the bush, trying to stride boldly like Simon. Thorns clawed her cloak. Ignoring the ripping sound, she felt a tug and realized the bush held her fast. She squared her shoulders, hoping the thief wouldn't know she was trapped.

"Stop," she said.

All three turned.

Her voice fluttered in her throat and came out with a squeak. "If you kill him, God will send his soul straight to heaven and yours to hell. *Deus misereatur.*"

"What?" The thief stared at Dominica with the bug-eyes of a trapped badger.

"He travels under God's protection." She nodded at Jackin, keeping her eyes firmly above his waist. "Show him your *testimonales.*"

Sickle still at his throat, Jackin waved his hands helplessly toward his crumpled garment.

The thief let go of Jackin and grabbed Gillian around the neck, letting the sickle hover at her neck. Lines of confusion scored his brow. He watched Jackin's every move as he opened the drawstring of his bag and pawed inside, searching with shaking fingers.

Dominica leaned forward, testing the hawthorn's hold. Then she tugged. The cloak did not budge.

Jackin finally pulled out the rolled scroll and waved it at in the thief's face. "Here. Look."

Behind them, Dominica saw Garren moving silently through the trees, Simon at his side. *Deo gratias,* she said to herself.

The thief peered over Gillian's shoulder at the scroll. "What does it say?"

Behind him, Garren stepped forward, touching the tip of his sword to the man's back. "Put the weapon down. Now."

Just in time, God, she thought. All the breath whooshed from her chest.

Beside Garren, Simon snickered. Jackin dropped the scroll and reached for his pants.

The thief pulled Gillian's head back. "Don't try anything or I'll cut her throat."

"The lady was right," Garren said, his voice as steady as his sword arm. "We are pilgrims. Entitled to protection."

The thief licked his lips, but kept his sickle at Gillian's throat. "You can pay for your protection. Give me some coin or I'll cut her throat."

Garren lifted his sword from the man's back to the dirty skin behind his ear. "Let her go and I will let you go. That is more payment than you deserve."

"There are two of us," Simon said, bouncing on the balls of his feet. "We can take him."

Garren ignored him, keeping his eyes on the thief. "Do you want to test your skills against a man who's been paid to kill?"

Dominica shuddered at the words. Paid to kill. But he was not paid to save the Earl's life.

At the tip of The Savior's sword, the thief was forced to watch Simon waving his sword before him and unable to see the threat behind him. "How do I know you won't kill me anyway?"

"You can believe him," Dominica said. "The man behind you is a messenger of God."

His bug-eyes swiveled to the limit of his lids, trying to look behind him.

"And before I let you go, I'll give you some food." The Savior held out the package over the man's shoulder, who sniffed it as if he were Innocent. "Come on. Let her go."

"Give me the food first."

He pitched it toward the trees at the edge of the clearing. "Now go pick it up and run before I change my mind."

"Bless you for a man of God's kindness." The thief scurried over to the package, snatched it up, and disappeared into the trees.

The Savior jerked his head at Simon. "Make sure he doesn't come back."

Simon strode off, smiling.

"And don't hurt him," Garren called over his shoulder.

Knees too shaky to hold her, Dominica sank to the ground as Gillian and Jackin fell into each other's arms. Rocking together, they did not look up until The Savior growled at them. "And you two. Satisfy your desires in the dark when we have a guard posted."

He stepped toward her and she turned away, tugging on her cloak, trying to get free before he reached her. The hawthorns held fast.

Kneeling beside her, he put his arm around her shoulders. For a moment, she wanted to lean on him and bury her head against his chest.

"Are you all right, Neeca?"

The sound of her childish name on his lips nearly made her cry. Only Sister, who loved her better than anyone except God, had ever called her that. She shook off the thought, pushing herself up to stand. "Yes, of course," she said, but her heart still thumped in her chest and the thought of Jackin and Gillian holding each other made her cheeks hot. She would say an extra prayer tonight.

When he stood, he towered over her. "Don't ever do that again."

"Do what?"

"Brave a man who holds a weapon."

She twisted around, yanking on her cloak again. It gave way, shredding into little fluttering banners along the hem.

She faced him again. "God was slow in sending you. I had to do something."

"God is a less than trustworthy messenger. You should have come to get me. It was chance that I discovered in time that all three of you were missing."

"That was not chance. That was God." She watched his stern lips fight the deep green relief in his eyes. "You called me Neeca. How did you know that name?"

He blinked. "Did I? I don't know. I must have heard Sister Marian call you that." Stepping back, he yelled to Jackin and Gillian, still rocking together. "Come on. All of you. Simon, come back."

He herded them ahead of him like sheep. "Don't ever get out of sight of the group again."

She kept her lips closed. She was no braver than she needed to be, but she had to write, to pray, to attend to her needs. She would be out of sight whenever she needed. He might be God's messenger, but Garren was beginning to try her patience.

And the feelings coursing through her when he touched her were beginning to frighten her.

Day Two

Watching God's glorious sunrise beneath the whispering leaves of his forest chapel, Dominica wondered what she could possibly write about yesterday.

Innocent curled at her feet, a cozy, warm weight across her toes. She flipped the feathered end of the quill across her nose. She had told no one about the feathers. Could she write about them? No, writing would be worse than telling. Written words did not float away on the air.

Fighting her thoughts of the feathers was the memory of Jackin and Gillian, rocking together, wrapped in their own world.

The joy they took in each other frightened her. What would it be like, to have that kind of joy on earth? How could God compete with such ecstasy?

She shook her head, wishing she could shake off the idea, but as she thought of Jackin and Gillian she felt Garren's hands comforting her. Heard Garren's voice call her Neeca.

Garren. She could not think of him as The Savior now. He was too big, too close, too real. Curly brown hair. Leaf-green eyes. Broad shoulders. Large hands.

She told him she had not thought of marriage. That was a lie. She had not known many men. The Prior. Lord William. The village boys.

Lord Richard.

Her quill shook.

They had talked of marrying her to Peter, the smith's son, who had cut off his right thumb with an axe. He was dull-witted, but pleasant enough, and no dirtier than most. The earth floor of the cottage was no harder than her Priory bed and a wife's work could be no more difficult than caring for a score of Sisters.

But there would be no words in his cottage.

She had begged them not to send her where there were no words. So the Prioress had agreed and Peter had married the carpenter's daughter instead and they had three children already.

It is better to marry than to burn.

She had always thought Saint Paul meant to burn in hell, but her skin caught fire when Garren touched her. Was that the feeling that drove Jackin and Gillian to mate in the middle of the day? If she had married, would she have those feelings?

She shook her head. God intended her to copy His words, not to succumb to the temptations of the flesh. It was instructive to see how tempting they could be, but that was not her destiny. This trip would prove it. To God. To the Prioress.

To herself.

Cool breeze, she wrote. *Many sparrows.*

Innocent's happy tail banged against her leg, announcing a visitor. Dominica looked up.

"Excuse me." Gillian stood before her, fully covered now. Dominica had never seen the woman without her husband. She had round cheeks and a small nose and little brown eyes that nearly disappeared when she smiled. She was not smiling now.

"I didn't mean to disturb your meditations. But I told Jackin I had to find you and apologize for what you seen yesterday. I know it's a sin and all to enjoy it so much and it's not right for a convent girl to see, but sometimes, the heat just comes over us and we have to lie together."

Dominica hoped the leaves' shadows hid her blush. "Well, thank you. It's all right. What I mean is, it's true I had never seen, seen..." She did not know a word that would finish the sentence.

Gillian looked down at Dominica's quill and paper and her eyes and mouth formed perfect *O*s. "You can write."

"Yes," Dominica said, forbidden pride streaking through her.

"Will you write something for me?"

"Sister Marian writes much better than I do. She is in charge of all the copying at the Priory."

Gillian ducked her head. Bright pink spread from her round cheeks to her ears. "This isn't something I could ask a nun to write."

A quiver of interest tickled her fingers. "Well, I'm almost a nun. I mean, I hope to be."

"Oh, it's nothing bad," Gillian said. "It's just, it has to do with...what you've already seen. Please."

What could Gillian possibly want to write about that? And what words did Dominica know that would describe it? But her writing was a gift from God. "I would, but this is all I have to write on," she said, turning over the parchment scrap that would have to last the whole of her journey.

Gillian's eyes widened at the sight of the letters trooping across the page, then narrowed, as if trying to understand them. "You could buy some more. I could pay, if it isn't too much."

The woman sat next to her on the log and gripped the hand without the quill before she could answer. "It's a message to the Blessed Larina, you see," she whispered, "so she will know why we've come. I don't want to talk about it in front of a priest. I mean, I pray and all, but I thought if you could write it down, it would be clearer to her. I don't want to come all this way and have her misunderstand."

"She will understand what is in your heart if you pray," Dominica said.

"But sometimes when I am in confession the priest tells me I don't say the words clear enough for God, and I don't know Latin and all. I am afraid that when I get there I will forget something or say it wrong. And this is too important."

A flash of anger at the nameless priest shot through her. This was why she wanted to write the Bible in the common tongue. So a woman like Gillian would never be ashamed to talk to God. She squeezed her fingers. "Of course, I'll do it. We will find a parchment seller somewhere."

"Oh, thank you. Thank you. If you write the words, I know they will come true."

She watched Gillian go and stared at the words she had written on her scrap of parchment.

Thief. Hungry. Love. Neeca.

Chapter Eight

"You should have seen him," Simon said to the Miller brothers and scar-faced Ralf, as Dominica picked up a biscuit and perched on the log beside him. She pretended to listen, looking for Garren.

The others were scattered around the clearing. Gillian, sitting next to Jackin, smiled at her. Daylight shone between them this morning, but each ate with one hand, their fingers laced together, as if each did not exist without the touch of the other.

Swallowing his mouthful of bread, Simon waved his hands, sculpting his foe. "A tall man. Brawny. This big. Holding a blade sharp as a Saracen's."

Tall, Dominica remembered, but scrawny as a starved chicken. "Actually, Simon, all he had was a rusty sickle."

He frowned at her, leaning toward the Miller brothers. "And there stood Jackin, pants around his ankles..."

Elbows on their knees, the brothers stopped eating, waiting for his next words. Even Innocent cocked his head, as if listening with his good ear.

Simon snickered through his nose, "...his shrunken thing hiding behind his balls for fear it would be cut off."

Howling, both brothers slapped their thighs. The younger

one, whooping, fell backwards off the log. Ralf's barking laugh dissolved into a hacking cough.

Jackin lifted his head at the laughter. Gillian patted his hand. Maybe they cared for each other overmuch, she thought, but Simon cared for no one at all. She hoped they could not hear his words. It was not right to make fun of something that should be as private as a prayer.

"Of course," Simon continued, "I confronted the serf and demanded he unhand him. Naturally, he quaked in fear. The peasant had no place holding a weapon against me, though it was a sharp blade, sharp enough to cut my hair. And meanwhile," another laughing snort seized him, "there stands Jackin, his member limp as melted—"

"Simon." Garren's voice sliced Simon's sentence. His shadow fell across her fingers. She shivered, as if his fingers, instead of his shadow, touched her.

Simon ducked his head as if he were a turtle retreating to his shell. "Sir."

"Have you no better training in how to converse before a lady?"

Dominica scratched Innocent's ear and watched a small black ant in the grass hoisting a fallen crumb from Simon's bread. Garren, she thought, smiling, needed training in the art of conversation as well.

Red splotches stained Simon's baby-smooth cheeks. "But she was there, she saw it all."

"If she saw it, there is no need for her to hear it as well." Garren kept his eyes on Simon, never looking at her. "Particularly as you embellish it."

Simon slumped at the reproof as Sister walked toward them, steps slower than yesterday. Dominica prayed briefly that she had not been near enough to hear Simon's story. Dominica had not worried her with the whole truth. The thief was bad enough.

Garren clasped the young squire's shoulder. "Simon, guard the rear today. Make sure everyone stays together. You can keep watch for Saracen steel."

Beneath the pressure of Garren's hand, Simon squared his shoulders. "Yes, sir."

"Gather your things. We'll be leaving soon," Garren called out, as the Miller brothers and Ralf slunk away. At least they would not laugh at Jackin again, Dominica thought, satisfied.

Sister joined them as Simon rose, gobbling the last of his bread. "Simon," she said, "I noticed yesterday you did not know all the words to the third verse of 'The Song of Larina.' I'll be riding Roucoud today. Walk beside me and I shall teach you." She smiled, sweetly as ever, but Dominica recognized the look in her eyes. Usually, it preceded twenty Hail Marys.

"Yes, Sister. Just let me gather my things." His shoulders sagged as he walked away.

"He's young," Sister said, shaking her head, and turning the Hail Mary eyes on Dominica. "But I think you did not tell me everything about yesterday."

"I did not want you to worry." She covered Sister's cold fingers with hers. "Just as you did not want me to worry so you did not tell me how tired you are. From now on, you will ride."

"I'll be fine. Don't worry about me. Now turn around, let me see your cloak." She picked at the fluttering shreds left by the hawthorn bush. "I'll mend it for you this evening," she said, patting Dominica's arm. "Did you get enough to eat? Did you say your morning prayers, Neeca?"

Neeca. At the sound, she could feel Garren's hands on her shoulders again. "Sister, did you use that name in front of Garren?" His name quivered in her mouth.

"Is it Garren now instead of The Savior?" Troubled lines

scored the pale skin between Sister's eyebrows like the knife rules on parchment. "Neeca, he may not be what you think. He is a soldier, not a saint."

Dominica nodded. "Did you know he nearly took his vows?"

Sister's eyes widened in surprise. "He told you that?"

He told me he carries Larina's feathers, she wanted to say, but she had promised. "Yes, but you haven't told me the answer to my question. Did he hear you call me Neeca?"

Sister blinked, thinking. "I guess he did. Why?"

"He called me that." The memory of her special name in his voice, rough, yet soft, wrapped around her like a blanket. Special. Private. Like God's voice, a sign of favor for her plan.

Yet instead of thinking holy thoughts, she thought of Garren's hands touching her. Strong. Gentle. And instead of seeing poor Jackin over his shoulder, she wondered what Garren would look like naked. Somehow, she did not think his member would melt like candle wax.

Sister watched her with a puzzled frown. Dominica hoped her jumbled feelings didn't show. Perhaps the encounter with the thief had disturbed her more than she thought. Time alone would quiet her thoughts. "I'm going to start walking. I won't go too far."

"But the thieves—"

"Don't worry." Picking up a stick, Dominica flung it as far as she could. Innocent ran after it, and she followed, the thump of her staff a comfort.

The road was straight and smooth. Sunlit green meadows stretched on either side, full of larks and free of hiding places. Yesterday's aches blew away in the sweet air.

Don't get out of sight of the group, he had said. She didn't, though she was safely out of sound of it. When she finally sat to wait for them, the band was still in sight, but small, like the figures painted on the church ceiling.

She out-walked the worry in Sister's voice and the boredom of the Widow's endless stories, but she could not walk away from her feelings about him. She had to be able to look at him without blushing. Without thinking sinful thoughts.

Looking at the daisies, she hugged Innocent. "What is God trying to tell me?" she whispered into his ear.

One of the tiny figures strode toward her a few moments later. It was an angry stride. She stood, waiting for him to come, filling her mind with holy thoughts.

"I told you yesterday not to get out of sight." Garren took her arm as if she were still walking and he wanted to stop her. His lips thinned and he breathed heavily, angry, she thought, for such a short walk could not have winded him.

"There are no thieves here." His hand on her bare arm made her think of Jackin and Gillian, skin to skin. She had thought the halo of his holiness touched her. Now, she was not sure.

"None you can see." He dropped her arm. "Did Simon's story upset you? Is that why you ran?"

She couldn't tell him that it was not Simon's story, but her own thoughts that made her leave. "He laughed at them. At something that should be private."

He started walking and she fell into step beside him. The harmonies of the singing brothers floated faintly behind them. Their staves thumped companionably in the dirt.

"You saw something private yesterday," he said.

She searched the fields for the distraction of a butterfly, but they all seemed to be fluttering in her stomach. She shrugged, trying to slough off the feeling, the terrible awareness of him beside her. She picked up a stick and hurled it as far as she could. Innocent scampered after it, scattering a flock of birds in the meadow. "'Tis something dogs do."

She had seen them, once. Found Innocent humping Sister Margaret's fluffy white dog beneath shaking purple blossoms on the thyme bush. Even after Dominica separated them, the dog mounted her again and again, urgent and driven, but it was not like yesterday. Dogs did not cling with such longing that surely they would die if parted.

Garren spoke softly, but his eyes darkened to evergreen. "Did what you saw distress you?"

He mustn't know how much. "I thought you told Simon this was not a topic appropriate for ladies." She shrugged, as if she saw naked couples every day. "Jackin and Gillian enjoy each other overmuch."

"Overmuch?" A smile threatening to crack his face open.

"'Tis a sin to take excessive pleasure in the flesh."

"And you recognized excessive pleasure?" Laughter lurked in his voice.

Her cheeks burned. Of course she couldn't recognize excessive pleasure. But that led to a frightening thought. What if the delirium she witnessed was not unusual? What if all lovemaking were like that? "Saint Augustine was quite clear on this point."

His jaw dropped out of a smile. "What do you know of Saint Augustine?"

She knew she had used sixty-two goose quills in one day, painstakingly copying a section of *The City of God,* but she was not ready yet to share the secret of her writing. "I told you I want to join the order. As a nun, I will need to know the doctrines of all the great Church fathers."

"And the Church fathers disapprove of taking pleasure in joining?"

"Of course they do." Only a heretic would question Saint Augustine. And God would not have entrusted Larina's feathers to a heretic. *He may not be everything you think.* Suddenly all the warmth drained from her cheeks. "I understand now. God sent you to test my knowledge of doctrine. He wants to be sure I am worthy to take the vows. I should have expected this." She squared her shoulders beneath the heavy cloak and rested her clasped hands on her stomach as Mother Julian always did. "I am ready. Test me."

No longer softened by amusement, the lines dug deeper around Garren's mouth. "All right," he said. "Explain the doctrine. Tell me what is wrong with a man and a woman enjoying each other."

His breath seemed a little unsteady. Shaken to be discovered, no doubt, she thought. God did not realize she would be so clever as to discover His plan.

Light air lifted a strand of her hair to tickle her ear. "Very well," she said.

She took a deep breath, imagining herself safely draped in her black habit. Beneath the weight of her cloak, dampness pooled under her arms. This seemed to be a very intimate topic to discuss with a man, even for the sake of doctrine.

"Let me lay out the argument. 'Nothing is so much to be shunned as sexual relations.' Saint Augustine said." She wished she could write it down. Writing let you think of the exact word. "God's only reason for creating the act between men and women is so that the woman may conceive."

His gaze held hers like a relentless inquisitor. "How do you know that?"

"Everyone knows that. The only reason for man and woman to join is to create a child."

"The only reason?" Other reasons danced in his green eyes. Reasons that would hold all the ecstasy that Jackin and Gillian felt.

"The only reason," she said, firmly. She struggled to concentrate. "So if they join for selfish pleasure, instead of only to reproduce, the joining for pleasure, that is a sin." Her tongue tangled in her mouth. This had sounded much simpler when she learned it.

"Why does God intend for us to be miserable?"

"Abstaining from carnal relations should make us joyful. God intends us to be happy in heaven, instead of here in the temporary illusion of the earth."

"Why is it sinful to enjoy the earth God created for us?" His eyes challenged her.

She knew what he said was not right, but she couldn't figure out why. She looked over her shoulder for the comfort of Sister's face, but they had walked over a small rise and the others were out of sight. "You are trying to trick me."

"Did you enjoy the sunrise this morning?"

"It was beautiful."

"An earthly creation of God. And what about this flower?" He bent over as if to break off the yellow and white daisy, but instead, knelt in the dust, tugging her to her knees beside him. Then holding it under her nose. "Do you enjoy its scent?"

She closed her eyes and breathed the brisk scent until she was dizzy with it. He drew her hand toward him and trailed his fingertips over the blue veins of her wrist and up to the bend in her elbow. "And when I do this, isn't the feeling pleasurable?"

His fingers on her skin seemed to have the odd effect of speeding up her heartbeat. "Yes, but—"

"How can that feeling be anything but a gift from God?" He turned her arm over and stroked her bare skin until her entire arm tingled and when he took his hand away, her skin felt cold as an empty room.

She traced her own fingers up and down her arm, as lightly as he had done.

He shook his head. "It won't feel the same."

"No. It doesn't," she admitted.

He lifted his head and bared his right arm, fist clenched as if ready for the barber's bleeding. Deep brown curls ran thick across his arm. "Touch me. You'll feel something different."

Her fingers tingled as if she were about to handle the sacred feathers. She brushed a fingertip over the fine hairs, not daring to touch his skin.

He gasped. Uncurling his fist, he stretched his fingers toward her. She stroked the lines that crossed his palms, wishing, for a moment, that his blunt fingers would close over hers, tightly as yesterday.

He pulled his arm away and she gasped in relief. In disappointment. Her breath came strong, quick, and fast.

He gripped her with his gaze. "You see what joy two people can make together, Neeca?"

Behind them over the rise, she heard the Widow bleating to the Physician. "And the man threw away his crutch and ran, not walked, ran, I tell you. As God is my witness. I saw it. He kissed the bone of the little finger of Saint James and the next moment, he was cured."

Miracles, she remembered. Miracles were beyond theology. She stepped away from him. "You cannot fool me with false logic. *Fides quaerens intellectum.*" Her voice quivered.

"Latin again?"

"You didn't spend enough time in the monastery studying Saint Augustine. It means 'faith before understanding.'"

"I learned all the Latin I need. *Carpe diem.*"

"Seize the day?"

"It's the only thing God cannot take away." His fingers

brushed her cheek. ''Seize today, Neeca. There may not be a tomorrow.''

She shivered at his touch, afraid to ask whether she had passed or failed the test.

Chapter Nine

For Garren, there was a tomorrow. While God snatched away those dearest to him, between a bitter past and an empty future, He allowed Garren an eternal today.

He inhaled the taste of sunshine and wondered how best to seize it.

The girl, frightened, avoided him. He regretted scaring her. He intended only to open her eyes to the world as it is. Yet stubbornly insisting he came of God, she retreated, clinging to the words of that reformed reprobate Augustine. Garren was no scholar, but he knew the stories about Augustine. Before he converted, the man succumbed to a lifetime of temptation.

And now she felt it. He heard the catch in her throat at his touch, felt the flutter of her pulse matching his. Oh, yes, she was tempted and that scared her. A tiny crack in her wall of innocence.

But it cracked her trust, as well, trust he needed not as a man of God, but as a man. Better not to rush her, he thought, looking over his shoulder to find her in the group.

She walked, dutifully, beside Roucoud, who carried Sister. Behind them, the Miller brothers snapped at each other. Garren sighed. When he agreed to lead them, he thought only of food, shelter and safety. That was enough for soldiers. It was not enough for pilgrims, despite the Church's strictures against comfort on the journey. After three nights, they needed a bed with a roof and a meal that wasn't cold. Perhaps Exeter's comforts would stop the Miller brothers squabbling and give the lusty couple some privacy and let Sister Marian regain her strength.

If the monastery had no beds left for pilgrims, their keep would fall to him, unless they begged for alms. Food and beds in an inn would total more than a day's pay. But of course, no one paid him now. The only coin he had was William's.

No matter how futile the pilgrimage, he had promised William. It was a small enough gift for all William had given him. He would repay any coin he spent. Through Dominica, if necessary.

The thought of her nudged his loins. Foolish, brave girl. When he saw her caught between the sickle and the half-naked couple, he wanted to swive her as well as save her. Of course, he had never thought he would find the task unpleasant. Only the pain of its aftermath.

Slow down, he thought. We have days to go. Let her come to you next time. She would.

The sun still climbed when they reached Exeter. It was the Feast of Corpus Christi. Rolling wooden platforms littered dusty streets, clogged with happy people who would do no work this day. Instead, they would move from wagon to wagon, each one a stage for a guild to present its own retelling of the stories of God.

The excitement gave them new energy. Before he let them scatter, he gave strict instructions to reconvene in front of the Cathedral by vespers.

Jackin and Gillian vanished first. The Miller brothers set out to find the sign with a wine barrel. Ralf disappeared into his own underworld. The Widow and the Physician wandered off to watch the plays together, which he retold into her good ear. Simon begged for leave to ride Roucoud, and Garren relented. The horse needed a good workout.

Only Sister Marian and Dominica were left.

Let her come to you, he reminded himself, feigning fascination with a wagon draped with a flag featuring a large fish. Around him, a crowd gathered for the next performance.

Sister and Dominica whispered to each other, each one stealing a glance at him. When Dominica crept close, he gave her a smile of deliberate surprise.

"Sister said I might watch the plays with you while she goes to the monastery to beg our beds. If it is all right. If you are not doing something else."

"Certainly. Nothing would please me more." Relief, stronger than expected, washed through him.

Sister, holding the dog, saw his nod. She waved, hesitantly, and walked slowly toward St. Nicholas.

They watched a huge whale, concealing three fishmongers, swallow a hapless Jonah. She laughed with the crowd, her eyes wide with wonder, as if she were trying to inhale every sight, sound and smell.

"Have you never seen a miracle play?" he asked, wishing for a moment that she wanted to see him instead of just the plays.

Her happy dimple flashed. "At the Priory, we celebrate the feast of Corpus Christi a little differently."

A house of chanting women circumscribed by a wall and a gate. Untouched. Protected. He shrugged his shoulders to shake the stain of the world that clung to him, that would sully the pure, clear pool of her life.

"How did you come to be raised there?" he asked. Her story, he guessed, would differ from the Prioress's.

"God left me there."

"God Himself?" This woman knew God's first name, he thought, amazed at her conviction that the Almighty personally managed her life.

The happy glow in her eyes stabbed him. "God arranges all things. He left me at the gate like an offering of apples." She puffed out her cheeks and held her arms in a round circle. "Don't I look like an apple?"

He must have looked startled, for she dissolved in giggles, happy and carefree and windblown and he wanted to touch her and hug her and kiss her funny nose for reasons that had nothing to do with the Prioress and everything to do with her.

Slow, he reminded himself, keeping his arms at his sides. He fabricated a frown, as if considering her question. "An apple? No. More like a plum."

She doubled over with glee, her laughter drowned in the applause from the crowd as Jonah and the Great Fish bowed. The little bow of her lip was uneven and he stared at it so long and hard his lips could feel hers beneath him.

He let his hand hover at the base of her back as he led her through the crowded streets. He bought two chewet pies from a street seller for lunch, holding them out of reach of an aggressive goose, and gulped his in two bites.

Dominica nibbled the pastry, delicately, without biting into the filling.

"Don't you like it?"

"We eat little meat at the Priory. I am not accustomed to the taste."

The goose, honking, nipped at Dominica's cloak. Garren waved him off, and she squealed, wolfing the pie down. The goose nipped at her fingers and she dropped the last bite.

The goose lunged for it, leaving a shower of white feathers in the dirt as he waddled off in triumph.

She picked up a piece of goose down. "They look very much like the Blessed Larina's feathers, do they not?" Dominica said.

He nodded, the reliquary case weighing on his neck as well as his mind, hoping she would never find out how much alike they were. "It is amazing how little difference there is between the feathers of a goose and the feathers of a Saint."

"There is little, sometimes, that keeps us from being as good as we might be. It should teach us to be compassionate to those who have fallen."

To sinners like me, he thought, but he knew there would be no forgiveness for the sin he would commit.

Late in the afternoon, the western front of Exeter's golden cathedral rose before them. Scaffolding covered the facade, still under construction, a new monument to the current bishop's ambition. The stonemasons' tools lay abandoned for the day. The arched door was crowned by a row of statues of saints, some finished, some still struggling to emerge from the stone. Above the door a vast hole yawned empty, waiting for its stained glass.

In front of the cathedral, another performance began. Dominica's eyes widened in wonder at the man dressed as God. Towering uncertainly on stilts hidden beneath a long, white robe, he wore a blond wig and a gold mask. At his feet, a horned Satan fought a lively battle for the soul of a cowering sinner.

She tugged at Garren's sleeve. "That's not in the Bible."

"Of course it is." He wondered why he argued. He had left the Church because the God they worshipped seemed less authentic than the man on stilts.

God now gripped the Devil in a knee lock, whacking his padded bottom with a long-handled paddle. The crowd roared.

"Two pence on the Devil," a drunken bowman yelled.

"No," she insisted, her voice Priory-still. "It isn't."

Garren scanned the laughing crowd, hoping none of them heard her blasphemy. "What do you mean it isn't in the Bible?"

She took his measure in a silent, defiant glance, eyeing him warily before she leaned over, her lips brushing his temple. "I've read it."

Her whisper roared loud as the crowd's laughter in his ears. Stunned, he couldn't speak. He knew she wrote and read a little. The bump on her finger told him that. But the Bible was written in Latin. Only the Church's chosen could read and interpret it. Though the nuns raised her, there was no reason to teach Latin to a poor orphan. "You read Latin?"

"Yes." She nodded, transformed by square, stubborn shoulders. "And I write it, too."

And he knew the trust it took to say the words aloud.

He rested his hand on her back, steering her away from the laughing crowd and into the cool quiet of the half-built cathedral, where no one but God would hear her sacrilege. The west nave, under construction, would nearly double the size of the church. Inside, columns grew from the floor, arching into a roofless ceiling like a grove of trees tall enough to reach heaven. Tall enough that God might be watching from the clouds, ready to strike him dead for impersonating a holy man.

Her echoing steps halted. She looked skyward, her braid swinging free away from her back. "The Castle and the Priory and the village could all fit inside. This truly is God's house."

To Garren's eye, it was carved and gilded for a dead bishop instead of a living God. The late bishop lay entombed to the left of the high altar. He wondered what poor fools, like his family, gave their life's wealth for the bishop's greater glory in death.

But as the waning golden sunlight poured through the huge hole still unstained by colored glass, it shimmered around Dominica as if she were an earthly angel. And he wanted to believe all over again.

He took her fingers, gently, and led her to the steps beneath the arch of a carved wooden screen that walled off the Quire in the center of the church. Rubbing his thumb over the little bump on her middle finger, he sat next to her, waiting.

"Now, tell me everything, Neeca," he said, finally, not sure he was ready to hear.

Worry lines furrowed her brow. "Is this another test?"

Yes, he thought, one I must not fail. "There is no right answer but the truth."

"I believe you." The eyebrow like a broken wing looked poised for flight. "Well, you know the Readingtons support the work of the Priory."

"Of course." William's prize possession, clutched all the way across France, was his father's psalter, the work of the Priory's nuns.

"Sister Marian is our chantress, responsible for the copying and the singing. She always took special care of me and let me sit at her knee when she copied. She taught me my letters with leftover ink and parchment scraps." Dominica giggled, looking over her shoulder when the echo bounced off the stone floor. "I think she decided I would never be a singer."

He smiled, relishing the trusting feel of her fingers. Even though he had neither the patience nor the talent for it, he respected the brothers who produced beautiful and lasting testaments.

"I love the smell of the ink, the feel of the quill, the way

God's glory is revealed when the page is complete. That is what I want to do with my life.'' Lit with joy, her face needed no sunlight.

No wonder she had no thought of marriage. Only a nun would be allowed to spend her days copying sacred texts.

She ducked her head closer and a stray hair tickled his nose. It smelled of tiny violets. ''I copied some of Saint Augustine's *City of God*. And there is a page of Matthew in our library that I copied myself, even the capital with red and gold. Sister put on the gesso to make the pattern, but I laid on the gold leaf and polished it.''

She had a mite of pride about her talent, he noticed, grinning. Barely enough to make a sin with. ''Which part of Matthew?'' he said, more interested in watching her lips move than in the Bible verse.

'''Ask and it shall be given to you; seek and ye shall find; knock and it shall be opened to you.' I will show it to you so you can read it and see what a good job I do.''

Now, he knew he too must confess. ''Even at the monastery, I left Latin to others.''

She smiled in delight at his words. ''That is just the reason I want to copy it into the common tongue.''

''English?''

Cold lightning shot through him as she nodded, smiling.

Even he could read such a Bible, he who could read English only slightly better than Latin, which was to say, not at all. It could be spoken, could be quoted, would belong to the people, not just to the Church.

He wondered what William, clutching his psalter in a death grip, would think.

''The Prioress knows this?'' he asked.

''She disapproves.''

Of course she does, he thought. Such heresy might

threaten the Priory's very existence. That's why she was willing to jeopardize Dominica's immortal soul.

She squeezed his fingers. "But even the Sisters slur through words at service because they know them by rote. I want to make them real, so everyone can understand. Do you…" she closed her eyes and then opened them to look directly into his. "Do you think it is wrong?"

Her blue, bottomless eyes blazed with the fervor he remembered from the first time he'd seen her. Until now, he thought of her as a bird, waiting for his touch to free her from the Church's cage so she could soar, joyous, into the real world.

Now, instead of freeing her, he realized that what he planned would make everything she cared about lost to her forever. He was not brave enough to do that yet. Even for William.

"I think that if you want to copy the Scriptures into English, that is what you should do."

"You are a strange man of God. Sister Marian has said I must never speak of it. Will you help me?"

"How could I help?"

"Tell the Prioress it is all right. When we return. Maybe she will listen to you, since you are so close to God."

He floundered, wanting, for a strange moment, the help of a higher power. "Perhaps we should leave this in the hands of the Blessed Larina."

Her smile glowed with faith. "That is why I am on pilgrimage. I know Larina will help. Surely God will not condemn me for spreading His word."

His chest ached as if with an axe blow at her misguided belief that God sat on her shoulder and that with his words, she could change the world. He cupped her soft, warm cheek in his palm. "You are more holy than I shall ever hope to be. Any God who would condemn you deserves no allegiance.''

But the God he knew deserved no more allegiance than the stonemason wearing the fake beard. By the end of this journey, when she learned where her faith had led her, she would be as bitter and as lonely as he. No God worth worshipping would let this happen.

As he looked into her eyes, deep blue with trust, he had a crazy desire to shield her shining flame of faith from the world's cold winds.

Instead, he would be the one to blow it out.

And he realized, suddenly, that he could not blame God for his own sins.

Richard held the clove-studded orange close to his nose as he walked into William's room for his daily duty visit. Today, he thought, he would ask about the message. The question had itched at his bowels for days.

William's skin sank into a skull that had lost chunks of shining gold hair. His pale hands curled into scaly claws, just as the Italian had promised and even the pomander could not drown the stench.

He shuddered. Niccolo had warned him, but it was taking longer than he thought. He would have to bathe the solar in rosewater before he moved in. ''And how are you feeling today?''

''Don't hover waiting for my death, brother. It does not become you.''

''I only seek to have you free of pain.''

''And yourself free to be heir.''

Gasping for a clean breath, Richard turned to the window. In the west meadow, sweating serfs scythed the new hay. The collier's wench, her neckline open to cool her generous breasts, carried ale to her husband in the field. She'd given

herself away before. Like the women his father had liked.
Certainly she was not pure when she married, like his
mother. Yes, his father would have liked her. Maybe he
would summon her tonight. "The weather has been fine,
William. Our little pilgrim band should be nearly to Exeter
with your message."

William closed his eyes. Closed him out.

"What did you write, William?"

"Naught of interest."

"Strange. That's what the mercenary said."

"He's not a mercenary."

Defending him. Always defending this man who was not
even related by blood. He was the one who shared their
father's seed, not that nameless, homeless knight. "He fights
for money. He even goes on pilgrimage for pay. What else
would you call him?" He snickered. "Savior, perhaps?"

"I call him more a brother than you."

Richard still heard his father's scorn in William's voice.
Why aren't you more like your brother? "What else do you
think he will save you from? Me?"

"It's too late for that."

Richard gritted his teeth in the long, hollow silence. So
William knew. Well, what of it, now?

William stared at him, eyes bright with mad fever. "You
want to know what the message says? Well, I'll tell you."
He struggled to raise himself on his elbows. Richard backed
toward the door, afraid he might develop a madman's
strength. "It tells the priest at the shrine that if I die, it is
by your hand and to hang you so God can send you straight
to Hell."

Richard's fingers suddenly felt numb as William's. He
sagged against the door. He should have known. He should
have stopped them before they walked over the first rise. If

that message reached the shrine, all his plans were for naught. "It says what?"

"You and your Italian. You thought I wouldn't know and I didn't until too late."

"Does Garren know?"

"Isn't it enough that God knows?"

"Of course he doesn't know." Richard spoke to himself, pushing himself upright again. No need to talk to William now. William might as well be dead. "If Garren knew he would have killed me already. And since all these fools think Garren is some holy man, they'd hang me themselves if he told them to." He paced, trying to think. "But you can scarcely hold a spoon." He paced, trying to think. "You didn't write it. You had a scribe. Who was it?"

William made a small noise. A laugh.

Richard grabbed his shoulders and shook until his head hammered the pillow, a loose, thudding sound like sacks of grain dropped by the miller. "The scribe, who was the scribe?"

William's eyes rolled back in his head. Richard dropped him and recoiled from the stench of the sheets. A twinge of remorse pinched his relief.

The numbness cleared Richard's brain. "The girl. Of course. Dominica." He smiled at the limp sack of bones that used to be his half brother. Plans would have to change. "It is not just your own death sentence you have signed, brother. It is theirs."

The sound of William retching followed him down the hall. Still alive. Too bad. He had other worries now. Pack a bag. Make sure Niccolo knew what to do in his absence...

"Niccolo!" he yelled, his voice shaky as William's fingers.

The man slipped out of a doorway as if waiting for Richard's call. "Sir?" The man made him nervous. Something about the flash of his eyes. Maybe he would have to get rid of him when his work was done, although, if he really could turn tin into gold, he would be worth keeping.

"My fastest horse. Have him ready before noon."

The orders should have gone to a page, but Niccolo glided without comment toward the stables.

The pilgrims left three days ago, but if he beat the horse, he could catch them before they reached the shrine. And if he took only a small guard…

No. He couldn't just ride up and kill them. He had to go as a pilgrim. Alone. He would figure out a way once he got there. One of Niccolo's poisons perhaps. Now what was the claptrap about cloaks and staves?

"Lombard!" he barked. Halfway down the stair, the Italian floated to a stop. "Get me some belladonna. And find me one of those gray cloaks and a cross to wear."

The man's overlarge lips twitched. "Like a pilgrim, Sir?"

Laughter burst from him like a waterfall. "Yes, you witless fool." He tossed the orange at the man, smirking as he fumbled and it bounced down the stairs. "I go on pilgrimage."

This could turn out well. Many accidents happened on the road. The mercenary and the girl could die along the holy path and go straight to heaven for their pains.

Pity about the girl, though.

Rising from her desk, speechless, the Prioress watched Sir Richard, costumed as a pilgrim, kneel before her. He never visited the Priory, never acknowledged any of her requests except to offer her his Devil's deal. Did he think she would have word so soon? Did he not trust that she had done what he asked? She was beginning to have a pang about Dominica. Almost missed the girl.

"Bless me, Prioress, I go to the shrine of the Blessed Larina."

"What change of heart sends you on pilgrimage, Sir Richard?"

"I have discovered an unfortunate occurrence." His eyelids twitched. "It seems my brother, near death and delusional, no doubt, has been seized with the idea that I have been trying to poison him."

Poison. Her stomach cramped at the word. "Why would he think such a thing?"

"Because Garren carries a letter to the priest at the shrine telling him so. My brother wrote it, or, I should say, Dominica wrote it for him."

She knew as clearly as if God told her that the Earl of Readington had no delusions. She had not only jeopardized Dominica's immortal soul. She had condemned her to death.

"Of course," he continued, "These are the ravings of a dying man, but I must allow no misunderstanding, don't you agree?"

She touched her forehead, chest, and shoulders with cold fingers to ward off his evil. *Forgive me Lord. Forgive my arrogance in thinking I could lie down with the Devil only in small things.*

He bowed his head. "So bless me, Prioress. I ride to right a great injustice that will be done if I am wrongly accused."

"Wouldn't you prefer to wait for the Prior?" It would take a day at least for the message to get to him. Another day for him to come. Perhaps that delay would save them. "He must bring you the official *testimoniales*."

Head bowed, he looked up at her through fluttering lashes with eyes as calculating as a weasel's. "No need, dear Prioress. You are close enough to God for me."

She waved her hand over his head and murmured "Lord forgive me" in Latin.

Chapter Ten

Chin resting on her hand, elbows on the table of the common room of Exeter's Inn of the Hart, Dominica stifled a yawn. On the bench to her left, Sister Marian dozed, cradling her head in her arms atop the table. On Sister's left, the Widow Cropton slept upright, head dangling toward her ample bosom.

Sister found no beds for them in the monastery's guest house, full of visitors for the Feast of Corpus Christi. Now, in the third inn they tried, Garren cornered the grumpy, round-bellied innkeeper, insisting he find a bed for the women. Gillian and Jackin, not waiting for a room, had disappeared. The men, wrapped in their cloaks, already sprawled in sleep on the common room floor.

Stories of Jonah and Jesus and Noah jumbled happily in Dominica's mind, clamoring to be written. And Garren approved, a sure sign of God's favor. She floated from the Cathedral of Saint Peter through fruitless stops at overflowing inns, smiling.

Garren did not smile. A black mood perched on his brow as they left the cathedral. Now, it settled around him like a mantle. Perhaps he worried about finding beds for all of them, she thought, watching him negotiate.

Though he dwarfed the bantam innkeeper, Garren never raised his hands or his voice. She could not see his broad, square palms and blunt fingers as threatening. When he touched her cheek and laced his fingers through her hair, she felt treasured.

What a strange man for God to choose as His messenger! But the Earl chose him, too, and the Earl's message was a matter of life and death. The joy of the day almost made her forget. It was probably the day's delay that burdened Garren's brow.

Underneath the table, Innocent lay across her feet, feasting on dropped scraps. Dominica wiggled her toes, poking his belly until he unwrapped himself and begged for her lap. She lifted him more easily now, his pampered haunches turned lean by miles of trotting.

The innkeeper mounted creaking stairs and Garren slid onto the bench across from her, stretching his long, muscled legs under the table. His calves brushed the edge of her cloak. Too close, perhaps, but the inn was crowded. Where else should he sit?

She held her legs very still, so she would not touch him.

He filled his tankard with ale and drank deeply. "You'll have a bed," he said, lips narrowed. "Whatever the cost."

She and Sister had no money for inns. Monasteries and the sky cost nothing. "I'll be all right. If there is only room for one, let Sister take it," Dominica whispered. "We can pay you when we return."

"I'm not letting you sleep among the men," he said sharply, then looked at the Widow and Sister, slumbering, and whispered, "Any of you. I have some coin."

"I don't feel sleepy."

The corner of his mouth twitched. "Then why are you yawning?"

"Maybe I *am* tired, but this is the best writing desk I've

seen since we left the Priory." She ran her hand over the table, not slanted and smooth as the scriptorium desks, but hard and flat. "If I sat here all night and had enough parchment, I could write down all the stories we saw today."

He cocked his head. "What would you do with them?"

"I would write them down so people would not have to wait for feast days to see them acted."

He snorted and sipped his ale. "People can't read."

"Some can," she insisted. "If they can understand, they can believe."

Perched on her lap, Innocent twitched his cold, wet nose. Someone had eaten a fine roast chicken tonight and the smell hung in the air. She whispered into his good ear. "Did you get enough to eat, boy?"

"Do you think if you wrote the Bible in 'dog words,' Innocent would believe, too?"

"Perhaps." Was his question a test or a jest? He did not smile. "God created dogs, too."

"But dogs have no souls."

She caught a gleam of triumph in his eye. The man could argue theology when he chose.

"I know. So they cannot go to Heaven." It did not seem fair. She would miss Innocent in Heaven. Perhaps that part of the doctrine was wrong. "If Saint Augustine had a dog, he would have written differently," she said, twirling her fingers in his fur.

Garren chuckled. Good. She was glad to have lifted his spirits, even for a moment.

Below the table, his calf touched hers.

Her whole body quickened, as if the crackle of lightning shimmered around her.

His lips curved into a smile.

She smiled back, wondering how it would feel to let her

fingers play in the dark curls hugging Garren's sun-warmed neck.

He spoke as if nothing had happened. ''What will you do if you don't get what you want?''

She pulled her legs back under the bench. ''But I will.'' Niggling doubt shadowed her words. *God does not always answer our prayers the way that we want.*

He did not follow her legs with his. ''How can you be sure?''

''Jesus said 'Ask and it shall be given to you.' I asked very clearly.'' She stretched out her legs, clutching Innocent so he would not slide off her lap. ''What do you want of the Blessed Larina?''

He sat up, folding his legs under the bench and tossed back a swig of ale. ''Something impossible. For William to live.''

She squared her lap, chastened. She was thinking of touching him while despair over Readington's health preyed on him. He might be the Earl's palmer, but his devotion was beyond price. ''Nothing is impossible to God. But do you want nothing for yourself?''

His frown returned, cutting deeper lines. ''Nothing the Blessed Larina can grant.''

The innkeeper stomped down the stairs. ''Three women?'' His gruff bark stirred Sister and the Widow awake. ''There's a bed. Only one other person in it. Up-stairs. On your right.''

Dominica put Innocent down to help Sister rise. The days on horseback had added new pains to her familiar ones.

''No dogs in the bed,'' the innkeeper grumbled. ''You keep that animal on the floor.''

She opened her mouth to say Innocent had no fleas, then realized she could no longer be certain.

''That's a crown, then, for the lot of you.'' He snatched

Garren's silver coin, turning it over to be sure none of the sterling had been shaved off. ''And another shilling for the horse's fodder,'' he added. ''That dog does any damage and it'll be extra.''

Grim-lipped, Garren dropped more clinking coins into the man's damp palm. ''That dog has better manners than you.''

Did it take so many? she thought, counting one, two, three. She hoped the Earl had provided generously for his palmer.

She turned to the innkeeper as Innocent raced up the stairs ahead of the Widow and Sister. ''Please, what is the fastest road to the Blessed Larina's shrine?''

''Most take the road around the moor and up the other side to Tavistock. That's three days. After that, it's another three days.''

''Six more days!'' she cried. Would the Earl be alive so long? ''Is there no faster way?''

The man stared as if a toad had spoken. ''What's your hurry, lass?'' His eyes lingered on her chest and she was glad there would be four of them in the bed tonight.

''She asked you a question,'' Garren said, looking up from his ale. ''Is there a faster way?''

''Oh, so that's the way it is.'' He winked, broadly, at Garren. ''There's a road straight across the moor. Saves a day or two.'' He dropped the coins, one by one, into a drawstring bag. ''But the old gods still lurk up there and if a fog rolls in…'' he shrugged, jingling his bag as he called over his shoulder. ''Some that go up don't come back.''

His chamber door rattled shut behind him.

''A day, Garren.'' She sat beside him on the bench. He must not have heard or he would not still gaze at the fire. ''If we cross the moor we could save a day. Maybe two.''

''What difference will it make?'' he said, never turning his head. ''You'll be a nun or not.''

My brother kills me by inches. The Earl's words still chilled her. "The day is not for me, but for Lord Readington. A day could save his life."

"William is most likely dead already." He drained his tankard and slammed it down.

He must be in the grip of melancholia, brought on by an excess of black bile. And no wonder. Garren had already worked one miracle. He must despair that the Lord would grant another. Perhaps if she reminded him of his duty. "But he trusted you with his message…"

His eyes narrowed on her. "Message?"

Had the Earl kept it secret from his messenger? "I saw a folded parchment with his seal," she said, carefully, watching his eyes. "I thought it must be a message."

"It proves the feathers are authentic." Neither a smile nor despair haunted him now.

"Then I was mistaken. But to pray for his life, don't you want to fly to the shrine?"

"Fly like the Blessed Larina?" He laughed, a bitter sound. "I am responsible for all these souls as well as William's prayers. Should I lead them onto a trackless moor?"

"You do not lead alone. God is beside you."

He turned his head to either side, taking in the floorfull of snoring men. "I see no God beside me."

"He is with you always." He might not be a saint, but how could he deny the God who so clearly worked through him? "He helped you save Lord Readington."

"I have saved nothing that God did not take from me." Anger, bitterness and loss creased his face. "Shall I save you, Neeca?"

She licked her lips and opened her mouth, but no words came. A little flame wavered in her stomach. His eyes became the hard, dark green of malachite. "Save me from what?"

"Save you from what you want." Both his hands hovered above her shoulders. The tingle crept around her. "Right now, you want me to touch you."

"That is not what I want."

"Isn't it?"

He nestled one large, square hand in the curve between her neck and her shoulder. Her skin pulsed. Her heart beat in her throat. She could barely catch a breath. Angry. He was making her angry. That was why she felt so hot and flushed. "I want to get to the shrine as quickly as possible. And so do you."

His other hand cupped her shoulder, and he ran them up her neck to hold her face in both hands, leaning close enough that she could feel his breath. Close enough that she wanted to feel his lips.

"Are you testing me again? Since I bested you on theology do you want to attack me through the flesh? Very well." She gritted her teeth to stop the quaver in her voice. "My faith is stronger than your temptation."

He stroked the line of her chin and traced the arch of her throat with his thumb until she swallowed against it. "Stronger than this?"

"Yes." Her very bones melted and she wondered for the first time if it were true.

She wanted to watch his eyes change from leaf to emerald with his moods. She wanted to hear him laugh when she said something clever. She wanted him to show her the smell of a flower and the arch of a bird's flight and the shape of the stars and how to seize all the wonder from each of God's days.

She wanted to curl into him and never move from the sanctuary of his arms, to heal something she didn't even know was broken.

And then he no longer touched her. Her skin shivered with his loss.

He threw back his head to finish the dregs of the ale. "You have a bed," he said, staring into his empty tankard. "Use it."

The smell of leftover chicken, the fire's smoke and the smell of sour ale all rushed into her chest. It was as if she had not breathed while he touched her.

"I want to join the order so I can copy the Bible into English. You said I should. My faith is strong enough to bear any temptation God sends through you until He sends me a sign."

Pushing herself away from the table, she rose, not sure with each step her shaking legs would hold her. He did not call to her and she did not look back, afraid, like Lot's wife, that she would turn to a pillar of salt for gazing back at the wickedness of Sodom and Gomorrah.

But when she stood with her foot on the bottom step, listening to a roomful of snores, wanting to hear him, she turned. "Is there no boon the saint could grant you?"

He refilled his mug, staring as the fire flickered through the golden stream of ale like sunshine through stained glass.

"To forget," he said, finally.

She climbed the stairs in a world where even the ground seemed unsteady.

In darkness, she followed the Widow's snores to her bed beneath a window that let in the smell of old hay and fresh manure from the stable.

Sister's voice startled her. "Neeca? Where were you?"

"Discussing tomorrow's route. I hoped a bed and a roof would give you a night's rest."

"I am not blessed with the Widow's deaf ear."

Sister said it with a smile, but Dominica heard the pain of her hip and back and knees in her voice. Sister had always taken care of her. What could she do in return? "Can I get you something? Do you need more covers?"

"I'll be fine."

Dominica rolled up her cloak and stuffed it under her head as a pillow, teetering on the edge of the bed, clutching the linen sheet. It was the same feeling she had with Garren, as if she were about to fall off of, or into, something. Beside her, the straw mattress rustled as Sister turned from side to side, searching for comfort.

"Are you still awake, Sister?"

"Yes, child. What is it?"

"Tell me," Dominica asked, made brave by darkness, "about men and women."

The rustling stopped. "What makes you ask?"

She could not say Garren. "Gillian and Jackin." She rushed on. "Why would God make it a sin for a man and a woman to join if that's the way He created for us to conceive?"

"It is not the joining that is the sin. It is the wanting that turns us away from God."

She knew the argument. She had given it to Garren. "But they seem so happy." Happy. What a poor name for the joy she witnessed.

"A happy marriage pleases God. The love between a man and a woman is like the love of Christ for his Church."

Dominica had heard this all before, but now, the image seemed sacrilegious.

Outside, an owl screeched in the silence between the Widow's snores.

"Neeca, have you been tempted?"

Yes, she thought, but I resisted. That's what matters. No need to worry Sister. "It is just that the world beyond the Priory is more confusing than I thought."

"The force that attracts man and woman is the most powerful on earth. Before you take your vows, be sure..." Sister's whisper trailed off. "Be sure you can resist."

"Of course I can." But for how long? She looked up into the dark, thatched roof and wished for the comfort of a skyful of God's candles. "Were you ever tempted?"

The owl screeched in warning.

"Each of us faces temptation."

Of course, that was part of God's plan. Sister had been tempted, and resisted. So had Jesus in the wilderness. Dominica rolled over, leaning on her elbow, trying to read Sister's face in the dark. "How did you recognize it?"

"You will want him more than food or drink or life itself." The words sounded like a curse. "More than your immortal soul."

She was strong, Dominica thought, closing her eyes for her nightly prayer. She would resist, just as Sister had. She would prove to God through all his trials that she was worthy.

Send temptation if you must, she prayed, and the will to resist.

But instead, God sent her a night of irresistible dreams.

Garren stood between two paths the next morning, head pounding, feeling like Moses about to lead his flock into the desert. Mercifully, clouds shielded the sun, but every footfall echoed in his head, throbbing from the excess of ale he had drunk last night while he tried to forget.

To forget how he would ruin her life. To forget that William most likely lay dead already. To forget the choice he must make today.

Less than an hour west of Exeter, the time had come. To his left, the comfortable, well-traveled path toward the sea. To his right the straighter, shorter path toward the moor, a day away.

"I've always taken the southern route," Sister Marian said.

"Take the moor," said Simon, pawing the ground, restless as Roucoud. "I'm not afraid."

"It's not a good idea," the Widow warned. "On the way to Santiago we were lost in the Pyrenees for weeks."

Dominica stood silent.

He squinted toward the moor, wondering if he could see the twisted spirit rocks that crowned the hilltops. *The old gods still lurk up there.* What difference did it make? Old gods were no different than new.

A west wind swirled across the grass, smelling of peat and cold granite. Should he risk all their safety? William would be just as dead.

But he had made a promise. To deliver a message and bring back a feather. And maybe, just maybe, if this Larina might sway God, if there were any chance to snatch William back again...

"Carpe diem," Dominica said.

If he could not give William life, at least he could give him peace in death.

Garren nodded to the right. "This way."

Chapter Eleven

God had no sense of direction, Garren decided the next day, as the flat sun hovered heatless in a tin-colored sky. Moses wandered the desert for forty years. How long would He let them wander the moor?

Since sunrise, they climbed every slow step cushioned by peat over stone, hard as the bedrock of creation. Miles ago, sheep dotted the slopes. Now, wind whistled through ancient, abandoned houses. Barren ridges rippled like waves without end. Nary a tree broke the desolate horizon. Instead, chunks of tall, twisted rock thrust through the spongy cover, like solid smoke swirling up from the pits of hell.

The west wind coated his cheeks with the damp of the unseen sea. Innocent chased every rustle, his bark, the clop of Roucoud's hooves, and the Widow's dire warnings of disaster the only familiar sounds in a foreign landscape.

"What think you?" he asked Dominica, on his left.

"It looks like the top of the world," Dominica said, eyes wide, as if to memorize the vista.

The top of the world or the end of it, he thought, looking west again.

As quickly as he turned his head, mist erased the horizon. The damp cloud rolled toward them, chased them fast as the plague of darkness across Egypt, surrounded them, wrapped them close and thick as sheep's wool. Veiled by the mist, the sun looked pale as the moon.

And then he could not even see the sun.

"Hold hands!" he yelled. Mist clogged his eyes, his ears, his lips and absorbed his words. He heard himself through the bones of his jaws instead of his ears. He wondered whether the others could hear him at all.

"Where's Sister?" Dominica, her voice shrill with fear. "I can't see."

He groped toward her voice to his left. His hand disappeared in the fog, but he found her head, cupped it in his hand, then slid his fingers to her shoulder, arm, and finally to lace them with hers, relieved to feel her hand's pulsing comfort.

Roucoud's reins chafed his right hand. The horse, though battle trained, whinnied, trying to pull away from an enemy he could not see. Garren stroked his neck, then spoke to Sister, a ghostly shape on his back. "Don't worry, Sister. I have his reins."

Barking surrounded them.

"Innocent, come." Dominica loosened her fingers, as if to run after the sound. "Where is he?"

He grabbed her back. "Neeca, you can't look for him now. If you let go you'll be lost as he is. He will find us. He knows how."

He hoped he did not lie.

The mist settled around them, as if the old gods, angry, sent down their wrath for trespassing on the moor.

"Listen, all of you," he called into a swirling nothingness. "Everyone take the hand on either side. I will squeeze and the next person will pass that on. When you feel it, call out your name." He groped Roucoud's flanks. "Sister?"

"Yes."

"Garren," he called out, defiantly, then gripped Dominica's hand. It was cold, but trusting, in his.

"Dominica."

"Gillian."

"Jackin."

And so on until Ralf grumbled his name, faint, from the end of the line.

"Now what do we do?" Gillian's voice. High pitched.

A babble of voices surrounded him like the fog.

"We should stay here until it lifts."

"And rot? We should turn around."

"When I was lost in the Pyrenees…"

"Go back the way we came. Take the south road. We should have done that in the beginning."

"That's madness. We've been walking for hours. We'll never find our way back. We might as well go on."

"How can we go on?" Dominica said, fingers clenched on his. "We can't even see."

God will lead us, she had said. He rippled with anger at the Almighty for disappointing her.

"We go on," he said. "Together. Whatever happens, do not let go of each other."

Voices jabbered in protest.

He took a step, straining his shoulders to pull an unmoving line like an ox straining against the dead weight of a plow.

Dominica stepped beside him.

Gillian must have followed, for the tension eased. Hands clasped, the line straggled like an awkward snake moving sideways across the moor. They shuffled, afraid to trip over an invisible stone or fall in a hidden hole.

I see no God beside me. Prophetic. Turned blind and deaf by the fog, he saw nothing at all. If not for Dominica's hand, warm in his, he would have felt completely alone.

Deprived of sight and sound, his eyes and ears created their own visions. A hellhound howled. A spirit screeched. A maiden in a long white dress floated before him. A ghost's cold breath chilled the back of his neck. Garren snorted softly to himself. He believed in ghosts no more than in God. Although up here, it was possible to believe in both.

With each step, he told himself they were not real. Only the solid ground beneath his feet, the leather reins, and Dominica's hand were real. The rest, the ravings of his mind, must be ignored.

There was no sun, only a fading light withdrawing. He led them toward it. How long would it be until they were alone in the dark?

He did not know how long they walked, or how far, but he kept walking, not because he had faith, but because he knew nothing else to do.

Down the line, someone stumbled.

"This is madness." Ralf's voice. "I'm going back."

"No, wait," Garren called, but he felt the emptiness through the human chain. The fog devoured Ralf in its maw.

Well, there was one man who did not burden him with the title Savior. Loss pricked him, strong as if the man had been his brother, but he could not jeopardize the rest for a futile search.

"Sister," he called, "lead us in a song."

From the horse's back, her clear voice surrounded him, louder than the screeches of the spirits.

"Faith gives you wings to fly like Larina
Fly like Larina, fly like Larina;
Faith gives you wings to fly like Larina
Into the arms of the Lord."

Garren lifted his head and seized the song.

His chest swelled and his throat opened and the notes flew out of his mouth into the fog. He threw back his head and sang for the joy of still being alive, defying old gods or new ghosts to strike him dead. If they did, he would die singing, madly, wildly, clearly.

The Miller brothers chimed in with overeager voices. Simon sang fast, so everyone would know he knew all the words. Gillian sang clear and high. The Widow lagged a beat behind.

Dominica's tuneless hum buzzed in his left ear.

And their voices soared into a chorus more beautiful than he had ever heard in church.

A soft thump and a yowl from the middle of the line broke the song.

"What goes there? Is everyone all right?"

Through the fog he saw a large stone, damp, cool, hard, solid, and nearly as tall as Neeca, thrusting out of the ground. Jackin had walked right into it. "Are you hurt?"

"No." Jackin's voice shook. "What do you think it is?"

"It's just a rock," he said. "Maybe a guidepost."

"Here's another," Simon called.

On either side, more stones curved into a circle.

"Maybe it's a warning," Jackin said.

"Pilgrims have nothing to fear," Dominica said, but her voice quavered.

"I was told of this place," Sister said, softly. "The story is that the maidens who danced here in a circle on the Sabbath were turned to stone."

Fear, palpable, shot through the linked hands like an arrow. He squeezed Dominica's fingers. He must keep the fear from chasing them into the fog.

"God will protect us," he called into the mist, a lie he wanted to believe. Prove yourself, damn you, he challenged the God who had protected neither his grandparents, his parents, nor William.

A dog's bark surrounded them. Urgent. Exited.

"Innocent, where are you? Come!" Dominica called.

For the first time, the sound had a direction. Despairing of anything else, he stumbled after the sound, dragging the others behind him.

As they walked, the fog shredded, revealing the ground for the first time in hours. Relief rippled through the line.

He saw the low wall just in time to stop. It curved in both directions, waist high, tall enough to keep cattle in, but not to keep soldiers out. But then, there was nothing up here worth dying for.

Inside, Innocent yapped, merrily.

He dropped Dominica's hand to grope along the top of the wall, looking for an opening where the ancient stones had crumbled.

He found one and stepped over the wall.

Inside, a stream gurgled. Small, round, roofless stone huts were scattered before him. A large pile of charred rubble marked a long-dead fire.

A resting place.

The knots in his shoulders loosened. "We'll sleep here the night."

A few twigs lay buried in the charred circle, a mystery, for he had not seen a tree since the sun was high. With shaking fingers, he struck a spark with his flint. The twigs flamed into heat and light, enough to hold the leftover spirits at bay. They ripped peat from the moor and flung it on the fire until smoke dense as fog spread into a night sky, now miraculously clear.

Watching the fire, Dominica let her eyes blur. Innocent, a smelly hero, lay across her feet. The pure, thin air numbed the inside of her chest.

Garren sat just behind her, a shield at her back, just out of reach. She pressed her lips on her right palm, which had clutched his all day. Deprived of his touch, it ached, empty.

Once again, with God's help, Garren saved them. From her this time. She had insisted they cross the moor, and now they were truly lost. Why had she thought a day would matter? Garren was right. Perhaps the Earl was already dead by his brother's hand and the parchment only the words of a corpse.

Through the flickering flames, she watched the Miller brothers and Simon throw the die. Simon whooped. "It's my lucky day! God saved us from the demon fog and now this!"

She shuddered. Somewhere out there, Ralf was alone.

"Throw again," the older Miller said. "I was as lucky as you today."

"God watched over all of us today," Sister said, loudly enough to be heard over the dice. "Perhaps this would be a good time to tell the story of the Blessed Larina, to remind ourselves why we take this journey. And as you listen, pray for Ralf."

The gamblers, chagrined, quieted like children ready for a bedtime story. The Physician shook the Widow awake to listen.

Dominica knew the story by heart. She never tired of hearing Sister tell it. Someday, she would write it down.

"Larina believed in God," Sister began, "and had perfect faith that God would protect her. One day, while carrying food to a poor family in the woods, she was set on by a pack of wild boars so she started running."

The words were the ones she always heard, but they sounded different tonight. If God wanted to save Larina, why didn't he just let her tame the wild boars? Saints did that all the time. Saint Ambrose held a swarm of bees safely in his mouth while he was just a baby. Saint Patrick commanded the snakes to leave Ireland. It should have been a simple thing for God to arrange.

"So she ran and ran as fast as she could," Sister continued, in a singing rhythm that made the night a little less frightening, "tripping over roots and branches. Heavy branches lashed her eyes and scratched her cheeks, but still she ran. And the sun sank lower and the day grew older, and she did not know where she was or where she was going, but still she ran."

Sister paused, waiting, stretching the silence until Dominica remembered her part. "And then what happened?" she asked, with less than her usual enthusiasm.

"She burst out of the woods to a clear place and ran and ran, but in front of her, the cliffs dropped straight into the raging sea! If she kept running, she would tumble into the churning foam crashing on the rocks below. She was lost!"

The Miller brothers leaned forward. The Widow turned her good ear squarely toward Sister's voice.

"But then, she turned her eyes to heaven and said to our Heavenly Father, 'I put myself into your loving hands' and she ran toward the cliff as fast as she could and when she jumped off the cliff, she sprouted wings…"

"Like an angel!" Dominica chimed, making up for her previous lapse.

"Like a bird. She soared off the cliff, skimmed over the surf and landed safely on the rocks where the boars could not follow. Because she had faith in God," Sister concluded. "She leapt and her wings appeared."

"Because she had faith," Dominica murmured. Perhaps her eagerness to cross the moor had been stubborn pride instead of faith. In fact, at the first sign of difficulty, she had lost her faith in Garren. And in God.

"God put Larina down on a rock and protected her with water all around. And that's where the shrine is today."

"On an island?" Behind her, Garren sounded surprised.

"Barely a rock, just big enough for a hut that holds a few feathers from her wings. You can walk to it when the tide is out."

"How often is that?" he said.

"Once a day, perhaps. Otherwise, you must go by boat."

A wisp of fog clung to the full moon. Silence turned to snores. The gamblers spread out their cloaks. Jackin and Gillian slipped away into one of the stone-walled huts. The Physician and the Widow fell asleep on each other. His snore, on her deaf side, matched hers.

Dominica felt a chill at her back. Garren was gone.

Garren followed the curve of the stone wall until he escaped the sounds of the snores and the light from the fire. Then he slumped to the ground, head in his hands, stone against his back. The reliquary and his lead shell were cold weights against his chest. A mist-smudged moon mocked him, round as the sun that had deserted them.

God still conspired against him.

He had believed for one wild minute. That one more prayer said in one more place might soften God's heart so He might let William live. For one foolish moment he had believed so he decided to cross the moor, to snatch a day that might save William. This was the result. Ralf was missing, or worse. The rest of them were lost.

He was farther from home than ever.

His promise to William seemed impossible. *You can walk to it when the tide is out.* He fingered the reliquary and the shell, dangling on his chest. If, by some miracle, they reached the shrine, how would he sneak onto an island?

Savior, Dominica called him. He was no one's Savior.

Dominica appeared before him as if he had wished her there, one of the dancing maidens come to life in the moonlight. The full moon, glowing behind the leftover fog, shone on her brightly enough that he could see her eyes, no longer fierce, but full of pain.

"I do not want to disturb your prayers," she started.

Prayers, he thought, derisively. When had he last prayed? On the field in France. For William.

"What do you want?" Her very presence condemned him. He wanted no reminders tonight of what he had promised to do.

She knelt, looking down at her clasped fingers, which still carried the smooth fullness of youth. Life had not yet stripped away all she had to give. "I must ask your forgiveness. I urged you to cross the moor because I wanted to save a day. Now we may have lost that day and more."

"The decision was mine."

"I was guilty of pride." She looked up at him, despair in her eyes. "I always think that if I just give God a little push that He will do what I want."

Only those who have seen nothing of life can have such faith, he thought, but he could not ridicule her. She reminded him too much of the time when he, too, had believed. "God has disappointed both of us, I see," he said.

"No, I disappointed God. The failing was mine, not His. I compounded my sin of pride by lack of faith. I should have known you would save us."

"Save you?" His words tasted like rocks. "I was the one who led us into a sightless fog. I should have waited instead of pressing forward blindly."

"You did the right thing. We are safe now."

"Tell that to Ralf."

"He did not follow you."

He shook his head. "Neither should you."

The lead shell lay heavy on his chest. She reached for it with reverent fingers, pushing it against his breastbone. "Why do you have so little faith, you who should have so much?"

"This is not a badge of faith. It is a reminder of faith's futility."

"But you made the pilgrimage to Compostela."

"No. My grandfather did." He closed his hand over hers and the shell, feeling the cold lead fight her warm fingers.

"And Saint James did not grant his request?"

"I told you. There are more pilgrims than cures."

She dropped the medal, but sat, her knee pressing his thigh. "Tell me the story."

Better she know now. Better she be prepared for the dis-illusionment waiting at the end of this road.

"It was in the first Edward's reign," he began, "before I was born. My grandfather returned home from fighting in Scotland to find his wife very ill." His sweetest wife, his grandfather always called her, Garren remembered, sadly. "The priest said 'Make a pilgrimage. God will cure her.' So he left his worldly possessions and started the long road to Spain.

"It took him six months to get there and six months to get back and by the time he returned, she was dead. He gave to God that last year he could have spent with her." He waved the scallop shell in front of her nose. "And all he had left was this little lump of lead."

"But they are together now. In heaven," she said, in a voice less assured than before.

"Heaven?" he snorted. "No invisible Heaven can right all the wrongs of this earth."

He thought of William, of his parents and grandparents, and of all the knights left on the fields of France. To breathe, to be alive, to see the round, full perfection of a pale cream moon set in a black velvet sky seemed unbearably sweet. Each day snatched from death was a miracle. To be relished.

She gazed at him while he savored the sight of her eyebrow, arched like a bird's wing, her high, broad brow, still a blank page waiting for the lines of life's cares, her wide-set eyes, blue as midnight. He wanted her to know the delight of living before a jealous God snatched it away.

He grasped her hands, drew her close, wrapping his arms around her until he could feel her breathing. "Don't save all your joy for death, Neeca."

Her chest pressed against his. Faster. Responding. "I have been thinking about what you said. About saving me from what I want." She spoke into his heart, but he could hear every word. "It is only right that God should send you, as He did to Jesus who was in the desert for forty days and tempted by the Devil."

"Would you like to wander the moor for forty days while I tempt you?" Her pulse beat in her throat and he rocked her in his arms, protecting her from the specters that walked in the moon shadows.

She nestled against him. Warm. Alive. He could feel her chest rise and fall. Feel her heart beat. Feel a lazy wind curl around them, unable to cut through the warmth between them.

Something surged through his arms. Throbbed in his palms where they touched her back. A life force. A spirit. He wondered if he imagined it, but then she stirred.

"What was that?"

He turned her face to the moonlight, stroking a stray hair from her cheek and behind her shell-shaped ear before he put his lips close and whispered. "The spirit of the moor."

She turned and he found her mouth. Whatever haunted the moor flowed between them, hot, alive, more real than the hard stone at his back.

Her lips were soft and sweet and clung to his. She smelled of peat smoke and heartsease. He wrapped his arms around her and drew her atop him, cushioning her from the cold ground with his body.

He would show her the joy of the now. The joy that could be made on earth. The joy of the sun and the moon and the sparrows and fresh spring water and a man and a woman. The thought made him clutch her more tightly.

Lost in her as in the mist, he did not let his lips or his arms break away.

She pulled away, gradually, reluctantly, but her hands clung, as if her fingers kissed him. "I think my penance for that will be at least three days of fasting."

Swift anger surged through him. "This stone is not carved into saints," he answered, his voice raw as the wind. "Your God is not on this moor."

She scrambled to her hands and knees, backing away, and he heard bitterness in her voice for the first time. "I was wrong. God did not send you to test me. You have come from the Devil himself to ruin me."

It was true, he thought, standing while she backed away, but he wanted something more. "Why do I have to be saint or devil? Why can't I be just a man?"

She crossed herself against him. "You won't succeed. My faith is strong enough."

"Is it?" He shoved shame aside. "Are you sure you want a life in the convent now that you have seen the world?" He slid his hands up her arms and tangled his fingers in her hair. "Now that you have felt it?"

She shook her head, as if trying to shake off everything she had felt. "I believed you. I believed in you."

Impaled by guilt and self-loathing, he let her go, but a life force still flowed through him, seeking her and spilling into the chill night air.

"Don't put all your faith in others, Dominica. In the end, you will have only yourself."

"And God." Her voice, rose, frantic, as if she teetered on Larina's ledge. "I'll have God."

"No. Especially not God."

"He was here all the time. Even when I didn't believe. He led us here." She allowed no doubt, as if any doubt would destroy her.

"A barking dog found this place," he snorted. "Not God."

She stilled, as if his words had opened a window and let the sureness flow back. She shook her head, looking at him with pity. "Do you recognize God only when He appears as a burning bush?"

He opened his mouth to mock her. It was by chance that they stumbled onto this ancient shelter. Just luck that there had been wood to start a fire. Nothing to do with his talk, it could hardly be called a prayer, with God. Nothing at all. Despite all evidence, her faith allowed no doubts.

The thought stopped him cold. Despite the evidence, did he doubt his disbelief?

He looked back at the dying fire.

"Tomorrow they will look to you to lead them again," she said. "What will you tell them?"

"God alone knows."

"Yes," she said, over her shoulder. "He does."

Fingering the well-worn lead shell around his neck, he did not watch her leave. It was only a souvenir. Only a memento of a family snatched away by a God who would not save them, even though they paid the price.

But what if it were something more?

He took it from his neck and tied it on the tip of his staff. It dangled, comforting, in wind that carried a scent of heather.

Chapter Twelve

Dawn bloomed before Dominica's eyes pink, gold, orange, and blue, as if the Lord had said ''Let there be light'' for the first time. It spilled across the far edge of barren land no longer shrouded by fog, ground that could not be retraced.

Blocking the wind with her back, she propped her elbows atop the rough rock wall. Far enough from the fire that she could no longer smell the smoke, she unrolled her parchment, placing stones on all four corners to keep it from flapping in the wind. Cutting a fresh, sharp slant on her quill, she dipped it into the inkhorn. She stroked slowly, with shorter lines than usual, for there was no smooth stone on a wall men built before they could write.

Moor. Mist. Moon.

The words mocked her. She wanted to write a guide for pilgrims. Now she was lost. Last night, with Garren's arms around her, she felt God. Or something older than God. *Aliveness* flowing between them.

The rest of the night, she looked up at the full moon touching a body that seemed no longer hers. Remembering, her skin shimmered and her humors raced again.

Exstasie.

There. Her sin in one word. But she felt like no sinner. The maidens who violated the Sabbath turned to stone. What if God punished her by withholding His sign?

What if she no longer wanted it?

She forced the quill over the bumpy stone. *Quo vadis?* Whither goest thou?

A shield at her back cut the breeze. Garren. She knew without turning.

"How are you this morning, Dominica?" He leaned his staff against the wall between them. The little shell hidden against his chest last night now dangled cheerily from the small branch at the top.

She wondered what changes God had wrought in his soul last night. "I am firm with faith," she said, folding the parchment with trembling fingers so he could not see.

Too late. He laid his large, square palm atop the precious words and frowned. "What is this? What do you copy?"

"I copy nothing. I create. I write of our journey." She held her breath for his approval.

He nodded. "So others will have a guide," he said, then grinned. "And not be lost on the moor."

She nearly giggled with relief. "I shall recommend the southern road."

"Perhaps that would be wise." His eyes darkened and she thought she still saw the moon reflected there. "Not many are strong enough to brave the spirit of the moor." He turned the paper toward him, following the knife scored lines with a blunt finger. "English?"

"Most of the words, yes."

"Here. What is this word?"

"Neeca," she said, swallowing.

His brows crunched. "That will guide no pilgrims. Why did you write it?"

A large lump lodged in her throat and she shook her head,

neither able nor willing to speak, staring at the black letters until they blurred.

He put his hand on her chin and forced her eyes to his. "Why, Neeca?"

Unable to add lying to her list of sins, she told him. "Because you called me that."

"It was so important?"

She pursed her lips and nodded, braving his eyes.

He looked at the parchment again, following the words with his finger, hovering over the last few. "And what did you write of last night, Neeca?"

She bit her lip. He was too close, too close to knowing how important he had become.

He cupped her head in his hand and tilted up her chin to force her to meet his eyes. Even her lips quivered, wanting to feel his again.

What if she wanted Garren? Garren, who could save everyone else but would destroy her.

She shook his hand off and stepped away so that he could not reach her, grabbing the parchment and holding it behind her back. She felt stronger when he did not touch her. "God tests us every day." The sun had climbed high enough to bleach the sunrise colors away. God brought light to chase the demons of the night away. "We must resist the Devil's temptations in daylight and darkness if we are to be worthy."

In daylight, leaning on his elbow, he still tempted her. A rim of darker green circled his eyes. "Am I still the Devil this morning or a saint again?"

She no longer knew. She only knew that her skin, her blood, her very soul felt alive next to him. *God have mercy on a poor sinner.* Praying for God's protection, she reached out her hand, flicking his lead shell with her finger, setting it happily swinging. "Whether you are Devil or Saint, you are His instrument."

He wrenched the staff away, making the St. James shell twist wildly on its leather cord. "How many times must I say it, Dominica? God does not work through me."

His anger was easier to brave than his touch. "Does the Devil?"

Surprise, guilt and an expression she could not name chased across his face. His mouth opened and shut. No words came out.

He does not deny it. She knew she should feel fear. Instead, her heart ached for his pain. "Do not worry. I will pay the penance for last night. Three days of fasting should suffice."

Foolish words. Carved stone and stained glass were a memory. Here, she touched the stone God made when he created the world. Stone still inhabited by spirits.

"I forbid you to fast. I won't have you faint with hunger."

"God will keep me strong."

"God," he said, grimly, "needs a little help. Did you break fast yet this morning?"

She shook her head. "I am not hungry."

He reached into his sack and thrust a soggy biscuit into her hands. "Eat."

"No!" She fumbled for the biscuit, not wanting it to fall to the dirt, and dropped her parchment and quill on the ground instead. The quill rolled crazily atop the page, splattering ink like a crouching spider. "Look what you did. Here, take it back." She shoved the biscuit toward him, but he had already turned his back.

"Help! Help me!"

The cry came from beyond the wall. Out in the heath, a shock of white hair bobbed above the bushes.

Ralf.

"Help," he cried again, and stumbled and fell.

Garren scrambled over the wall and ran to him before he called again. Looping Ralf's left arm around his neck, Garren dragged him into the camp. Ralf's other arm waved wildly up, down, left, right. A large sign of the cross to ward off a large evil.

She blew on the spilled ink, then threw her supplies in her sack and ran back to the smoldering fire, clutching the biscuit.

Garren dropped Ralf, sobbing, beside the smudge of smoke that drifted into the morning air. His red-rimmed eyes, wild, saw none of them, but looked at a world they could not see.

Sister laid hands on his shoulders. "Are you all right, Ralf?"

The rest clustered around, but kept their distance, as if he were a ghost returned from the dead.

Garren waved his hand before Ralf's vacant eyes. "Do you know who we are?"

"I spent the night alone with God on the moor."

Dominica shuddered at the dead look in his eyes. Had he been alone with God or with the ancient ones?

Ralf squinted at Sister. "And He gave me back my soul."

"God is merciful," Sister said. Her arms encircled him like a child, rocking.

Innocent jumped on Ralf's chest, licking the tears from his cheek with a little pink tongue. Dominica reached to rescue him. Ralf had never even petted Innocent before, but he did now, rubbing his head with long, awkward strokes.

No one spoke. Yesterday, the fog had swallowed every sound. Today, the air carried Ralf's sobs halfway back to Exeter.

Ralf's eyes cleared slowly, as if he woke from dreams.

He reached out a hand to touch Sister's face and Garren's arm. "Are you real? Am I here?"

"You are safe. Tell us what happened." Garren said.

"When I broke away there was nothing but fog. Nothing to see. Nothing to hear. I was alone," Ralf intoned with a voice empty as death. "Then I saw shapes, heard screams and I realized it was all the poor souls in Hell. Flesh ripped by the Devil's claws. Burning. Screaming. Forever. Damned for eternity." Tears rolled down the crags lining his crooked nose. "God showed me. That would be me. That was where I was going."

The cold earth numbed Dominica's feet and crept up her legs. Her chest tightened, watching him struggle for breath. This was not the God whose still, small voice guided her heart. But Ralf knew what he saw. It was real.

"And I prayed," Ralf cried, "I said 'God tell me what to do.' And He told me to repent. To truly repent." He hung his head. "You see, Sister, I came because they told me to, but only with my body. God told me that wasn't enough."

"No, my child." Sister's voice, always soft, sank to a whisper, as if she spoke only to herself. "God requires true repentance of the heart."

"I know that now. I got down on my knees and I told Him I was sorry I beat my wife. That I was sorry I crushed her hand. That I would never let drink take me over again. And He forgave me." Ralf's wonder-rounded eyes, she noticed for the first time, were blue. "He forgave me and led me back to you."

"How did you know He forgave you?" Dominica said. Was this the same God she knew? "There was no priest to hear your confession."

A sweet smile blessed his battered face. "I felt a peace all over. In my bones." Then, eyes wide, he looked at Garren, clutching his sleeve. "And I heard Him say 'Follow The Savior. He will lead you to safety.'"

Garren tried to pry the man's gnarled fingers from his arm. "He meant Our Lord Jesus, of course." Over Ralf's head, he looked to Sister for help.

"Yes," she said, quickly. "Our Savior Jesus Christ."

Too late. The rest, awestruck all over again, stared at Garren.

Ralf looked from Sister to Garren, shaking his head like a stubborn child. "No, no, He meant you."

Dominica crossed herself and begged God's forgiveness for her doubts. She must hear and follow the voice inside that had never failed her.

She had promised God this pilgrimage. She must not waver or doubt. She knew His plan for her, felt peace in her bones as Ralf did, when she was on the right path. Garren was part of that plan, if only she knew which part. God would show her. If only she had faith.

She dropped the biscuit in the dirt.

By noon, Dominica wished she had eaten the biscuit.

God followed the sunrise with a cloudless day. Scrubbed clean by the fog, the land lay open before them. To either side, piles of twisted rock, shaped strangely as foreign letters, peered down at them. This morning, she knew they were signposts, pointing the way to something, if she could only tell what.

They found no road, but everyone felt as if God had re-blessed their journey. Innocent ran ten miles for every one they walked, dashing after every rustle in the underbrush. At least she no longer worried he would get lost.

When the sun was high and they stopped to rest, Innocent trotted over to her, tail quivering with pride, and dropped his catch at her feet—a limp, bloody, long-earred piece of fur.

"Rabbit stew for dinner!" Garren said, scratching him behind his good ear. "Good boy! He's a hunting dog, after all."

Dominica petted him, too, but for once, didn't let him lick her face. The sight of the poor, dead, brown-furred animal roiled in her stomach, but she couldn't tell whether she felt sick or hungry.

"Go get the pot, dearie," the Widow said. "Gillian and I will get the fire started. I think I have some dried thyme tucked away for a special occasion." She opened the first of several pouches that swung from her ample girdle while Gillian picked up the limp, bloodstained fur and pulled out a knife. "Get your wits about you, girl. Get the pot off the horse and fetch some water."

She had promised God three days of fasting. This was just another of His tests.

Garren unpacked the pot and three sprouting onions from the horse and walked her to the small stream, full and flowing merrily westward. Sometimes she thought the moor was only rock and water, disguised by the green peat.

"Fog yesterday. Who knows what tomorrow?" he said. "Enjoy the stew today."

"I told you, I am fasting."

"If God used Innocent to lead us to last night's shelter, He must also mean for us to eat today's catch."

Dominica could almost smell the stew, bubbling, onions nestled against the meat. Her stomach growled. "Stop tempting me."

"Pride is a sin, too, Neeca."

"Just hand me the onions." She turned and water sloshed over her feet from the pot as she walked back to the fire.

She would prove her devotion. She would cook the stew for others to eat.

"Marriage," the Widow was saying when she returned, "only works when the woman is clearly in charge."

Gillian shook her head. "The man rules in all things."

Dominica had no interest in hearing talk of men and women. It had no bearing on her life, she thought. She dropped the pot in the middle of the fire, splashing water on the coals.

"Careful!" the Widow said. "Don't drown it!"

"I'm sorry." She slashed at the onions as she would sharpen her quill. At least the half-deaf Widow would not hear her growling stomach.

The Widow continued to lecture Gillian. "I know. I've had five husbands. Ralf's wife could have asked me. You let him think he makes the decisions, but in truth…" She shook her head. "Helpless without us."

Dominica whacked the onion so hard the pieces flew into the fire. She plucked them out, sucking on her onion-flavored, ash-covered fingers, singed by the coals. "Marriage," she said, through gritted teeth, "is like the love of Christ for his Church."

The Widow chuckled. "Don't believe everything they tell you, dearie." She winked at Gillian. "Unless, of course, you believe that as a nun you really will be the bride of Christ."

The Widow whooped and Gillian blushed. The image that flashed into Dominica's mind was so sacrilegious, she was ashamed to ask God's forgiveness. "The bond is mystical," she said.

Mystical. The heat crept up her neck and into her ears. Like what she felt with Garren.

The Widow wiped tears from her eyes that did not come from the onions. "I'm sorry, dearie. There's a lot you don't know." She waved her hands in front of her. "I'll stop now," the Widow said, "before I blaspheme too loudly and disturb the lovely Sister over there." Crossing herself, she nodded toward Sister Marian, listening patiently to Ralf recount again his meeting with God. "There's one the Church is lucky to have. Too bad they are not all like her."

This seemed blasphemous enough. Hunger gnawing at her stomach and guilt clawing at her soul, Dominica grabbed old certainties. "You cannot doubt God and still go on pilgrimage."

The Widow stopped stirring, resting her spoon on the edge of the pot. "You know what I really want from God, dearie?" She patted Dominica's cheek. Dried thyme stuck to her fingers and the sharp smell clung to Dominica's nose. "Oh, yes, it would be nice to hear again, but I've learned to live without hearing. But I haven't learned to live without a husband. That's what I want. A new husband." She looked over at the Physician. "And so far, God's doing just fine."

A husband, she thought. What an unworthy petition. "But God requires true faith, like Larina's!"

"Look at Ralf," the Widow said. "Sometimes faith comes after the miracle."

The chunks of rabbit bobbed happily in the boiling water. She could almost taste the steam. The Rule, she remembered, allowed the eating of young rabbits even on fast days. She peered into the pot, wondering whether God had been thoughtful enough to give Innocent a young rabbit, just so she could eat one bite.

As the pilgrims lined up to be served, Jackin jerked his head toward the west with a ferryman's practiced eye. "New clouds coming."

She followed his gaze. How far could they get before the rain?

* * *

The pilgrims were farther ahead than Richard had thought. Two days of hard riding and he had not yet caught a glimpse of their dust. He didn't know yet exactly what he would do when he found them. Only that Garren must not live to deliver that message.

And the girl? He shook his head. She would have to die. But he would taste her first.

He laughed to the sky, the thought of it rising stiff between his legs. Maybe he was the one more truly his father's son. The father who had shunned him since that night so many years ago.

Richard, a newly minted squire home to swagger, had heard the footsteps that night, footsteps intended to be secret. Hefting his sword in his shaking twelve-year-old arm, he filled his chest with air and stepped into the hall.

"Who goes there?"

His father, tall, lion-like, stood frozen in the candle's light. His chausses drooped. His tunic sat crooked on his shoulders. His hair was ruffled. He looked like a man who had just come from a long duel with a skin of Gascon wine.

But instead of the roaring anger or swaggering happiness of drink, guilt glittered in his fierce blue eyes.

"What are you doing, boy? Why aren't you abed like your brother?"

Why aren't you like your brother? That was always the question. His brother William. Son of the first, golden wife.

He lowered the sword, glad to rest his shaking arm. "I heard a noise. I thought I ought to see what it was."

"Don't you know better than to poke your nose into things that are not your affair?" His father clutched his sagging pants with one hand, running his other through his hair.

Richard's eyes widened, taking in the long strand of honey-colored hair on his father's shoulder and the damp spot between his legs. The words slipped from his lips before he could stop them. "You've been with a woman."

"Hold your tongue, boy." The Earl looked toward the solar door.

The door opened.

Richard's mother stood in the doorway, her brown hair tumbled around her shoulders. Her sallow cheeks and narrow chin sagged slightly, then she stiffened, looking at her son and her husband. "It's all right, Richard. He was only practicing his writing. Come to bed, husband."

He let himself be led into the room. The smell of woman hit Richard's nose as he walked past.

"But, Mother, he—"

"Good night, my son," she said.

The door shut with a sad, final thud.

Richard, astonished, stared. So this, he thought, was his father's honor. Respect for William's mother. Dishonor for his. Well, he could understand such dishonor.

His father sent him away the next day. He never spoke to him again.

Now, Richard had made William pay for the sins of the father. William, who was so much his father's blond-haired, blue-eyed child. Richard would be the master soon.

The midsummer sun had turned to sodden showers by the time Richard arrived in Exeter. Wet banners drooped over empty wooden platforms. He picked his way through them, determined to find a real bed, pilgrim's suffering be damned.

By the time he found the Inn of the Hart, rain fell in sheets.

Richard dripped from his nose, from his fingers, from the staff between his legs. "You there, I want a dry bed and hot wine." He paused. "And information."

"I've beds aplenty tonight." The innkeeper's girth spoke

of success and his eyes screamed of avarice. "What information do you want? And what's it worth to you?"

"Nothing if you don't have it." He flipped the arrogant peasant a farthing. "I'm looking for a band of pilgrims. Leader is a broad-shouldered knight with a fine horse."

"You're a pilgrim?" The innkeeper looked skeptical.

"Can't you see the cross?" Richard thumped his soggy chest. "I am supposed to be with them. I got separated."

"Pilgrims? Well, my memory isn't what it used to be...."

Richard dug out a tuppence and slapped it on the table. "Now talk, damn you."

"Pilgrims? Well, I think they were here two, maybe three nights ago."

"Which is it, man, two or three?" He grabbed the man's throat and squeezed.

Fear cleared the squint from the man's eyes. "I remember now. It was the night of Corpus Christi."

Damn. He let the man go and rubbed his hands on his tunic. *Still two days ahead of him.* He was going to have to get a new horse to keep this pace. "There was a maid with them? Tall, blue eyes?"

"Oh, yes," he winked. "I remember her."

Richard twitched at the smirk in the man's voice. Had he seduced the girl already? "Shared a bed with the leader, did she?"

The innkeeper looked at the tuppence with disgust. "That information's worth a shilling."

"Oh, then she did," Richard said.

The innkeeper's lips curved into a "don't-be-so-sure" smile and Richard knew that Garren had not yet seduced the little virgin. The innkeeper was right. That information was worth the shilling he had not had to pay for it.

"Well, never mind. Which way did they go from here?"

"There's two ways. Across the moor and over to Tavistock or down south by Plymouth and up. The Plymouth way is longer, but safer. I told 'em that, but I don't know which way they went. They were fighting about it when I went to bed. The girl seemed to be in a hurry.''

The girl wrote the message, Richard thought, but apparently she had not told Garren yet or he would be hurrying to act the Savior again. ''Now bring me my wine and show me the bed.''

Two nights. He was gaining. Even if they had been fools enough to cross the moor, he didn't need to. The rain would slow them down.

Chapter Thirteen

Dominica welcomed the rain when it came. Unending drops plopped on her head, slithered down her neck, and dripped off her nose. One sinful bite of rabbit and onion clung to her tongue, tempting her stomach to growl.

Every step was a penance.

"When I was on pilgrimage to Compostela, there was a rainstorm on the plain in Spain," the Widow began. Thunder snarled, followed by the hush of falling rain. She sighed. "But it was not as bad as this."

Sister huddled on Roucoud's back, shoulders raised against the rain. Dominica heard her rattling cough over the thunder. *She needs a fire and dry clothes,* she thought, with a flash of anger at God. Must even the good be punished?

Garren walked ahead, alone. Rain slid off his curls as from a stone and he accepted it all as if it were natural, raising his face to catch the fresh drops from the sky. *He can take joy even in the most miserable of God's creations,* she thought.

They rediscovered the beaten path after their meal. A sturdy bridge of flat stone slabs slick with rain carried them across the first river. Nothing guarded its edge and Innocent, sniffing for any scent not washed away, nearly slipped over the side.

But streams and rivers riddled the moor, each filled higher than the next. Finally, they came to a river with no bridge. A stone marker, cross-shaped, taller than the Physician, hunched near the road. They clustered around it.

"It says Tavistock," Dominica said, grateful it was not a stone left by ancient spirits. "We must be on the right road for the monastery."

Sister's teeth chattered. "I have never been this way, but if we can get across this river, we may find dry beds there for the evening."

Garren ran wet fingers through wetter hair. "Sister, I am glad your God does not require us to sleep in the rain as well as walk in it. I'll carry each of you across on Roucoud's back."

"Take Sister first," Dominica whispered, so she could not hear.

He nodded.

He mounted the horse behind Sister, his body engulfing hers. At the first step, Roucoud slipped on the rain slick moss. Dominica clasped a hand over her mouth to stifle a cry. Garren patted his flanks and soothed him, but Dominica let her breath go only when his hooves cleared the water on the other side.

He came back for Ralf, the Physician, the Widow, and Jackin and Gillian, who argued for five minutes that they should be able to go across together. Finally, only Dominica, Simon and the Miller brothers remained.

"Your turn," Garren said.

She hurt for the weariness pressing on his shoulders. Tucking the top of her sack over, a final protection for her oilcloth-wrapped scroll, she picked up Innocent. She would be sure, she thought, to write of the rivers in her guide for pilgrims.

Glaring down from his seat on Roucoud's back, Garren frowned. "Put the dog down."

Innocent licked the rainwater from her cheeks. "He can't swim across."

"I'm not leaving him, but you can't mount with your arms full of dog. And I can't lift you like a sack of wheat. Now give him to Simon."

She did, but she felt like a sack of wheat anyway as he hoisted her up in front of him in the saddle. His arms circled her with none of last night's gentleness. Well, why should he? she thought. She had accused him of being the Devil.

She perched uncertainly on the moving mountain, legs dangling to the left. The horse shifted and she grabbed Garren's arms. "He's very big, isn't he?" she gulped.

"Have you never ridden a horse?"

She shook her head. "The Priory has only asses."

"He is the best," he said, patting Roucoud's thick neck. "This horse did not flinch before the French chevaliers. He'll not fail us now."

"Nor will God," she said, although she was unsure whether God was in a mood to aid or punish her.

"I have more faith in the horse," he said, grimly. He jerked his head to Simon. "Give her the dog."

She crushed the wiggling bundle of wet, black fur to her chest, squeezing her eyes tight against the water gurgling angrily beneath Roucoud's hooves. The horse lurched with each step.

She turned her face into Garren's chest. Beneath two layers of wet clothes, his warm, comforting scent wiggled up to her nose.

"Steady, I've got you," he said. She wasn't sure whether he spoke to her or the horse.

The steady thump of his heart merged with the sound of rushing water.

Roucoud lurched to the right.

She fell backwards, squeaking a scream before she realized that Garren's arm encircled her. Innocent, jarred, pushed against her with his short hind legs and launched into the swirling river.

"Innocent! No!"

Her eyes flew open and she reached for him. Too late. The splash was followed by a soggy bark.

Her reach carried her forward after him. She grabbed for Garren, but lost all balance and slipped off the saddle. Rushing water tugged at her feet.

Her last coherent words to God were to look after Sister Marian and Garren when she was gone.

Chapter Fourteen

Rushing water sucked Dominica into the current. She grabbed for Garren, but clutched only a handful of soggy cloak.

Clutched it and never let go.

Water filled her ears, her eyes, her nose. She was blind and deaf. Her body screamed for air and inhaled water.

The cloak slipped from her fingers. No need to touch it anymore. She could touch the hereafter. And she wasn't sure whether her voice or just her mind screamed "Save me."

Something pulled her, sputtering and gulping, flailing, above the water.

"Hold on. I won't let you go."

Her saturated cloak weighted her down like a shroud. Even with her head above water, she could not breathe. She thrashed, gasping for air, beating the water away.

"Stop!" he said, sharply. "Float or I'll lose my grip."

Sputtering, she felt Garren's arm around her. She opened her eyes and forced herself to bob like the sticks and branches sailing by on top of the froth.

The horse, battle trained, stood like a rock amidst the swirling waters, waiting for his master's command.

"Roucoud will pull us to shore."

Garren's right arm clung to Roucoud's left front leg and the horse took one step, then another, pulling Garren and Dominica with him. Relief flooded her like water. Safe. Cold and wet and still halfway across the river, she clung to Garren. Safe.

Coughing, her chest finally clutched air. "Where?" She couldn't talk and breathe. "Innocent?"

Garren jerked his head. "Swimming like a duck."

Looking to shore, she saw Sister with her hand on her heart. Jackin ran back and forth, shouting something she could not hear, and splashing into the shallow water near the bank. Ralf kneeled in the mud, face to the rain from Heaven, hands clasped in prayer.

And Innocent's one-eared head bobbed happily above the water, swimming toward them.

She laughed but coughed instead. "Why do I worry about him?"

Garren chuckled in her ear. His arm, solid, warm, carried her through the rushing water, holding her just a little more tightly than necessary. It was wet above the river and wet in the river and she was not sure she felt any more soaked below the water than above, but she was safe. Saved.

Thank you, Heavenly Father.

As the horse dragged them step by step through the river, she felt her sack bouncing on her back, still there, but full of water. Oilcloth was no match for the river. All the wonderful words she had tried to write must be washed away. Tears mingled with the raindrops on her cheek.

He squeezed her. "No need to cry. I've got you."

"Not for myself," she sniffed. "My writing. It's ruined." A worse thought seized her. "The message." she pressed her fingers to his chest, searching for it. "Where is it?"

"Tied to Roucoud's saddle."

Above the water. Better, but not sure. "It may be damaged, too."

When she looked back at him, she saw his silver reliquary submerged in the river. "The feathers! They're soaked!"

"It rains on the birds."

"But these are holy!"

His left arm gripped her more tightly, though he kept his eyes on the riverbank. "I have saved you. God can save His own relics."

And she knew it was probably sacrilegious, but she smiled anyway.

The sheets of rain had tapered to threads by the time Jackin and Ralf pulled them the last few feet to shore. Innocent raced up and down the riverbank, as if the whole thing were a wonderful adventure and he thought everyone enjoyed the water as much as he did.

Separated from the comfort of Garren's arms, Dominica was smothered in Sister's wet, black robes, as if she were still a child.

"Shh, shh, God protected you," Sister said, breaking into coughing.

Dominica lifted her head from Sister's shoulder to look for Garren. All the pilgrims stood back as if he were surrounded by a halo that set him apart from them.

Mounting Roucoud, he rode back into the river to bring the last three across.

"Pardie," Ralf muttered. "He really is a Savior."

Dominica shivered. *And now he has saved me.*

The rest of the pilgrims settled in the monastery's pilgrim's quarters, but Sister insisted Dominica receive a room reserved for important guests. She basked in the heat from the hissing fire, sipped the hot spiced wine, and when the beans came, mixed with a bit of bacon, she ate. Finally,

Sister tucked her under the blanket, hands outlining her body, bouncing her on the bed as if she were still giggly Neeca.

Dominica did not smile tonight. Even Innocent could not cheer her. When Sister took the bowls back to the kitchen, she burrowed under the covers, cozy and warm, but her soul was adrift. Everything she thought she knew about God's purpose for her life was washed away.

When, with trembling fingers, she had finally opened her scroll, she saw no words. There was only a blur of unrecognizable black blobs and dark streaks. She slapped it down, as if she could beat it flat, but it cracked and then rolled right back over her hands. Every touch destroyed another word until she couldn't bear it and threw the poor thing to the floor, shaking her hands to rid them of the dead dreams.

How could God save her and destroy her work?

Garren tempted her and she sinned, but instead of punishing her, God sent Garren to save her from the river.

She closed her eyes and listened to the familiar bedtime echo of the compline hymns, sung tonight by monk's voices.

She wanted to hear the nuns sing. She wanted to go home. To the Priory, to her quill, to the comfort of each day going forth exactly like the one before. To the peace. To the sureness. To the belonging. Where each day helped build a place in heaven. A place without doubt.

Sister's cough and the slap of wet robes broke her prayer.

Warm and full, she watched Sister drape the soaking contents of her sack across the bench and bed. *She is as soaked as I am. Why did I not notice?*

She climbed out of bed. ''Come now. It's your turn to be warm in bed.''

''I'm fine. I'll join the others. You are the one who was

almost lost today." She laced her fingers tightly with Dominica's, as if wanting to be sure she was still alive.

"I'm bigger than you now," Dominica said, peeling Sister's wet wimple off and draping it on the bench by the fire. "You'll do as I say. Let me take care of you."

She let herself be led to the bed and covered with a blanket. Dominica tucked her in, bouncing, but it brought on a coughing spasm and she stopped.

"Thank you, my child," she said. "I guess I am tired."

"You must keep up your strength. We are almost there, aren't we?"

"A few more days."

"God saved my life today."

"Yes. I've always thought God brought you for something special."

"I am ready to be home. To start copying like you do."

She waited for Sister to tell her, as always, that God intended her to do it.

Instead, she saw her confusion reflected in Sister's eyes. "That is what I have always wanted, but make sure that is God's plan and not just your own."

She did not want doubts tonight. She wanted to be a little girl in the Priory. "Tell me again how I came to the convent." It was her favorite bedtime story. Like Larina's legend, she knew all the words by heart.

"It was a summer morning," Sister began, as always, except this time she lay in bed and Dominica sat on the edge of the narrow mattress. "I was still a novitiate, sent to open the gates for travelers. The sun had been up for hours when I did my morning chores. I went to the gate and there was a basket covered with a cloth."

"Like Moses in the rushes!" Dominica said, reciting her part.

"Perhaps." Dimples creased Sister's cheeks.

"And what color was the cloth?"

"Blue. Blue like your eyes." She looked at Dominica and smiled. "But I thought it was an offering of apples."

"Apples," she said, suddenly not wanting Garren to think of her as a round, red fruit. "And do I look like an apple?"

Or more like a plum.

Sister laughed and pinched her cheeks. "Well, you had round red cheeks. But when I picked up the basket, the apples kicked and cried!"

"And it was me!"

"Yes, it was you. And I loved you immediately and said I would take care of you."

"And what did the Prioress say?"

Sister looked down at her clasped hands. "She was not sure at first."

"But you persuaded her?"

Sister stroked Dominica's forehead, just as when she had been a feverish child. "We all did. We all love you dearly."

"Who do you think my mother was?" She had never asked before. Somehow, tonight it seemed important.

At her back, the fire's wood creaked with heat.

"I think," Sister said, finally, "she was a young, foolish woman alone who could not keep a baby."

A foolish woman alone who succumbed to the temptation of earthly pleasures. She traced the line on her palm, wondering whether her mother's hands were broad and square or slender and graceful. What had happened to her, afterward? "Do you think God forgave her?"

"Remember what Ralf said. It takes true repentance to gain God's forgiveness."

True repentance. Did she truly repent those minutes in Garren's arms?

But as Sister Marian slept, Dominica lay on the floor by

the fire, hands wrapped around her own body, and wondered about the young girl, her mother, who had been so foolish.

With her eyes closed, the river rushed back at her. She had almost died. Garren had been her Savior. Surely that was a message. God must have sent Garren for a reason. Maybe he was meant to be her teacher, not her tempter. What lesson did God save her to learn?

And as she thought about the way her body burned when she was next to Garren's body, she began to understand how that young girl might have felt who must have wanted someone more than her immortal soul.

The Widow's snores, rattling through the guest house, did not waken Garren. He had not slept.

He rolled over on his pallet, turning his back to the large room where the men slept and closed his eyes against the fading fire.

But when he closed his eyes, he felt Neeca slip from his grasp again. Felt his heart pound and sweat on his skin heavy as rain, felt the sickening sense of the world slipping away. Felt his arms reach for her.

You truly are the Savior.

How God must laugh.

He had almost lost her today. Tonight, he shook with what that meant. She ached in him like an old wound. Day did not begin until he had seen her. Night could not fall until she lay safe. He felt her hunger in his stomach. His body screamed to join hers until he could barely walk beside her.

A live presence flowed between them. The spirit of the moor, he had told her, as if they could touch each other's souls.

Of course, he had no soul left.

Near death, she worried about William's message and

Larina's feathers. He forgot it all, forgot everything he promised everyone except to save her from her God.

She clutched her faith tightly as a shield. As if she would die if she let it drop. As if she had nothing else. Well, what else did she have? No family. No future except the one she demanded God give her.

The one Garren would take away.

What will happen to her afterward?

Her life will go on much as before.

Much as before. Washing, gardening, a servant without standing. An orphan accepted on sufferance. He knew that life. It had been his until William had opened his arms and made a homeless squire his own. For that, he owed William a debt no pilgrimage could pay.

He lay on his back, looking sleeplessly into the thatched roof of the guest house. What he would do would not ruin her. He would save her. Yes, save her from a life chained to this ridiculous God, trying to create justice in the here-after with words in the here and now.

Don't lie to yourself. This isn't about saving her from the Church. It isn't even about the money. This is about what you want.

He rolled to his side, shrugging off his guilt. Things in life happened. No justice. No pattern. Only a series of trials to be borne. Enjoy today. The past is too painful.

God promised no tomorrows.

Certainly not to William, whose grave would accept the feathers and the coin, if he could get them.

Certainly not to him.

God had taken enough from him already. He wanted to care for no one new. He would initiate the girl into life's disappointments. She would learn to bear hers and grab what scraps of joy she could. Like all the rest.

He would do no more caring. He would suffer no more losses.

Tomorrow, he would pursue her in earnest.

Chapter Fifteen

With a grimness unsuited to wooing, Garren gazed over the booths gathered around the gray-stoned monastery, gauging his battlefield terrain. Tavistock market day, a forest of canvas-covered collapsible stalls, seemed an unsuitable site, but a commander could not always choose. Today he would launch his campaign to capture Dominica.

After Sister whisked her away to a private room last night, he had not seen her again. Now, he filled his eyes with the wonder of her alive beside him in the morning sunshine, kneeling to wave a forbidden tidbit for Innocent to gobble.

Following the rigors of the moor, he had called for a day of rest. The others already scattered to the market except for Ralf, who knelt in the chapel, giving thanks to his newly found God, and Sister, still abed with a hacking cough, lodged in her lungs by the drenching rain.

"How is Sister's cough this morning?" he asked.

She stood, brushing her hands on her skirt. "The Physician gave her lungwort and I have prayed to God. She'll be better tomorrow."

He doubted that. Sister's strength faded with each step.

But Dominica didn't want to see. And he didn't want to show her.

"You were right to insist we rest," Dominica said, gazing at him again as if he were The Savior instead of the Devil of the moor. "Sometimes, I am too sure of God's will."

"And you?" He stopped his hand from touching her cheek, just to make sure she was there. "Are you all right?"

She did not look like a woman who had touched Death. Days of walking had tempered her like steel. She stood taller, her shoulders straighter than when she left Reading-ton. Sun-ripened freckles sprinkled her nose, but no longer did she thrust out her lip and raise her chin in defiance. Life's lessons had pounded her, as he predicted. He missed the fierce woman who never doubted herself or God.

"Oh, yes." She turned her head and he barely heard the next words. "But everything I wrote is gone."

All those painstaking, hidden words washed away. His chest twisted with her grief. "Can't you start over?"

"All I had to write on was a scrap, and now it has cracked." She looked at the sack slung over his back, "That's why I'm so worried about the message you carry. Is it with you?"

"No. Why?"

"Was it damaged?"

He hadn't thought about it since yesterday. "I don't know. It is sealed."

"Let me look. I can get some idea without breaking the seal." She dropped her voice to a whisper. "Tonight. After compline. The chapel will be empty."

Watching her whispering lips and thinking of being alone with her in the dark, he nearly forgot to wonder at her con-cern. "Why are you so interested in a letter about the rel-ics?"

A nail-bitten finger worried at her pursed lips. "I only

thought to help because I know something of these matters.''

''Doesn't Sister know more?''

She turned white behind her freckles. ''I don't want to bother Sister with it.''

So wrapped up in Dominica and his own foolish promise to steal a feather, he had not thought of William's message for days. What had William written? And how, with hands that shook like one with the palsy.

Someone must have written it for him.

He looked again into her eyes, eyes that burned with what could only be knowledge.

Neeca. Neeca had written it for him.

And what she had written frightened her.

''Tonight then,'' he said, watching her droop with relief.

And before he let her go tonight, he would find out what William would trust him to carry but not to know.

But now, the wooing.

''You need a token of this journey,'' he said, as they strolled by the cloth seller. ''What would you like?''

She stroked a length of scarlet wool and sighed. ''I have no coin.''

She is even poorer than I am, he thought. Every scrap of food had been a gift from God. No wonder she believed God would provide whatever she needed.

''I've one to spare.'' It would be worth a few pence to make her smile. He looked at a pile of small, round decorations. ''A button, perhaps?'' He picked up one carved from a shiny sheep horn and held it against her gray wool sleeve. Where did women put these things?

She pulled her arm away. ''A novice can't wear that.''

''You are not a novice yet.'' *And never will be.*

''Perhaps something to offer the Blessed Larina.''

"Perhaps something for yourself," he snapped. *Fool. Speak kindly.*

"Do you think it is allowed?"

Eyes wide, she was looking at The Savior again, instead of at Garren, but at least she no longer believed him to be the Devil. He seized his advantage. "Not only do I think it is allowed, I think it is required. Part of the reason for pilgrimage is to see more of God's world."

"Carpe diem?"

"Exactly."

She dimpled with a smile. "All right."

He couldn't stop his own grin, so delighted was he to have lifted her sadness. Victory won, he reached for a coin to pay for the button when he felt her hand, light on his arm. He fought the desire to cover her fingers with his.

"If I am to see God's world, then I should see as much as possible," she said. "I should visit every single stall."

"Every one?" He thought to buy the button and be done with it. The stalls—how many?—stretched endlessly around the monastery walls: furs, spices, fish, tin, cloth, leather, coal.

Surely she would not look at the coal.

"Pilgrims," a hook-nosed man whined from the next booth. "Would you buy a Sliver of the True Cross?"

Most likely a splinter removed from the seller's toe, Garren thought. One of thousands of pieces of the "True Cross" peddled to easily gulled pilgrims from England to the Holy Land. If you put them all together you could build a cathedral.

But she was already standing at the relic seller's table. "May I touch it?"

Garren sighed and put the button back on the pile. "Come on, Innocent," he said, ruefully to his shaggy companion. "Let's go."

She fingered the tightly woven Norstead cloth, cooed at the singing birds, tried on a pair of leather gloves and sniffed the cinnamon. She stopped at the collier's booth and assessed the coal, which when mixed with sap, became ink.

Without coin, everything was priceless, but when she slipped a gold chain over her head, his stomach lurched.

He would have to sell Roucoud to pay for it.

The heavy links nestled snug between her breasts, rising and falling with her breath. She looked down at the chain, then up at him through her eyelashes with the instinctively feminine glance of a woman who was never meant to be a nun.

Faced with a strumpet's eyes in a virgin's body, he laughed with joy.

She laughed, too, a wonderful sound that started in the curve of her throat and chased the blue shadows from her eyes. She laughed so hard she could barely stand. As she leaned toward him, he wrapped his arm around her shoulders. Enfolded against him, the soft heat of her breasts pressed his ribs. His heart thumped so hard she must have felt its beat. He caressed the gold links, as if assessing their craft, with fingers that ached to slide to her breasts.

He wanted to take her lips again. He wanted to be alone with her on the dark moor again.

She stiffened at the change in his eyes and pushed away from his chest. Lifting the clanking chain over her head, she handed it back to the merchant. Soft, sun-bleached strands escaped her braid and clung to her throat as she turned back to him. Puzzled blue eyes searched his, full of questions he did not want to answer. "Was this what I was saved for?"

She didn't mean the chain.

He wanted to say yes. Yes would bring her to his arms. Maybe to his bed. Yes would mean her capitulation. But he did not want her to say yes to a saint or a devil. He wanted her to say yes to Garren. He looked away, afraid she would see beneath his disguise to the truth.

"Perhaps," he said, "we should keep looking."

Trust and confusion warred in her eyes. Finally, she pointed to a booth at the end of the wall. "There's the parchment seller. Gillian gave me coin to buy some for her."

Relieved, he fell into step beside her. Beneath the cloak, he tugged at the chausses tight around the damp bulge between his legs. "What does Gillian need with parchment?"

"She asked me to write her petition to the Blessed Larina."

"She will pay you for the writing, as well as the parchment, I trust."

She tilted her head. "People get money for writing?"

Didn't William pay you? he wanted to ask. But in truth, Readington wealth had paid for every bit of food, cloth and ink the Priory used. "Yes. In the city and at the court, a clerk can make his way by scribbling messages."

"Look here! Fine paper," the parchment seller called out. Showing off his gap teeth with a smile, he plucked a piece from a pile on a small wooden bench at his knees. "Imported from Frankfort, made with Rhine water."

She shook her head. "Local parchment, please, but new, not used."

As she bargained for a price that fit Gillian's purse, he watched her finger the edges reverently. This was the gift she wanted. Why hadn't he thought of it? "Let me buy you a piece of your own. Other pilgrims will need your guide."

She dropped the sheet. "God does not intend for me to write it."

"How can you doubt it? He saved you from a raging river." At least that was what she thought. No need to remind her of his own strong arms.

"Saved *me*. Not my words."

"And because of that you think you are quit? What kind of faith is that, Neeca?" He bit his tongue. The kind of faith he would spoil soon enough. Why was he encouraging her? Better she give it up now. Accept that the Bible would not come to life beneath her patient fingers.

But the misery in her face was more than he could bear. If writing made her happy, then by God, The Savior would tell her to write. Let her mourn its loss after he was gone, when he would not have to watch her sorrow.

He snarled at the seller. "Show us some parchment."

Her smile was reward enough.

The seller thumbed through the stack on his bench, while Garren pulled out a soft, white sheet. "This one looks nice."

The seller pulled the sheet away with hands cleaner than a cook's. "Watch the fingers, sir. Staining, you know. But you have a good eye. That's a lovely selection." His lips twitched at the prospect of another sale. "Finest Cistercian lambskin. Nothing better than this."

"And much too dear for my needs," Dominica said. She plucked a piece from the bottom of the pile. Layers of faded ink stained the sheepskin. "What about this one?"

"Well, it's used, of course, but it's been cleaned well."

"Not well enough. I can still read the Twenty Third Psalm and the Beatitudes written on it before that."

Here was the woman who had no doubts, Garren thought, smiling. He stepped back to let her bargain. The seller didn't have a prayer.

"I'll have to rub it down again before I can use it."

"Well, perhaps I can take some off the price…"

At Garren's feet, Innocent sniffed imported paper with a damp nose.

Putting his paws on the bench, Innocent wobbled. The

bench tipped. Sheets of parchment and paper slipped toward the edge. The parchment seller threw himself atop the tilting pile. "Hey! Watch your dog!"

With a shriek, she grabbed Innocent just as the sheets slid off into Garren's waiting hands.

The seller snatched them back, dusting each piece, squinting at imaginary stains. "Look at this now! Nearly ruined…"

"Not ruined," Garren said, tossing the seller a more generous coin than the parchment deserved. He waved at Dominica to run, grabbed the sheepskin, and followed her until they were far enough away to burst into laughter.

"You are a bad dog," Dominica said, wagging her finger at Innocent's nose, but her laughter spoiled the effect. Innocent's tail quivered in happy pride and he licked her finger.

Shaking her head, she plopped him down on the ground.

"Here. For you." Garren held out the parchment.

She took it, with trembling fingers. "Thank you." Some of the shadows had left her eyes.

"Neeca," he began. "Did you…" But he stopped. His questions about William's message could wait until tonight. Let her be happy for an afternoon.

In the meantime, he would try to avoid thinking too deeply about the question of what he wanted from Neeca now.

In the quiet after vesper prayers, Dominica sat across from Gillian and smoothed the sheet over the rough wooden planks of the table in the Monastery's empty pilgrims' quarters. Her parchment lay safely rolled at her side. She patted it again, just to make sure.

As she moved, the coin Gillian gave her clinked against the eating knife in her bag. She prayed for forgiveness for a twinge of pride. Besides, the coin wasn't really hers. She would give it to the Priory, just as soon as she got back.

"How do you start?" Gillian asked.

Dominica sliced the tip of the quill with the sharpening knife, squared the tip, and recut the groove before she dipped it in the inkhorn. She would have preferred a smoothly worn copy table, with its slanted top, but the monastery's scriptorium was not open to strange orphan girls. "I shall start by writing 'Greetings to the Blessed Larina.'"

A warm sunbeam streamed over her shoulder onto the page. She carefully drew two rounded shapes, one nudged off center at the bottom of the other. It was hard to keep the letters whole and the lines straight, even though she scored the page with faint, horizontal stripes.

She held up the sheet and blew on the ink. "See, this is a 'G.'" She looked at it with a critical eye, wondering how G-a-r-r-e-n would look.

Gillian frowned at the letters. "Is that the words you said?"

"Yes. 'Greetings to the Blessed Larina.'"

"The saint don't know those words. I thought you could write Latin."

"Of course I can." Pride pricked her upright. "But you don't speak Latin."

Gillian shook her head emphatically. "Saints only know Latin. That's why the priests must translate for us. They don't speak our language so they don't understand our prayers."

She wanted to argue that Larina lived in the West Country, not Rome, and that God listened no matter what the language, but how could she? Gillian might have misunderstood the Church's reasons, but she was right about the result. No poor soul on earth could speak to God without the Church.

''All right.'' She bit her tongue and dipped the quill in the ink. She added a Latin phrase, muttering in her head the things she dared not say aloud. The Church was just wrong about this. Like the dogs' souls. That's why the Bible needed to be in her own tongue. So this poor woman could talk to God herself.

She lifted the pen from the last stroke. ''There: *Salutem dicit*. That's 'Greetings' in Latin.'' Larina would just have to recognize her own name. ''Now we need an introduction. Something like 'Here come before you Jackin and Gillian of...''' She paused.

''Jack's Ford. Jackin runs the ferry.''

''But whose castle do you belong to? What lord takes care of you?''

Gillian laughed, a lilting trill Dominica had heard many times along the road. ''Our sheep take care of him, more's the like.''

''But everyone is taken care of by someone.''

''There's fewer of us than there used to be. We get to keep some of our own.''

Here was heresy, a violation of the rightful order of the world and God's laws. The Church took care of its own; serfs and knights owed fealty to their lords. Everyone belonged to someone. Except, of course, for the merchants she saw today. And mercenary knights like Garren. No one took care of him. And if the Priory did not take her in, no one would take care of her either.

But Jackin and Gillian clearly took care of each other. She rubbed the smooth shaft of the quill, stripped of its feathers. ''How long have you been married?''

''Two years last Christmas.''

Dominica pursed her lips, afraid to ask, but it might be her only chance. ''What's it like, being married?''

''Is this going in the letter?'' Gillian frowned.

"Oh, no." Dominica flushed. "I just wondered."

Gillian leaned forward, her rosy cheeks aglow. "Well, I wouldn't give up marriage for God. My man is as near to Heaven as I'll get on this poor earth."

Dominica wasn't giving up marriage for God, either. No one would marry her. "Your husband, what is it, I mean, what is he like?"

"He's a good man. He warms my toes at night and my insides in the morning. He bends his back to the work and knows how to have a hearty laugh. His temper is better than some, although I know my place, sure enough." Gillian shook her head. "Widow Cropton is right. I don't think I could learn to live without a husband."

Dominica wanted to ask whether Gillian felt a melting rush in her bones when Jackin held her. Whether she felt their souls link. "You seem to take such…" Dominica did not know what word to use. "…joy in each other."

Gillian blushed, looking around the empty room as if afraid she would be overheard. "You saw more than most ever see. But we're lucky. We've a fever for each other still."

"But you know it's a sin. Aren't you afraid for your souls?"

"I know the priest says it's wrong, but God created that wanting, too. He must have had a reason."

She cut her quill again and dipped it back in the ink. Her life must be writing or that wanting feeling with Garren. It could not be both. "What do you and Jackin want of Larina?"

Gillian ducked her head and spoke to her lap. "A child."

So, despite all their love, Jackin and Gillian were *sine prole.* Without issue. Based on what she knew of babies, they were helping God as much as they could. That meant

Gillian might be barren. A chill lodged in the base of her spine. Then they indeed needed a miracle.

"Ask for a boy," Gillian said.

Homo, she wrote. Pausing to look at it, she wrote, to be sure there was no mistake. *Non femina.*

"Anything else?"

Gillian peered at the page, which still had a handswidth of space. "There's more room." She waved her hand. "Ask for a red dress. And a gold ring with a ruby to match."

This sounded more like a Twelfth Night gift list than a pilgrim's request. "And you think God will give you all this if you only make a pilgrimage?" The dress alone would cost more than they would earn in ten years.

"Oh, yes," she said. "That is the bargain with God."

"But you still need to raise your sheep, birth the babies…"

Gillian wriggled, looking down at her clasped hands. "I'm much better in bed than in the fields." She shrugged. "God will provide."

Even among the nuns, Dominica had never seen such blind faith. "Sometimes God needs help from you."

"That's why we are on pilgrimage. Then it will be God's turn. Oh, also ask for a gold chain."

"A gold chain?" Neeca felt again the weight of the chain and the feel of Garren's fingers near her breasts.

"Yes," Gillian giggled. "I want to wear it naked. We did not tell the priest about that one when we asked permission to go on pilgrimage."

"When God answers your prayers, He may not give you the answer you want." She recognized Sister's words, but not the tart voice that spoke them.

"You sound as if you don't have faith."

"Of course I do," she snapped over the buzzing doubts in her head.

"What is it *you* want from God?"

"My request is somewhat less wordly. I want to be a nun." Her tongue tripped over the familiar words.

Suddenly she felt ashamed. Hadn't she thought just as Gillian did that God would give her exactly what she asked for? Was that faith or pride?

Gillian's eyes widened with respect. "I'm sorry. I didn't know. Of course you have faith. But it sounds like a life in jail to me."

"Oh, no, it's my whole world." She thought of Reading-ton Priory, so small and so dear. Of the small cloister yard. Of Sister's fingers guiding her first letters. Of the tiny bit of sky she could see from her window. And understood for just a moment how someone might see it that way.

"Of course, some folks say marriage is a jail, too." Gillian tapped the paper with her finger. "Write down about the chain."

Aurum, she wrote for gold. What would her wish list be? But thinking of meeting Garren alone tonight, she was no longer sure what she wished for. Or who she was.

She only knew she wished for the feel of his arms again.

Chapter Sixteen

Chanting haunted the monastery's chapel. Lying prone on the rough floor, Garren pretended to pray, waiting for the whine of compline hymns to cease. This was not the place he would have chosen to meet Dominica. Even for an unbeliever, there was something unholy about a tryst in a house of God.

Pillars soared to the darkness of an invisible ceiling where, for all he knew, God perched like a hungry vulture, just as he had when Garren was little more than a boy, pressing his cheek against cold stone praying for parents who died anyway.

Sunlight faded with the song's last note. At the other end of the nave, the monks shuffled dutifully up the night stairs to their beds. Garren's reliquary scraped the floor as he rose to his knees, alone in twilight silence.

He never heard her convent-trained footsteps before he saw her, holding a candle in one hand, clutching her parchment like a sacred relic in the other.

"Neeca…"

She shushed him, looking over her shoulder. Uncombed from bed, her hair ran riot over her breasts, gilding her like a statue. "Did you bring it?"

He nodded.

A ghostly chemise hid under her cloak and beneath the blur of white linen, her bare toes curled against the cold floor. She motioned toward a side chapel, where a single candle wavered before a statue of Our Lady. "Over there."

In the chapel, she set her candle on the floor beside her parchment like an offering before the altar. Reluctantly he put the folded message in her reverent hands. No doubt the fine calfskin carried the words of a man now dead, but he had promised William its safe delivery. "The seal must be unbroken."

Folded into a small rectangle, the vellum was doubly sealed. First, William's Readington ring stamped a red wax circle. Then, a thread, still unbroken, pierced the layers.

She rubbed her thumb over the wax imprint, now cracked where the Readington sword crossed the open book, then held the parchment carefully before the flame as if she could read through it.

"It looks all right," she said, handing it to him.

He slipped it beneath his tunic and held her shoulders so she could not turn away. He could smell the bed-fresh scent of her. "Confess, Neeca. You wrote this message."

The familiar defiance sparked her eyes. "He made me promise not to tell anyone."

Even you. The unsaid words hurt. Why would William not trust him?

She must have seen him flinch, for she laid her hand over his as if to heal a wound. "You care for him very much, don't you?"

"I am more his brother than the one God gave him."

Even in the shadows, Garren could see her pale at his mention of Richard. "Tell me, Neeca." He tightened his grip. "Tell me what he wrote."

She shook her head.

"Please."

Her eyes begged for understanding. "I can't. I promised him."

Look after her, Garren. It is one more thing I must ask of you. Had he kept his promise so well? He sighed.

"Keep your secret, Neeca." *I owe William that.*

Not wanting to let her go, he lifted a handful of her hair and draped it in front of her. Beneath his hands, she squared her shoulders. "There *is* something I need to confess to you."

He dropped her hair. "Go wake a monk." He wanted to hear no more of broken fasts.

"When will you accept what you are?"

Devil or Savior. She could not see him whole. "When will you accept what I am not?"

Candlelight caressed the curve of her cheek. "But my confession is about you."

Desire smoldered in his belly, not just for her body, but for her thoughts. Resolve tumbled into want. "Then," he croaked, "I must hear it."

"I shall stand with my back against yours so you will not look at me while I talk."

He wanted to tell her he was a Devil not a saint, but when she pressed her back against his, he could not make his lips move. Her heat warmed his skin and facing the accusing eyes of the Virgin Mary, he felt like a martyr about to be burned.

"Now, ask me what I have to confess."

"What do…" The words stumbled over the stone in his throat. "What do you have to confess?" Surely two Paternosters would cure any sins she might have committed.

Except the ones with him.

"I have thought of you in the night."

He clenched his fists, as if he could grasp control. ''What have you thought?''

She uncurled his closed fingers, lacing them with hers. ''I have lain in the dark on my pallet and wished you lay beside me.''

He shifted his legs to allow room for the stiffness that threatened to poke through his chausses. ''Neeca...''

''You cannot absolve me yet.''

''I cannot absolve you at all.''

''It must be you or God.''

A drop of melted wax oozed onto the altar. In the unsteady flame, the Virgin's painted blue eyes filled with tears. *I saved her, God,* he thought, shocked at the anger that surged through him. *You shall not have her.* ''Then it must be me.''

Her damp palms pressed his. ''I feel your hands. I want you to touch me. I have even...'' She squeezed his hand. ''I have touched myself, wishing my hands were yours.''

The blood stopped moving in his body.

Rigid, feet apart, he looked down, helpless, as his body reached for her. ''How?''

''I put one hand on my breast and one...'' she seemed to speak inside him, ''one between my legs.''

His entire world stopped. Desire and something more screamed in his veins. He wanted to hold her. To touch her. To take her and leave her before it was too late. Before God took her from him. Before he could not leave her at all.

She sagged against him and her fingers slipped away, as if telling had drained all the strength from her body. ''Garren, what does it mean? What should I do?''

He turned and lost himself in her eyes, no longer fierce or defiant, but tugging at him as gently as her fingers. ''Close your eyes. Show me.''

''I can't.''

He wrapped his arms around her, stroking her hair with shaking fingers. "Show me."

She hugged herself tight against him, as if afraid to let his hands find her secret places. "I can't," she mumbled against his heart.

"I will help. But don't open your eyes, whatever you feel." *I cannot face what I will see there.*

His thumb nestled in the hollow of her throat, he slipped his hand under her cloak, spread it across her chest, careful to avoid her breasts, swelling just out of reach. "Here?"

She shook her head.

"Show me."

She pushed his hand lower, gasping as he brushed the linen over her breast.

"Here?"

Eyes shut, she nodded.

Her hand still lay atop his. He let the tip of her breast slip between two fingers and then squeezed, gently. She squeaked and her breath, fast now, pushed her against his hand.

He dropped his left hand beneath her cloak and cupped it over the linen covering the warm place between her legs. "And here?"

She stiffened, but didn't answer except to cover his hand with hers, trapping it between the warmth of her secret center and the coolness of her fingers.

"Show me how, Neeca."

Scarcely breathing, he waited, letting her get used to his hand. Then, instead of guiding his hand, she pushed her hips against him.

He pressed the damp linen chemise into her hot center. "Like this?" He slid one finger into her and found her wet.

She dropped his hand and threw her arms around his neck, jerking her hips away from his touch. True to her promise, she did not open her eyes. "Not as wonderful as that."

He leaped in response. "Let me make it more wonderful."

Slowly, gently, with a hand on either side, he pulled the linen up, past her calf, over her knees, finally running his hands over the white curve of her thighs, reveling in the feel of her skin. His finger found her again. Her legs opened to him. Wet, full, she tightened around him, breathing in rhythm with his soft strokes, whimpering deep in her throat, arms thrown around his neck for her legs would not let her stand.

All he could hear was the catch of a moan in her throat and the thump of his heart in his ears. All he wanted was to carry her away and never let her go. And he no longer thought of who he was or where they were or what he had promised to do but only his wanting. And hers.

When she pulled away, abruptly, he did not know at first what had happened. Slowly, he saw the world again, where he was and what he had nearly done, glad he had not taken her too far, too soon, right here on the cold, hard floor.

And wondering when the pleasant means to an end had become an urgent end in itself.

She staggered to the altar rail, then slumped against it as she slid to the floor. Her eyes fluttered open, as she returned, as slowly as he, from the secret place he had taken her.

"The spirit," she whispered, voice full of confusion and fear and wonder. "Like on the moor."

He nodded.

A sputtering candle pulled shadows from the Virgin's grieving eyes.

Wide open now, Neeca's eyes never left him, as if expecting him to sprout horns or wings, unsure which it would be until she saw them grow.

He sat beside her, back against the wooden screen, and cupped her chin in his palm, willing his fingers to patience.

Searching his eyes, she stroked his cheek. He hoped his beard was not harsh on her fingers.

"Kiss me," she said.

He felt ashamed that he had not done even that.

His tongue sought her mouth. She offered it until he was dizzy all over again. Strands of honey silk clung to his fingers and when the kiss broke, he tugged a hunk of hair, hoping to tug forth a smile.

Her smile, when it came, was sad. "This is not what I felt with Lord Richard."

The name stabbed his gut and slammed him into the real world of promises and betrayals. Hands still tangled in her hair, he forced her eyes to his, remembering Richard's hands on her at the chapel door. "What do you mean? What did he do?"

She looked at the floor, but then faced him, full. "He tried to kiss me and…touch me."

"And you let him?" Jealousy licked at the fog in his brain.

"No," she said. "I knew then what I wanted."

Jealousy dissolved into self-loathing. Could he call himself a better man than Richard? "I am no saint, Neeca." He let her go, letting her speak without the distraction of his touch.

"If you are not, then what am I? And what did God save me to do? I thought He sent you with an answer." She rose, twisting her hips to smooth down the rumpled chemise. "Instead, you have given me parchment and damp linen. My life cannot hold both. Now, I must find which God wants me to choose."

She tangled her fingers in his rough hair and he wished it were flowing, like William's honey locks. He wished he could offer her the choice of a life outside the Priory. He wished he were everything she deserved instead of a miserable, lying, homeless mercenary who would ruin her life.

She picked up her parchment and candle. "Confession requires penance. What penance must I pay?"

"None." He could scarcely bear the pain in her eyes. "The penance should be mine." And he knew whatever penance he would pay for spoiling her life would not be enough.

"I think," she said, "that God will find a penance for us both."

As he watched her leave the chapel, he realized God had already ordained his punishment and the price would be much, much too high.

He would lose her. As he had lost all the others.

Dominica fled the chapel, hurrying through the arched cloister as if she could hide from life the way she hid from death as a child. Stumbling on legs weak as melted wax, she knew Garren was right. He was no saint.

Neither, she was discovering, was she.

She thought she was above the snare of earthly pleasures. Strength and luck were enough to resist Lord Richard's groping fingers, fumbling under her skirt on the dark stairs.

But she needed more to resist Garren. She needed to resist everything that made him a man, both bitter and kind, one who loved people more than God, loved today more than the hereafter. Last night, she had promised God to open her heart to what this man could teach her. Today, he led her to writing. Tonight to sin.

To wanting more than her immortal soul.

She leaned on a slender column, gasping for breath. The smell of leather and ink drew her through an open door into the sanctuary of the scriptorium.

She knew, as if coming home, that the desks would be set near the windows to catch the light. That the black ink would be on the right and the red on the left. That the copyist's place in the master text would be marked with a weighted string.

She cupped a hand under the candle, straining her ears for the sound of the monks waking for matins. Bad enough she be found in the scriptorium; worse to be careless with a candle.

But the temptation was too great. Unrolling her parchment on an empty desk, she brushed the shabby surface. It was not vellum worthy of words for the ages, but it was her own. She would prepare it as it deserved.

She set the candle down carefully, ignoring the excitement that still fluttered between her legs and the guilt that clawed at her stomach. Here, she would atone for her sin.

She found a pumice stone and scrubbed until her arm ached and the old text was a faint shadow. Next, she covered her palm with chalk and smoothed it across the page. Then, using a string as her guide, she ruled the page with thin black lines.

Finally, the parchment awaited her words. She dipped a quill into the ink. She would write no record of this dark night of sin and doubt. Only of the future.

She slashed a black, bold, *I*. God would have to speak English.

She succumbed to the small temptation of decorating her bold *I* with red shadows before she moved on. She hummed as she worked, unaware of the night flying by, of the rise and fall of matins music, of the moon looking over her shoulder. And if a wave of feeling swept through her when she pressed her legs together, she ignored it.

At last, she admired her handiwork.

I renuwe mi vowe.

It was written. It was real.

That was the lesson. God sent temptation. She resisted. She would repent. She would tell Garren her choice tomorrow and he would understand. Surely Larina would forgive her one transgression. Or two.

Prodding the tight muscles of her neck, she glanced at the copyist's page carefully set aside. Approving of the workmanship, she read the first line.

She blinked, sure her tired eyes had misread. Even in Latin, the words were shocking.

Let him kiss me with the kisses of his mouth: for thy love is better than wine.
He brought me to the banqueting house and his banner over me was love. Stay me with flagons, comfort me with apples: for I am sick of love. His left hand is under my head and his right hand doth embrace me.

She dropped the page. God had looked down from heaven and given words to her thoughts. The heat of Garren's hand warmed her breast again and swirled between her legs.

She turned back to the page. *Song of Solomon.* One of the books of the Old Testament.

The nuns had never read that one.

She capped the ink with shaking hands. *Lead me not into temptation, Lord.* Here was where she belonged, in this quiet peace. When they reached the shrine in a few more days, Larina would give her a sign.

Blood beat warm in her chest and her toes curled on the cold stones of the Tavistock monastery floor as she left the scriptorium.

What penance must I pay?

She paused at the door, remembering the sanctuary of the

Priory's scriptorium, the joy of learning each letter and building words with them. What could be a greater penance than being locked out of this room forever? What could be worse than to lose the life she had always wanted?

She shuddered.

To lose the desire for it.

Chapter Seventeen

The next morning, Dominica searched for Garren in the guest quarters, the warming house and even the chapel, where her determination wavered like the fresh candle burning before the Virgin's statue.

She found him in the stables, surrounded by the warm smell of well-fed animals. The sight of his blunt fingers stroking Roucoud's bay mane sent a fresh wave of weakness from her center through her knees.

No more doubts, she reminded herself, sternly.

A yawn cracked his face as he folded a blanket carefully across the horse's back. She smiled, peevishly pleased he had slept no better than she.

A matching yawn left her mouth wide open just as he saw her. "Did you sleep well?" he asked, with a sad smile.

She swallowed her yawn with a frown. "As well as you did," she answered, doubting it was true. After she returned to the room, Sister's hacking vied with thoughts of him to keep her awake until prime.

"Then you slept not at all." He bent to lift the saddle. "How is Sister this morning?"

"It will be hard for her to keep a seat on Roucoud." She petted the horse's soft mane where Garren's hand had been.

He nodded, as if expecting her answer. "That's why we are borrowing a cart to carry her and an ass to pull it."

"Thank you." She stifled further gratitude. She did not want to think kindly of Garren this morning. What she must say would be hard enough. "I would speak with you alone."

He hoisted the saddle to Roucoud's back, making sure it sat comfortably. "Only the animals can hear." He turned to a long-eared ass in the nearest stall. "Good morning, friend," he said, stroking its nose. "Are you ready for a journey? Where did they put your bridle?"

"Last night...." She spoke to his broad back, as he searched the neat line of nails pounded into the timbers. She swallowed. "Please look at me."

When he did, she was sorry. Something like hope lit his eyes like sunlight shining through green leaves.

God was making this very difficult.

She pushed out her practiced words in one breath, before her courage failed. "With God's help, you saved me from drowning. I thank you. But I was confused because God saved me, but not my writing. I did not know what He meant for me. I thought He sent you to give me answers. That is why..." She ran out of breath. "That is why I came to you with my confession."

His eyes deepened a shade, but did not leave hers. The ass, ignored, nudged him in the ribs. Garren rubbed its nose with one hand, still looking at her.

She talked faster now, afraid she could not finish the most difficult part. "I was foolish to doubt the answer I have always known. My place is at the Priory. God will give me a sign. No matter whether you are a Saint or a Devil or just a man, you can tempt me no more." Her body, vibrating at the touch of his eyes, called her a liar. She raised her voice to shout it down. "I will not fail."

Cheeks hot, she scowled, daring him to speak.

"Is it a failure to be a woman instead of a nun?"

"It is for me."

"Perhaps I am the only one who knows who you really are and what you really want."

Crisp straw crunched beneath her feet. "You don't know what I want." Did she?

He lifted her hand, stubbornly kissing each knuckle, one by one, and teasing the sensitive skin between her fingers with his tongue until a moan tangled in her throat.

She wanted his arms around her. She wanted to feel his soul flowing into hers, making her not quite so alone. And she could not let herself want these things.

He pressed her fingers to his lips. "What will you say when you must confess to a real priest?"

He knew. As if he felt the humors surging through her body. Knew she melted at his touch. "Why do you want to destroy me?"

"I want to save you from a life you no longer want."

"But I do want it!" She snatched her hand away and stared at her fingers, afraid his lips had stained blacker than ink.

"What temptation is there in toneless chants to a thankless God?"

"God offers calm, peace." Neither of which she felt right now, writhing beneath his relentless gaze. "A place in heaven." And one more thing, the most important. She whispered now. "A place to write."

"You write now."

"It's more than that."

"What more, Neeca? Tell me." He gathered her hands, covering them gently with his large, square ones, but his eyes stripped her soul of its protections. "What do you want?"

She ripped her hands away. "To belong!" Shaking, she turned her back, arms wrapping her waist, trying to hold the pain inside. Tears clawed at her eyes.

He enfolded her from behind, curving his body around hers. For just a moment, she laid her head back against his heart. "Neeca, there are places other than Readington Priory. The world is wide."

"What does that matter to me?" Wrapped in his arms, his body shielding hers, she fought his comfort. This confession was harder than the last. "I have no money to travel like the Widow. I have no husband to take care of me like Gillian. The only thing I have is writing. The only place I can write is in the Priory. And the only way I can write is to become a nun." Her voice rose with each word. "The only home I have is within those walls. Do you know what it is like to have no home, to belong to nothing and no one?"

In the silence, the ass in the stall in front of her chomped on a mouthful of straw, flicking his ears.

Still holding her, Garren neither spoke, nor moved. Finally, she felt his brow pressed atop her head. "Yes," he said, his breath warm on her scalp. "I know." The arms cradling her stiffened and fell away.

She heard him lift the bridle and murmur to the ass as he slipped it over the beast's head. When she turned, it was as if he had dropped a visor over his face, snuffing the light in his eyes. *Of course he knows. He is Garren of nowhere.*

As he led the ass out of the stable, he stopped in front of her, his eyes bleak. "Do not seek your answers from me or from your God or anyone else, Neeca. Find them in yourself." He did not look back.

How could she find answers in herself? she wondered, shaking her head. The only sureness came from the still, small voice that was God.

But as she watched him hitch the ass to the cart, she felt as if she had just lost a home she didn't realize she had.

Garren walked alone at the end of the line, Roucoud's reins slack in his hand, Sister's coughs pounding his ears. Two cups of lungwort tea had done no good. Beside the squeaking, two-wheeled, coffin-shaped cart, Dominica and the Physician conferred in whispers.

Despite everything, he couldn't keep his eyes from resting on Dominica. She had ripened with his touch, her breasts fuller, her blue eyes darker under arched brows. He had made her older, sadder, wiser. And when he had done what he must do, she would be sadder yet.

And he would do it anyway, because he couldn't bear to owe William any more than he already did.

Her life will go on much as before, the Prioress had told him. A lie. Oh, they would still let her do the Priory's dirty work, but she would no longer live within its walls, surrounded by a bevy of loving Sisters. They would marry her off to some village lout, if they bothered with marriage at all. She had no dowry, no family alliance to bring to a marriage. Nothing but her good name.

He would deprive her even of that.

Do you know what it's like to have no home?

He did. Too well. And the pain he recognized in her cry was almost enough to stop him. Almost, but not quite.

She would survive, as he had, one day at a time, for when he had done his worst, today would be all she had left.

The sound of horse's hooves broke his thoughts. They came from behind him.

One by one, the others lifted their heads as if catching a whiff of a fox.

"Robbers?" Jackin asked, stepping in front of his wife, still holding her hand.

Garren turned his ear away from the wind to listen. "Probably not. It's only one horse." And the horse was faltering.

Simon drew his sword. "I'll go."

"No," he said, mounting Roucoud. "You get everyone hidden. I'll see who it is."

He mounted Roucoud and wheeled the horse around to ride over the road they had come. Glancing back, he saw Simon and Dominica struggling with the teetering cart, too large to hide. He drank in one last sight of her, wanting to tell her to hide, to save herself, that he was no one's Savior. Not even his own.

Over a rise and out of sight of the rest, he saw the rider, thin, dark and breathless as his exhausted horse. Garren pulled up Roucoud and drew his sword, resting it across his saddle.

The strange man slowed his mount to a walk. His hand hovered over his own sword for a moment, then he waved. "Garren, is that you? It's Lord Richard."

Fury, visceral, throbbed in Garren's sword hand. He did not return the wave. Richard dropped his hand.

This is not what I felt with Lord Richard. If he let go the rage roiling through his gut, he would tear off lips, fingers, tongue, any part of the man that might have soiled Dominica. He quelled the anger. Surely Richard had not ridden so far just to slake his lust. He could do that in the comfort of his own bedchamber.

Within speaking distance, the heaving horse slowed to a walk. Richard's cloak, painted with a rain-splattered, blood-red cross, fitted him ill. Why had he come? Did he bring news that would confirm the futility of this trip? Garren's promise weighed heavier than the message that lay in his sack. Was he too late?

"Where are the others?" Richard called out.

"I sent them ahead in case you were a robber."

"You are the one in need of money, as I recall." Contempt smeared Richard's voice.

He must know. "How fares William?"

"Alive. When I left."

Thankfulness flooded his veins. Maybe faith in a stolen feather's power kept him clinging to life, Garren thought, realizing he still harbored secret hope that God would pity an unbelieving pilgrim and spare William's life. "Alive and you are sorry of it?"

Richard's nostrils flared in indignation. "How can you say that? I have come to pray for his recovery."

Garren snorted. Richard, he wagered, had less faith in God than he did. He was just more willing to use those who did. "I hoped you had come to pray for your own soul."

"A mercenary couldn't understand. If I can do anything at all to save my brother's life, then, of course, I will."

Garren doubted that. "Strange you came to that decision only after the rest of us left." Why had he come? What had changed in six days?

Unable to force an answer, he reluctantly jerked his head to the west. He could not deny a pilgrim the right to join them. "Come. They are just over the rise." The horses turned in step.

Simon stood alone with drawn sword before the listing cart. One wheel sagged in the mud just off the road. Inside, Sister huddled over the dog, her eyes closed in prayer.

"Where is everyone?" Richard said.

"Hiding."

"It's all right," Richard said, waving to the invisible throng as if he were the King himself. "I have come to join you."

At a nod from Garren, Simon let his sword drop. Sister opened her eyes and lifted her head. Innocent, freed, jumped to the ground, yapping. Sister dragged herself to the edge of the cart, where Simon lifted her more easily than he had hoisted his sword.

"Ah, Lord Richard," she said. "We feared you were a band of robbers."

Beneath Richard's stirrups, Innocent leapt on short legs, snapping at his booted toes. Just jump a little higher, boy, Garren thought. You almost have him.

"I am but a humble pilgrim like yourselves." Richard's high-pitched voice competed with Innocent's bark. He glared at the dog. "While praying for my brother, it came to me that I should add my voice to your pleas to God and the Blessed Larina."

Disgusted, Garren watched them step forward, one by one, murmuring and bowing, offering the respect due the Readingtons to one who did not deserve it. Innocent, he thought, was a better judge of character.

"Where is the girl?" Richard said. "What have you done with her?"

Guilt bit Garren with teeth sharp as Innocent's. "I? Nothing. What did you do to her?"

Richard's cocked eyebrow feigned innocence. "Garren, I am expressing concern about all those under your protection. Or did William only pay you enough to take care of yourself and his letter?"

William's letter. The one Richard had tried to tear from his hand. What did the letter say? From the urgency in his ride, Richard now knew, somehow discovered after they left. And from the glitter in his eye, Garren thought the answer was a matter of life and death.

Richard had forgotten until he saw the girl among the bowing pilgrims, just how lush she was. Stingy lips, he thought, peering down from his horse's back, but the swell of her breasts tightened the stones between his legs. He shifted in the saddle, wondering whether Garren had swived her yet. "Dominica."

She ducked her head without the courtesy of a curtsey. "Greetings, Lord Richard. How fares your brother?"

His brother, his brother. Did none of them care that his bones hurt after too many days in the saddle?

"He still lived when I left." He twisted back a smile. It was difficult to sound sorrowful over a barking dog. "Of course, I have been on the road for several days."

"With God, all things are possible." When she was not smiling, and she was not smiling now, the girl's face looked as stern as the crow standing next to her. What was the old nun's name? Her holier-than-thou attitude irritated his bowels.

"Yes, of course, God works miracles." he said.

"We pray continually for his health," said the old nun. Sister Marian, that was her name.

"And mine, too, of course," he snarled.

"We pray for all God's creatures, Lord Richard." The coughing crow's bland tone told him he was no more important than the cur nipping unchecked at his heels. She'd taught that to the slut along with reading and writing. And pride above her station. She should be grateful that a titled lord would even speak to a foundling.

"It's time for the midday meal," Garren said. "Simon, Ralf, Jackin, let's lift that cart back on the road."

As they drifted out of hearing, Richard swung out of the saddle, boot hitting the dog's jaw with a satisfying crunch. The dog yelped and the girl cried out, falling to her knees to pet him.

Maybe now she would know he meant to be reckoned with.

She swept the animal into her arms, nuzzling him like a

baby while he licked her face. Disgusting. He should insist she put the dog down, but decided he would be safer if she kept her grip on the beast. "Tell me of your journey, Dominica."

She skewered him with those haughty blue eyes as if he were not worthy of her glance. His father had looked at him the same way. "I must help with the food, my lord."

"Don't make me command you, Dominica. What new things have you learned on pilgrimage?" He watched for a guilty flush that would signal her violation.

Instead, she smiled. "Oh, God's world is wide and wonderful, milord. And full of many things."

"What things?"

Stiff-backed, clutching the dog, she arched away when he tried to put his hand on her arm. "You trod the same path as we did, milord. The sun warmed us. The breeze cooled our cheeks. Buttercups stretch waist high. We walked nearly six miles and shall be able to say vespers in Liskeard if you do not delay us overlong."

Scorn dripped from her voice. He would turn that to respect soon enough. "And have you written during your travels, Dominica?"

"Nothing of interest, milord."

Nothing of interest. Did they know no other words, any of them?

"Words are magic, aren't they, Dominica? Words can make things appear or disappear. You've created some interesting words, haven't you?"

Her eyes flickered, wary. Good.

"I copy the Word of God, Lord Richard."

"Oh, that is not all. You copied my brother's words, too. Words the mercenary carries."

Her skin went pale under the peasant color she had ac-

quired on the road. She looked over her shoulder, then lowered her voice. "What did he tell you?"

First, he would tease her. "Or perhaps my brother never
said those words and you just wrote them down. That would
be a sin, wouldn't it? To lie."

"I didn't...I don't understand."

He smiled, gratified. Now that he had put fear in her eyes,
it was easy to face them. At least the shrew was smart
enough to recognize a threat when she heard one. "Oh, I
think you do." He draped his right arm around her shoulders
and let his hand dangle over her breast, keeping a watch on
the dog's teeth. "But you can help me forget what you
know, Dominica."

Before he saw her move, he gasped as her elbow jabbed
his gut.

"Ah, Lord Richard, even if I forget, God remembers. *Deo
gratias.*" She scampered away, the cur trotting at her heels.

"Richard," Garren yelled. "Come get some food. We
need to move on."

Food. The slut had punctured his stomach. Yet another
thing she would answer for when he had her on her back.

God, Dominica thought, eyeing Lord Richard from a safe
distance, had failed her this time.

She had escaped, but not far enough or fast enough. Only
when they reached the shrine would she and Garren be safe.
But there were miles and days to walk.

And now, Lord Richard walked with them.

She thanked Our Heavenly Father that she had told Garren nothing about the message. That was part of the Earl's
wisdom and she was glad to keep his secret. Glad for all
the Priory owed the Readingtons, of course, but there was
something more than that. Something she did not feel for
Lord Richard.

But as long as Garren carried the message, he could be in danger. Saint or Devil, she could not allow harm to come to him. Her promise to Lord William was reason enough for her to protect him, even if there were other reasons she didn't want to think about.

"Time to go," Garren called, holding both horses.

Lord Richard ignored him, walking over to her. "Ride with me. My tired nag can carry two."

Garren took the bridle and pulled the horse away. "Welcome to a pilgrimage, Lord Richard. We walk."

The hatred in his eyes as he looked at Garren strengthened her resolve. She would find a way to steal it tonight. Then she would tell Lord Richard she had it. That Garren knew nothing of it. Garren would be safe and she would be the only one in danger. Surely God would protect her.

She slid a glance to Lord Richard, stomping by himself ahead of the rest.

Or she would end up closer to death than Lord William.

Chapter Eighteen

As Dominica watched the waning moon rise over the trees, a dying fire warming her back, she thanked God they slept outside tonight. Stealing the message would have been impossible in a crowded guest house.

A chorus of sleep sounds drifted on the night air. The Widow's snore. Sister's wheezing cough. Ralf's garbled prayer as his night on the moor visited his dreams.

A new sound spoiled the familiar harmony. One that made her shiver.

Lord Richard's nasal rattle.

Garren made no sound at all. On his pallet in the shadow of the trees at camp's edge, he lay silent as one dead. Once he stretched out, she could not tell whether he slept or woke until the older Miller brother came to trade the watch. The Miller snores joined the chorus before Garren disappeared into the woods on his first circle of the camp.

She would not have much time.

As she scrambled to her feet, Innocent cocked his good ear and whined.

"Shh. Stay." She wagged her finger *no,* listening frantically for footsteps in the trees.

Sister lifted her head. "What is it, Neeca? What's wrong?"

"Nothing. Just a need to relieve myself. Go back to sleep."

Sparing only a glance at the sleeping figures, she scampered to Garren's pallet, flinching when a twig snapped beneath her feet. She held her breath, but the sleeping choir sang on.

Falling to her knees, she grabbed his sack, praying he did not carry the message with him tonight. Keeping watch for him in the woods, she groped inside. She touched a worn leather pouch full of noisy coins, a sheathed eating knife with a smooth wooden handle, and rough wool, warm on her palm like his skin. An extra tunic, perhaps. A pointed corner pricked her finger. The tunic was wrapped around a folded piece of parchment. She pulled it out, dropped the stack, stood and turned, poised to run.

Turned into the arms of a tall, broad, warm wall with strong arms, gentle hands, and a low, husky voice.

"So, have you come to my bed after all?"

Arms full of Dominica again, Garren's first thought was how she would feel between his legs. He wrapped her close, inhaling her scent of damp grass and tiny violets, feeling her breath fast and hard against him. It took a moment before he realized her hands clutched something against his chest.

He leaned away and looked down at a piece of folded parchment pierced by a thread and sealed with cracked red wax.

The scheming wench had plucked the message right out of his bag.

Disappointment vied with astonishment.

"What," he said through clenched teeth, "are you doing with that?"

She wiggled, which thrust her hips against his throbbing groin. He clamped down a moan. "Let me take it," she whispered, stilling her hips much too close to his. Her fingers tightened on the letter as if she had strength enough to keep it. "You will be safer."

"From whom?" A foolish question. Together, they glanced at Richard's sleeping figure on the far side of the fire.

Without letting go, he dragged her into shadows under the trees. A gust of wind rattled the oak leaves, blowing acorns skittering down the tree trunks.

Why did she want a message she had written? What did it say? Last night, he allowed her to keep the secret. Richard's arrival changed everything.

"Neeca," he gentled his voice, "I know you promised William, but now Richard is here. You must tell me what you wrote."

"He told me to tell no one."

He fought his admiration for a loyalty to William as strong as his own. He laid his hand in the sensitive curve where her neck met her shoulder. "He trusted me to carry it for him. You know I would never hurt him."

Or you, he thought, stroking her throat with his thumb, but he did not say it, afraid it might be the truth.

An owl screeched, hidden in the whispering leaves, but Neeca said nothing. He tipped her chin up, but darkness hid her eyes. "You are in danger. I want to protect you."

"God will protect me."

"God protects no one."

"How can you say that?" He did not have to see her shadowed eyes to know she accused his lack of faith. "God saved Lord William."

He grabbed her arms in frustration. "Dominica, stop this. Either tell me what William wrote to the Godforsaken saint or I will break the seal myself."

She gasped, curling her hands around the battered parchment. "No, you mustn't. He didn't write to Larina. It's for the monk who cares for her shrine."

"Can you remember the words?"

She nodded.

"Then tell me so I will not need to read them."

In the stillness, her blood pounded against his palms. Then she tugged the fingers of his left hand free. Cautiously, he let her match her right hand to his left, palm to palm, pointing to heaven in prayer.

And for a moment he stood in a candle-lit chapel again, and he wanted to hear her confess, wanted to lay his lips soft on her parted ones and draw out her truth with his tongue.

She closed her eyes and the words tumbled from her memory in the monotone of the mass. "'By the time this is delivered I shall surely be dead by my brother's hand.'

No. Not dead. "But Richard said he still lives!"

She shook her head, as if afraid to stop the flow. "'...dead by my brother's hand in spite of the miraculous efforts of my friend, Garren, who with God's help brought me home from the field in France when all others left me for dead. But in my own bed, I worsen. My brother kills me by inches. He poisons my food and he thinks I do not know. I write this so God and Saint Larina may be my witness to his treachery."

Poison. A coward's weapon destroying William from the inside, oozing out his skin in white spots and black warts. Now he knew what alchemy Richard's Italian practiced. Too lazy or cowardly to make a second son's way in the world, Richard, like a jealous Cain, slew his brother instead.

"I should have let him die in battle," Garren said. His gift of life cursed them both. But William knew he was being poisoned. Disloyal anger buzzed in his head. "If he knew, why did he let it happen?"

She laced her fingers with his. "He was weak and confused. Maybe some food was tainted and some not. Maybe he tried to keep up his strength. Maybe they forced him to eat. Maybe all he could do was ask God for help."

"Why didn't he ask me?" *Why didn't I see?* Guilt's teeth gouged deep into his heart. Richard murdered William before his eyes and he had been blind.

"How could he ask you to act without proof?" she said, her voice full of forgiveness he would not give himself.

"His word is all the proof I need." How could he atone? Should he go back to Readington now? But he didn't even know whether William lived or died. He gave his word he would deliver the message that would expose Richard. That was William's plan. But something had gone wrong. Very wrong. And if the Church didn't punish him? "I will make Richard pay."

She squeezed his hand. "That's exactly why William didn't tell you. Listen. There's more. Something to do with you." She tightened her fingers, cleared her throat, closed her eyes, and recited again. "'I ask the Church to punish Richard for his sin of murder. I also petition the King to give my castle, my land, and all that would have been my brother's on my death to my friend Garren, who has been more than a brother to me.'"

His knees buckled and he stumbled, nearly bringing them both to their knees. A home. Ripe English earth and hills so startling green they hurt the eye. A place to live, grow old and die.

But the price, William's life, was much, much too high.

"I never asked him. I wouldn't want it like this." He

tried to see her eyes in the dark, needing her to believe him. "Besides," he said as an afterthought, "the King would never agree."

But who knew what a King might do? Why had the King agreed to let Garren's home pass from royal control to the Church?

She touched his cheek. "None of that matters, don't you see? If you kill Richard, people will say you did it to get Readington, not to avenge William. We must let God punish Richard."

He laughed, bitterly. "The same God who let him kill?" God let Cain live. Garren would not be so generous to Richard.

She turned his chin and forced him to look at her. "Garren, if Richard knows what this says, he's come to kill you."

Her words cleared the fog of anger and regret. It was Neeca who was in danger. "And you, too." He tightened his arms around her as if as long as he held her, she would be safe. "I won't let him, you know."

"But don't you see? He must kill both of us *and* destroy the message. He thinks you carry it. Until he has it in his hands, you'll be safe."

He picked a leaf out of her hair, stroking the top of her head until she curled against him, hiding her face on his shoulder, the parchment cradled against his chest. It was a harebrained scheme. Richard would want them both dead in the end. "And what about you?"

"God will protect me," she said.

Her words were no longer defiant and he wondered whether her faith faltered as much as her voice. "So you think God will protect you but you have to protect me. Is that how your faith works?"

He almost laughed. No one had tried to protect him for ten years. But in the midst of flying arrows and flailing swords on the battlefield, he had never feared for his own life, only for William's. Was that what Neeca felt?

Was that what he felt for her?

"God will protect us both," she insisted, words muffled in his chest, "but sometimes, He needs a little help."

He rocked her, envious of the innocent faith that believed anyone could be safe in a dangerous world. "All right," he said, letting her go, reluctantly. No arguments would be won tonight. "Take it. I'll think of something."

Slipping away from his arms, she sighed, but he could not tell whether it was from relief or regret.

"And Neeca," he said, watching her tuck the folded message against her breasts. "I'm going to give God a lot of help."

He thought she smiled as she sprinted through the trees.

She held the message, but he'd make sure Richard never knew. In fact, he would tell Richard that William brought an unknown scribe to the castle. That would keep Richard's attention away from Neeca.

But as much as he hated to admit it, they were going to need a little help back from God.

Garren found Neeca huddled over Sister well after sunrise, arms around the frail, shaking shoulders. He knelt, absently scratching the sensitive spot behind Innocent's missing ear. The short, straight tail thumped happily against his thigh.

"How are you this morning, Sister Marian?" He knew he would not like the answer.

"She's tired." Neeca answered. "She did not rest well."

"I'll be fine," Sister said, her voice too weary to lift the words.

"Maybe a day's rest…" Neeca said, her eyes begging him for help. All her fears gathered in her gaze. Losing

another day for William. Risking another day with Richard.
Fear that rest would not be enough.

She must have forgotten their day of rest at Tavistock.

"Restormel Castle is just north of here." He had been
there with William before they went to France. A lifetime
ago. "I think we can be there by afternoon."

Neeca's eyes widened. "One of the Prince's castles?
Would we be welcome?"

"The Prince has more castles than he can count. He won't
be in residence, but the steward will remember me." He
turned to Sister. "We'll put some extra blankets in the
cart."

Sister nodded. "I'm grateful. I don't want to delay the
others." Her eyes met his and he saw Death in them. *Like
a soldier on the field, she knows her time has come.* He
glanced at Neeca, collecting the blankets to pad the cart.
Sister shook her head. *And she doesn't want the girl to
know.*

He shook a mental fist at God. *Not this one, too. She is
one of yours.* "I'll speak to the others," he said instead.
"I'm sure they'll be happy to partake of the Prince's hos-
pitality."

No one protested. They murmured and made the sign of
the cross and clasped their hands and shook their heads in
pity, each glad it was not them.

Richard was the last.

"I can barely walk this morning." He yawned in Garren's
face. How could two brothers be so different? William
hearty, blond, a warrior and a scholar; Richard, slight, dark,
self-contained. A weasel being eaten by a tapeworm. "I
can't sleep another night on the ground."

"Then you'll like my plan. Tonight, we'll sleep in Restormel. Sister needs a day of rest."

"Well, I need a night of rest after hearing her cough from

dusk to dawn. You carry that old nun like the queen and I can't even ride my own horse!''

Garren crossed his arms to keep from throttling Richard. ''Your sleepless night must have erased your chivalry lessons.''

Richard's thin nostrils flared and he dropped the mask of piety over his face, spreading his fingers across his chest in apology. ''Forgive me. It is only my worry for my brother. You still carry the message he gave you?''

So soon he showed his hand. Garren shrugged. ''Of course. Still sealed, as he asked.''

A slight scent of relief wafted from Richard's sloping forehead. Good. Maybe he could convince Richard he knew nothing of what it said.

''He gave it to you because I was not coming.'' Richard held out his hand. ''Now that I am here, I'll see that it's delivered.''

Clever. Maybe Neeca was right and he needed the proof in his hands before he killed them. ''Oh, that won't be necessary. I gave him my word that no one but the monk would see it.''

''Oh, when he said no one he didn't mean me. He wants me to carry it. He told me.'' Richard's eyes shifted, unable to hold Garren's while he lied, but his smile stayed painted in place. ''While we prayed together. Right before I left.''

''Well, I'm sure that's true,'' Garren said, sure it was not, ''but I gave him my oath. He was so secretive, he sent for a scribe from White Wood to write it.''

Richard's glance slithered around the camp until it found its prey. ''Dominica is the only scribe I saw.''

Garren kept his eyes on Richard's. In the habit of lying himself, Richard might be adept at catching others. ''Well, I only know what he told me. It's probably some secret penance.'' He forced his hand to a friendly slap on Richard's back. "We can only hope the Saint answers all our prayers, William's as well as yours and mine for him."

Richard's lips drew into a thinner smile. "And Dominica's."

Garren's muscles tensed like an archer's taut bowstring. "Dominica's?"

"Dominica's," Richard prompted. "For her acceptance into the order."

This was ground uncertain as the spongy soil of the moor. How did Richard know? And what else did he know? Garren crossed his arms again, wanting to wipe clean the hand that touched Richard's back. "She is a woman whose faith can move mountains."

Richard's nose twitched. "But perhaps better suited to other callings."

The girl was not made for the veil, the Prioress said. Disturbing, that Richard agreed. He cleared his throat, afraid to sound overly eager. "What do you mean?"

"Well, her birth can hardly be worthy. Daughter of a whore, no doubt, with nowhere better to drop her."

Garren strangled the urge to defend her. If Richard knew he cared for her, his motives for shielding her would be suspect. He feigned indifference and idle curiosity instead. "What calling might suit her?"

"She'll make some man an excellent bedmate." Richard's eyes defiled her. "Don't you agree?"

His body did, but Richard's insinuation made his blood pound in anger. Would the man dare to take her first and kill her later? "I don't know. I find her a little tall."

Richard cocked his eyebrows. "Oh? I thought I saw the two of you go into the woods together last night."

Dangerous, shifting ground. "You must be mistaken. Besides, why would I want to bed someone who loves God more than me?"

"She's not a nun yet, you know." A sultry leer simmered behind Richard's brown eyes. "I don't believe she ever will be."

And suddenly, Garren knew what would happen to Dominica. After.

His anger flashed like lightning at Richard and the Prioress.

Then, it struck him.

He was the one who had agreed to ruin Dominica for thirty pieces of silver. Before he knew her. Before he knew her dreams. He would be the instrument to destroy them. Not God's instrument or even the Devil's, but the instrument of an unholy alliance between Richard and the Prioress.

Richard waited, smiling.

Hot anger turned to cold fury. Yet another reason for Richard to die. He stuffed his guilt in a box, to wrestle with later. Right now, the game had become precarious. If Richard expected him to spoil Dominica, he must pretend he would or Richard might take her himself. He might anyway. He was not sure which Richard wanted more: her body or her life, but he would make sure he had neither.

"No, she's not a nun yet." He let his glance rest on her, as if considering Richard's evaluation. "You might be right. And she does have beautiful hair, doesn't she?"

Richard almost licked his lips. "Some man will have her, Garren. Mark my words."

His words were a threat.

Chapter Nineteen

Restormel Castle sat like a rusty crown above its moat, surrounded by a forested deer park. Straining to hear Sister breathing over the rattle of the cart, Dominica barely noticed. As soon as they crossed the drawbridge, she watched anxiously as Garren lifted Sister out of the cart as easily as if she were Larina's feathers. Trailed by the castle's steward and the Physician, he strode across the courtyard.

Lord Richard's skeletal fingers gripped her wrist before she could follow. Straining against his hand, she watched Garren carry Sister through an arched doorway.

"Don't worry, Dominica," Lord Richard said, with a pious sneer. "If Sister dies on pilgrimage, she goes straight to Heaven."

His words chilled her more than his touch. She had never admitted that Sister might die.

"I am certain, Lord Richard," she said, raising her voice above Innocent's growl, "that Sister will go straight to Heaven whenever God chooses to call her."

She pulled free. Clutching her sack, she pushed through the milling pilgrims at the gatehouse entrance toward the room where Garren had disappeared. Gillian thrust a dun-colored blanket at her chest. "Here, take it. In case she needs another."

The scratchy, home-woven wool was Gillian and Jackin's own. Dominica hugged it, blinking back tears. "Thank you for your kindness. I'm sure she'll be fine in the morning. I'm sorry to delay your journey."

The Widow squashed Dominica against her ample bosom. "The Blessed Larina can wait a day. Go on now, she needs you."

Innocent at her heels, she walked across the courtyard, ignoring the whispers behind her. Perhaps they whispered what only Lord Richard was brash enough to say aloud.

The Physician and the steward left the room, heads together, as she approached. She paused at the door.

Neither Garren nor Sister saw her. Eyes closed, Sister lay on a narrow bed, so small that only her black robes gave her substance. Garren's broad back still faced the door as he tucked another pillow under her wimpled head with awkward fingers.

His gentle care of Sister clutched at Dominica's heart.

Sister laid bloodless fingers on his strong right arm. The voice Dominica knew better than her own trembled. "Remember, my child. God doesn't wait for us to love Him first. He knows our secrets and loves us anyway."

"Ah, Sister," he said, a teasing smile in his voice, "I'll let you keep your secrets. Let me keep mine."

She held her breath to listen. Surely Sister had no secrets, but she wanted desperately to hear Garren speak of his.

Instead, Innocent raced into the room and hopped on the bed, setting Sister coughing again. She hugged his black, furry body with the shaking tail and waved Dominica into the room.

When Garren turned, the sadness in his eyes belied the smile in his voice.

So, he too thinks she will die.

"Thank you." They were the only words she could say.

"She deserves more."

She nodded, burying her face in Gillian's scratchy blanket, glad Garren shielded her so Sister would not see her cry. His hand, large and warm, cradled her head. At his touch, peace, deep and wide, surrounded her, the kind of peace she had expected when she first kneeled in Readington's dusty courtyard to ask his blessing, so many miles ago.

Then his hand, and the feeling, were gone.

When she lifted her head, he reached for her sack. She held it behind her back. "It's here. Safe." she muttered, slipping the message inside her chemise, where it lay next to her heart. "Just keep him away."

He frowned as if to argue, but she shook her head, glancing at Sister.

"I must see to the others." He spoke loudly enough for Sister to hear, but his eyes never left hers. "The steward will bring you food and build up the fire. I'll be sure you are not disturbed. By anyone. If you need me, I'll be at hand."

She wanted to call him back as soon as he left the room.

Stretched on a pallet on the floor beside Sister's bed, Dominica slept fitfully though a night alternately filled with coughs and rasping silence. When the Widow filled the doorway well after sunrise, Sister finally dozed.

"James is preparing a new remedy," the Widow whispered.

Dominica's yawn stretched into a smile. When had the Physician become James to Widow Agnes? "She's sleeping now."

"And never slept a wink all night, I vow. Go on," she said, waving her hands. "Take that dog outside. You both need fresh air. I'll sit with her. I raised five children and only lost one.''

On the bridge across the moat, Innocent at her heels, Dominica tried to draw a breath but a weight pressed her chest and she couldn't fill her lungs. The message branded her skin. The sunshine mocked her, streaming through the trees to casting shifting shadows on the deer park's green carpet. God kept every blade of grass clinging tenaciously to the earth. Why not Sister?

She slumped to her knees, ripping tufts of grass up by the roots and throwing them at an unfeeling tree trunk. Innocent chased each disintegrating clump, trying to fetch it back. Sobs thick as Sister's coughs rattled her chest until she bent over and buried her face in dirt covered fingers.

Please God, she thought, *do not let her die.*

''Is this a new form of prayer?''

She looked up, wiping her hands on her skirt, to see Garren leaning against the tree. Dappled with shadows, he belonged to the red and green and brown of the forest, deep, dark, full of secrets.

''He won't take her,'' she said, as if words were truth. ''He mustn't.''

''This is the first time God has taken someone from you.'' He did not ask a question.

''I have begged Him to spare her.''

''Begged? Not told Him what to do?''

She bit back the tears and shook her head. *Sometimes God needs a little push.* How bold those words seemed now. How far away that girl in the Priory who was always so sure of what God would do. Her useless hands curled in her lap. Would God listen if she pressed them together and pointed them to Heaven? ''I am willing to beg if it will change His answer.''

He sat beside her on the grass. "And if He doesn't answer your prayer? What then?"

She shook her head. "I do not know." Not a day of her life had been led without Sister. She tried to imagine returning to the Priory, donning a habit and picking up the quill day after day alone. The very thought left her lost. "It would be the first time He has failed me."

He crossed his arms, the bitterness in his voice shielding his secrets. "You will learn to live with God's failings."

She curled her hands around his arms, telling herself her touch was only compassion. "What did God do to you that you resent Him so?"

He looked at her for a long moment, then uncrossed his arms and spoke abruptly. "I had reached my seventeenth birthday." A slight burr blurred his words. "I had left home and was living in the monastery, concerned only with God and my upcoming vows."

She smiled, seeing him at Simon's age, shoulders not so broad, lips not so narrow, face still beaming with faith. Her heart ached for the boy long lost. "Where was home?"

"Near Berwick. English or Scots land, depending on the strength of the troops and luck of the day. All my father wanted was to be left alone. His loyalty was only to his land. It made him popular with neither side."

"You were a second son?" Only after the land was secure with an heir would a son be allowed to give his life to God.

He nodded. "My brother's name was James."

Silence followed. Each word from him was a gift. "How old was he?"

"William's age." He stared down at her hands, atop his knee. "He could always best me at arm wrestling."

"You were at the monastery," she prompted. "What happened then?"

"The Death came." Remembered pain flooded his voice. "I feared for my family, so I rode home. Death rode quicker. The plague felled James as I crossed the draw-bridge. Then his wife. Their babe."

She shuddered, still feeling the fear of a child hearing death cries echo from cloister walls.

"I sent word to my Abbot asking him to give comfort, to pray to God to spare them. The Abbot could not, or would not, come." Grim memories clenched his jaw. "Hours passed like weeks then. Death as sudden as in battle. But I knew, surely, the monks prayed for us eight times a day. I knew God would listen to their prayers." He spoke to him-self now, gazing into the trees as if into the past. "My mother fell ill the next day. My father would not leave her side."

Both father and grandfather, praying over a wife's death-bed. No wonder Garren still walked alone. She wondered what it would be like to be loved like that.

"Then, my father fell ill. Finally the Abbot sent a mes-sage. My father must sign over his property to the Church. Then, he promised, God would save us."

Dread pressed her shoulders. Not even an Abbot can make promises for God. "What did your father do?"

"He signed. I helped him make his X. Then I took the scroll to the Abbey, wearing my grandfather's badge and I made my own vow. When they were spared, I would tread the path to Compostela my grandfather walked. I spent hours with my forehead pressed against the stone floor be-fore the altar. 'Take me instead' I told Him." He whispered now, as if begging God again. "Take me instead."

God doesn't always answer our prayers the way we want. But she could not say the hollow words. They would choke her.

As if coming from a trance, he looked at her again, eyes

as bleak as death. "God killed them all. My brother, his wife, his son, my father, my mother. But He left me alive."

She laid her hands on his, wanting to pull him into her arms and hold him, but it was too late, much too late for comfort. She could not excuse or explain God's plan. The good died with the wicked and the Church's only explanation was that the entire race must pay for its sins. "What happened to your home?"

"The lying Abbot lounged in my father's chair and told me their death was God's will, but that their generous gift would shorten their time in Purgatory." Years of pain burned into his laugh. "The monks' fat sheep graze there now."

"How could the King allow it? The right to award the land is his."

He shrugged. "Perhaps he needed God's help to hold the Scots' border rather than mine." Beneath her fingers, his hands curled into fists. "The Abbot offered to sell it back to me if I had enough money."

"If you had chosen to bring back prisoners for ransom, instead of…" How could she ask it? "…instead of the Earl, would it have been enough?"

"To buy it back?" She saw again the face of the Garren she knew. The one forever at war with God. "I would not let God take William, too."

This time, he forced God to take him instead of a brother, she thought. This time, he traded his future for the Earl's, trying one more time to correct God's mistakes. She understood. Readington, Lord William, felt like family to her, too. She had never stopped to wonder why. "You would do anything for him, wouldn't you?"

He looked at her long, hard and deep, and tucked a stray strand of hair behind her ear. His fingers trailed down her cheek, soft as a whisper. "I thought, once, that I would."

She held her breath. Waiting. Wanting. Hoping.

His fingers slipped away, leaving her only the touch of the wind at her cheek. "Do you miss it, your home?" she asked.

His eyes looked puzzled and far away. "I barely remember it, but I miss having a home."

Do you know what it is like not to have a home? She had hurled those words at him, doubled over with her own pain, never knowing they were both homeless children. For the first time, she saw him truly as a man, neither Saint nor Devil. A man who carried sacred relics and wore ancient shells despite his disbelief. A man no more able to control God than she.

"So," she said, soft as a breath, "you believe in nothing now?"

"I have little use for vows and pilgrimages." He stood, as if trying to get far enough away that he could not touch her again. Alone. Terribly alone. Without the comfort of family or God. "You believe because you do not know. Once you've seen what God can do, faith will never be enough. I believe only in what I see."

Faith will never be enough. The empty world she feared yawned before her. "How do you do it? How do you stand it alone, without God?"

He smiled, sad and knowing. "How do you stand it with nothing but God?"

"What else is there?"

Her question seemed to wake him and he knelt before her, grasping her hands, squeezing her fingers with the urgency of life and death. "Each other, Neeca. Today. Seize today. We may not have tomorrow with those we love."

What if Sister died tomorrow? Had she seized every day? Had she seized every precious day with Garren?

She lifted her face, not even thinking why, until the air

between them trembled. Hope and despair warred in his eyes. She touched his sleeve, ran her hands over his shoulder to his back, hoping her touch could heal.

He took her face between his strong hands and took her lips with his warm ones.

She entered his kiss as if slipping into a familiar blanket, into that protected space where their souls met. The sun shone warm on her head and the breeze teased her ear like his fingers and the feel of him surrounded her, strong, warm and solid as the earth.

A cold, wet, jealous nose poked her fingers, clinging to Garren's back. Then Innocent jumped between them, barking for attention.

Garren laughed, sinking into the grass atop fall's leftover leaves, scratching the dog's head behind his one good ear. Then, with a whoop, he grabbed a stick and hurled it through the trees. Innocent raced off, short legs pumping, barking merrily at Garren to follow.

He jumped up, pulling Dominica to her feet. The gloom vanished from his face and he looked like that young man of seventeen again. "Run with me."

Gripped by his large, square hand, she had little choice. Breathing deep and hard, she ran as if she could escape the earth, light as a bird. She ran as if she could fly.

Her gulps of air turned to joyful laughter. Garren let go of her hand as she fell to her knees, nursing a stitch in her side.

"Are you all right?"

When she opened her mouth to answer a large hiccup erupted.

Garren raised his eyebrows and cocked his head.

She giggled. That brought on another hiccup, and another, until she dissolved in laughter and gasping, sank back onto the grass. Innocent, ready for a new game, dropped his stick and trotted back to lick her ears and nose. She shrieked with laughter. Above her, the green leaves, lit by the sun, glowed more alive than stained glass.

Garren stretched out beside her, leaning on his elbow, and holding the dog at bay with his other hand. "Innocent has the perfect cure." He leaned over and stopped her breath with a kiss.

Another hiccup escaped, but his lips clung to her, smothering the sound. She was full of the blue sky and the green grass and Garren's brown curls rough beneath her fingers and this time, they ignored the cold nose and rough paws nudging Garren's back.

He broke the long kiss, gazing down at her with a grin. "Better?"

She sat up. Air flowed in and out like life, but no hiccups followed, only her heartbeat. She nodded.

Hands gentle on her neck, caressing her arms, following the curve of her waist, he kissed her again, not just with his mouth this time, but with his whole body.

Maybe, she thought, lying back onto the grass with him, what rushed through her was not temptation. Maybe it was love. *Carpe diem. We may not have tomorrow....*

An arrow whizzed over Garren's back and buried itself in the tree with a thunk, quivering.

All warrior, Garren's body tensed, hardening into a shield over her. "Stop, fool. Who shoots?"

"Who's there? Garren? Is that you?" Richard's voice dripped with innocence as he emerged through the trees on horseback, dragging a dead roe at the end of a rope behind his horse. "And Dominica, too? I'm surprised. I thought I heard a deer."

Dominica stared into the roe's soft brown eyes, still open in death. Just a few inches and she and Garren would have been as dead as the deer.

It seemed they had not fooled Richard, after all.

Chapter Twenty

Shaking like the arrow embedded in the tree, Dominica watched Garren rise to shield her from Lord Richard. A wave of fear crashed over the trembling excitement that quivered in the pit of her stomach at his touch.

Garren towered over her, seemingly at ease, but taut muscles stretched up his wool-cased legs and coiled at the base of his spine. Lord Richard lounged in his saddle, but his thin fingers drummed the hard leather.

Garren grabbed the arrow with a hand no longer tender and snapped it in two, leaving the jagged shaft impaled in the bark.

"An unusual hunting method, Richard," he said. "No dogs tracking the hart. No bowman with you." He thrust the broken arrow at him. "And not a very successful one. You missed."

Lord Richard snatched the arrow and tossed it away like a toy he had tired of. Innocent chased through the trees after it, ready to play. "It's a deer park. I wasn't expecting to stumble on two lovers."

Lovers. Heat singed her cheeks at the thought of what she must look like, on her back, sprinkled with leaves and grass.

Dominica scrambled to her hands and knees. "We are not—"

Garren interrupted. "You should be more careful," he said to the man on the horse. "Things change quickly during the hunt."

She shuddered at the glitter in Lord Richard's eyes. "Yes," he said. "I can see they do."

"I trust you have permission to kill the Prince's deer," Garren said.

"They're breeding like rabbits. He'll thank me for it."

"Right after he fines you for the privilege."

"Always thinking of money, aren't you, Garren? But then, I knew that when I made my plans."

What plans could include Garren? She glanced sideways, but no flicker of feeling crossed Garren's face. Her stomach wobbled and she swallowed, turning back, forcing herself to look directly into those ferret-like eyes. "You are mistaken, Lord Richard. We are not lovers."

Not now, at least.

Slouching atop his horse, Lord Richard peered down his nose. "No? Pity. I thought you might have decided to spread your talents." A leer stained his voice. "And your legs."

Beside her, Garren surged to avenge the insult, but she held him back with a touch.

The sneer in Lord Richard's voice thrust her back to an empty stairway, trapped against a cold stone wall by a man twice her age and many times her strength.

She had escaped him then. She would again.

Heart pounding in her throat, she lifted her chin. "How I use my talents, Lord Richard, is more God's concern than yours."

To her surprise, the man laughed. "Perhaps she *does* love you more than God." He gouged his horse with his spurs and rode toward the castle, dragging the wide-eyed deer behind him, trailed by a yapping Innocent. "Good hunting, Garren," he called back, his grating laugh louder than the rustling leaves.

Good hunting. Did he mean Garren was hunting her? Distrust clouded her vision. Still shaking, she threw her words at him. "Why would he say that? Why did you let him think we are lovers?"

An iron-eyed warrior stood in the body of the laughing lover who had kissed away her hiccups. Fingers more tender than his eyes brushed the grass off her skirt and picked the leaves from her hair. "Neeca, Richard just tried to kill both of us. That changes everything."

"What he said changes everything."

With an exasperated sigh, he gripped her shoulders. "Neeca, give me the message. It's too dangerous for you to keep it."

She searched his eyes, but couldn't read an answer. "I took it because I knew you were in danger. This proves it."

"This proves your plan protects neither of us." He gave her a shake. "Now give me the message."

"No. You and Lord Richard," she floundered for a word, "...talked." *About me.*

"Don't change the subject," he muttered, grim-lipped.

"This was the subject. You changed it." It was a foolish fight. She knew it. But right now, knowing was more important than life. Or death.

He wrapped her in his arms and she wanted to melt into him, no longer certain she should. "You're not strong enough to keep it away from him alone," he murmured. "I can't always be there to protect you."

"God will protect me."

Instead of the anger she expected, he chuckled. "You didn't trust God to protect me without your help." He squeezed her. "Well, I don't trust him with your life, either."

She wriggled free from his embrace. "Maybe you are the one I shouldn't trust with my life."

He let her go, pacing a few steps, waving his arms in frustration before he glowered at her. "Neeca, stop pushing me! I'm trying to do what's best. For you, me, William. I want to keep you safe. Don't you believe me?"

"I don't know. Why should you want to?"

"Because I care about you!" His shout bounced off the trees. He clamped his jaw shut as if he could catch the words by the tail before they escaped.

Hope bobbed on the little swell of love still shifting through her center. "Thank you," she whispered over the fist in her throat.

He sighed, relieved. "Give it to me."

She slipped her hand inside the laces at the neck of her gown, fingering the folded missive tucked safely against her skin. "Nothing must happen to you," she whispered. *Or I will never forgive God.*

She wanted the warmth of his hands on her shoulders. She wanted to hide in his arms. She wanted to silence all the nasty questions inside her head and hear the still small voice that would speak louder than Lord Richard's insinuations. The one that said she could trust Garren.

He stretched his hand toward her, broad palm open and ready.

Good hunting, Garren.

Fool. Even now you trust him. But you know now he is only a man. You know he may be flawed as any poor sinner. The Earl had trusted him, of course, but his judgment was clouded by his illness. Maybe Richard had bribed Garren for his help to kill the Earl.

Her fingers froze on the parchment. To kill her.

With the message in his hands he could destroy it before they reached the shrine. No one would ever be the wiser about the Earl's death.

She left the folded parchment where it was. "Since you can't explain what Lord Richard meant, I'm keeping it until God tells me I shouldn't."

Anger darkened his eyes. "God doesn't talk to you," he snapped.

She bit her lip. "He used to."

She stalked away, no longer certain of God or Garren.

He did not run after her.

Sitting on the floor in Sister's room after the evening meal, Dominica jerked the sharpening knife across the quill. A large, ragged chunk flew into the fire, leaving the writing instrument jagged as Richard's arrow.

I knew that when I made my plans.

I care for you.

Which voice could she trust?

She slashed at the quill again, sending another chunk flying.

"Neeca, you know better!" Sister lifted her head from combing the day's twigs out of Innocent's black fur. "You won't have a quill tomorrow if you continue like that."

"Yes, Sister."

Sister's chiding comforted her. She missed the light fingers that picked dirt from her skirt and the sweet voice that nagged her to stop biting her nails.

"Neeca, what's troubling you?"

"Naught, really." She had told Sister nothing of today. Not of kisses or arrows or doubts. Worry about Dominica's life and virtue would not speed Sister's recovery. "I was just wondering, how do you know who to trust?"

"What do you mean?"

Too much understanding lurked in Sister's voice. She would have to be careful. "Lord Richard, for example. He is the son of an earl but...." She let the sentence hang.

"Somehow you don't trust him?"

She dipped the quill in the ink and let it hover over the parchment. "While Garren, well, we know almost nothing about him, yet somehow..."

"You believe in him?"

She nodded. Watching the flickering flames instead of the page, she let the quill glide over the parchment, undirected.

"Faith in people is like faith in God. It enables us to act in the absence of proof. Do you have that kind of faith in Garren?"

She looked down. Two new words screamed her thoughts on the parchment. *Garren + Dominica.*

The quill shook in her hand. She turned the page over to hide the evidence of her thoughts.

"Excuse me." The Physician's head brushed the top of the doorway as he glided over to the bed, carrying a goblet full of fragrant wine. "I brought something to help you sleep." He held his arm behind Sister so she could sit up and drink. "Not too much. You are very small."

Sister murmured her thanks. "The cough has made sleep difficult."

Your remedies make her no better, Dominica thought, as she waited at the door. "Is there nothing else you can do?"

"Medicine alone is not enough without God's help." He patted her shoulder, hooded eyes sad with the death he had seen. "God helps those who believe."

Did He? She thought, as she turned back to Sister. Why hadn't He helped a young Garren who believed so deeply?

Sister already breathed more easily. Tucking Gillian's blanket around her, Dominica molded her hands on either side of the tiny body. "Remember how you used to tuck me in?" she said. Sister nodded. "Now it's my turn."

The wine sent her to sleep, holding Dominica's hand. She looked near enough to death that the blanket hugged her like a shroud.

Dominica shuddered at the image. Remembering.

Like night-flying bats, cries of pain flew through the Priory and echoed off the wall. Six-year-old Dominica clung to Sister Marian's black skirts, afraid Death would catch her if she let go. Death had come for so many already.

"Come," Sister said, taking her hand. "Lift your head. Walk beside me."

They walked through the maze of stone corridors to the scriptorium, filled with scrolls and sheets of parchment and bound books that muffled the cries of pain.

On a desk by the window a sheet lay abandoned, the careful copyist carried off by the Death in midstroke.

Sister laid a small, clean sheet of paper in front of Dominica. "This could be a page of our songbook, or a leaf from Our Lord's words, or a prayer book. It is all in the copyist's fingers to create."

She curled Neeca's pudgy fingers around the shaft of a goose feather, stripped of its feathers. It swayed wildly in her grasp. "This is a quill. With this, you can create the words."

Dominica waved the feather over the page, expecting black marks to appear.

The page remained stubbornly blank.

Sister smiled. "It isn't magic." Holding her fingers over Neeca's, she dipped the quill in the ink. "Now write this letter," she pointed to a small shape on a large sheet, "on this page."

Dominica's lip trembled. She might as well have been asked to fly. "But I do not know how."

"This is how you learn." Guiding Neeca's hand, she traced a shaky *a* on the clean sheet.

"I have ruined it," Dominica said, tears threatening to blot the black blob further.

"No, you haven't."

"I can't do this."

"Neither could I the first time. This is how you learn. It takes patience and practice. Now, try it by yourself."

She did. Ink flowed down the page in a little stream. Neeca's tears threatened to follow it.

"Beautiful start. Next time, let your pen glide instead of pushing. Now, try again."

This time, she tapped off the excess ink and stroked a bold, slanted line and a circle attached on the left. It filled a quarter of the page. No rivers of ink escaped. She smiled.

"That's very good," Sister said. "But this sheet is all we can spare now. The best copyists fill the page with small, even letters. And smaller letters will give you more practice."

Neeca looked longingly at the thick, supple sheet of prepared calfskin. "Can I use that?"

"Later. After you practice many years. Now, show me another."

Humming, Neeca dipped the quill in the ink and drew three letters. Two of them were recognizable.

Sister hugged her, then knelt to meet Neeca's eyes. "I will be gone for a while. Keep practicing. When I return, I want you to show me you have learned to write the letters *a* and *b*."

A death scream pierced their sanctuary. Neeca buried her face in Sister's robes. "Don't leave me."

Sister scooped her onto her lap, rocking her on bouncing knees. "I must. I go on a pilgrimage to the Shrine of the Blessed Larina."

"When will you come back?"

"As soon as I can."

"How can I learn without you?"

"One letter at a time." She pointed to each one on the long list. "This one, then this one, then the next. Just work on one letter at a time. Later, I will teach you how to make words." She looked at the little girl on her knee. "Don't be afraid. Remember what Saint Bernard said?"

Dominica sniffed. "'Every word you write is a blow that smites the Devil.'"

Sister hugged her. "That's right. While you do God's work, He will protect you."

In the weeks that Sister was gone, practice protected her from fear. She learned patience and the letters *a, b, c, d,* and *f.*

She traced the letters, familiar now as all the others, with her fingers on the blanket covering Sister, who slept, fitfully. Years ago, God had brought her back safely. She had done nothing but God's work all her life. Why wouldn't He protect her this time?

God helps those who believe.

Two more days and they would be at the shrine.

Two more days and it would be time for her sign.

If there was to be one.

Her heart fluttered frantically as she realized she had doubted God. Distracted with Garren, she had picked up his disbelief. As a man, he was more dangerous than as a Devil. You knew a Devil would question God. In his despair for his family, he had made his doubt oh, so understandable, even to her.

Perhaps her qualms were killing Sister.

But surely, God would not abandon her. Of course she would have her sign. One that everyone would know. Clear.

Unmistakable. Something that would prove her faith. Something that would save Sister.

Something even Garren would believe.

She would prove to Him, to herself, that she believed. In the absence of proof. God would, must give her a sign.

Maybe He needed a little push.

Following the river to the coast the next day, Garren tried to think about Richard and the road and how he would repay William and why he had been so softhearted as to let her keep the message. He tried to think about anything except what he had admitted. And what it meant.

I care about you. Now he knew. Now God knew. And now God could take her as he had taken everyone else Garren loved.

Behind him, the pilgrims' caterwauling blocked the birds' songs.

"Wings to fly like Larina, fly like Larina, fly like Larina."

As if flying saints were any match for Richard's evil, he thought. Or my own.

The leaden shell swung accusingly from his staff. All through the afternoon, he tried to think logically about his choices.

The Prioress was right. Neeca was not meant to take the veil. But if he took her, he would destroy every dream she had. Oh, if William still lived, he could give him a final gift, to repay him in some small way. Maybe there would even be some money left over to help him start a new life all over again.

But to repay William, he would reward William's killer. And Neeca would end up as Richard's doxy, or worse.

His body ached with wanting her. Not just his shaft or his loins or those parts that could be fed and satisfied, but bone-deep. He hungered to hold, to cherish, to make her happy. To give her what she wanted.

He sighed. What she wanted was a home at the Priory, no matter how ill-suited. If he returned to William empty-handed, he would face his own disappointment. He would also face Richard's anger. He would be thrown out to make his way alone in the world with a strong right arm that grew weaker every year.

But if he were not there to protect her, Richard would have her anyway, sooner or later. And more cruelly.

And right now, Garren could offer her nothing except his fear that God would snatch her away like all the others.

"It was trees like these," Sister Marian said late in the day. The sun twinkled through the leaves and she let it rest on her frail face, paler every day. "This is the forest through which she ran."

Garren listened with half an ear. Maybe Larina's feather would be gift enough. But if Dominica ever knew he was stealing a relic, her last vestige of trust would disappear. Perhaps if he just showed William the goose feather, told him that was the real one. Why not? It would make no difference anyway whether he breathed his last breath on one goose feather or another, if he wasn't already dead.

The path finally broke out of the trees. Bare, windswept cliffs plummeted down to crashing waves. Seagulls' screeches pierced the howling wind, that whipped around his ears and sent the cloaks flapping.

"Look! The sea!" Dominica shrieked with joy. She threw her arms out and yelled to the sky. "I put myself in your loving hands."

And then she started running toward the edge of the cliff as fast as Saint Larina pursued by wild boars.

Chapter Twenty-One

Garren ran, legs churning, as if he chased his own life instead of hers. Salt air seared his lungs. The reliquary pounded his chest with each footfall. Fast as one possessed, she outran him, sprinting into the wind as if she had never walked ten days on pilgrimage.

As if she would not stop at the edge of the cliff.

He ran faster.

Near the high cliffs that dropped off to the sea, she flung out her arms, twirling, dancing, swirling, spinning, never looking where her feet fell. A wave crashed against the rocks and shattered into droplets, coating her honey hair.

Chest ready to burst with fear that he would be too late, he prayed.

Save her, God, and I'll let you have her.

She wobbled, no longer knowing up from down, sea from shore. She would never see the edge of the cliff until her feet hit air instead of land…

He lunged, knocking her flat to the ground within a man's height of the cliff.

"You idiot!" he yelled into the wind, hands gliding over her head, caressing her shoulders, exploring her back, searching for broken bones. "You could have killed yourself.'' He surrounded her with his body, listening for her breath, wanting to inhale her, to assure himself she was not lost.

She wriggled against him and he let her turn onto her back. Her breathing was ragged, her eyes closed, but she lived.

She lived.

"Don't ever scare me like that again," he whispered, pressing his lips to the soft, warm curve of her neck. Her pulse beat alive against his lips.

Above them, seagulls cawed like crows. Beneath him, she opened her eyes with a giddy smile, the wind whipping her hair in her face. He shifted his weight and let her sit up. When he looked in her eyes, he realized she did not see him. Nor any creature of earth.

"Why did you stop me? I was going to fly." She blinked and shook her head, confused. Suddenly, she saw him for the first time. "Oh, you're right." She slipped her fingers into the neck of her gown and thrust the crinkled message into his hand. "It might fall into the sea."

Against his chest, the worn parchment carried the warmth of her skin.

Before he could touch her, she pushed herself to her knees and staggered toward the sea again. He grabbed her hand, but her strength was nearly a match for his, as if God were helping her pull. Her hair flapped behind her like a banner in the wind and he tightened his grip, leaning against her, his shoulder stretched from its socket as she strained to reach the edge of the cliff.

She stumbled at the limit of his arm. "Let me go. Let me show you." The salt wind snatched her laughter, light as a feather. She raised her free arm like a wing, all faith and no fear. "The spirit is here. I feel it. I can fly."

His shudder had nothing to do with the sea wind. He

pulled her into his arms and laced his fingers behind her back, struggling to hold her, struggling to reach behind her eyes. "Neeca, you can't fly. No one can fly."

"Larina did!"

"It's just a story, Neeca. People can't really fly."

As if from years away, he heard Simon, or maybe Jackin, shout from the trees, words too weak to swim against the wind. She was his only reality.

Frantic, she shoved her palms against his chest, twisting to break free. "What do you mean? It's why we are here. It's why you bring her feathers." At the word, she stilled, stroking the dented silver case hanging around his neck. She curled her fingers around it and she looked up at him. All the fierce blue fervor the Prioress had ever feared was distilled in her eyes. "Give me a feather. Then I can fly."

He grabbed it out of her hand, whirling to block her path to the cliff. "These aren't from the saint's wings." He wanted to speak softly, calmly, but he had to shout over the wind, rattling the silver case in front of her nose, trying to will her to sense.

She tilted her head, as if he spoke Latin poorly. "What do you mean?" The stillness vanished and a shiver rippled through every limb as if she really did have wings and they were beating to take her away from this place. "Of course they are. I saw them."

Anger pounded his ears. Anger at her foolish faith, at the Church for its lies, at Richard and the Prioress for putting him on the edge of this cliff. At himself.

"Neeca, these are feathers." The unceasing wind tore the words away from him and hurled them in her face. He had saved her. He would keep her safe. No matter what he had to do. "Feathers. That's all they are. Nothing else. Nothing but what you see."

He let her go just long enough to wrench the battered sheath apart.

The wind flung the goose down to the sky. She cried out and jumped, grasping nothing but air.

The feathers skipped toward the sea.

He gripped her hand, but with the strength of belief, she dragged him toward the cliff as she chased the useless bits of down. The feathers swirled on an eddy of wind at the edge of the cliff, danced beside a seagull, and disappeared.

When she looked at him again, doubt sparred with the fierce, joyous faith in her eyes. "How could you throw Larina's feathers away?"

The screams of the gulls and the endless wind roared in his ears. "Don't you understand yet?" He gathered her cold fingers in his. "It was nothing but down I plucked from the mud of the goose pen."

"No." She jerked away, waving her hands to ward off his words. "You told me they were Larina's."

What did it matter now, that she had told him first. He had let her believe. "I lied."

She flinched as if he had stoned her. "The Savior lied?"

"Savior was never my word. It was yours."

"What other lies have you told?"

So many, he didn't know where to start. "Neeca…"

She clenched her fists, arms stiff at her sides. "Was it a lie that you cared for me?"

"No." She must know that. "Why do you think I kept you from leaping to your death?"

"You should have let me jump. If I could not fly, at least I would have died happy. But you had to play the Savior again." She laughed, a bitter sound now, like his own. "Is it not enough that you have no faith? Must you destroy mine as well?"

"God does not always answer our prayers the way we want." The platitude soured on his tongue.

"An easy phrase for a man who does not believe God answers at all." She slumped, to her knees, defeated. All the pliant strength of her faith had turned hard and brittle and he knew if he touched her, she would shatter.

Save her, God and I'll let you have her.

No, God did not answer as he'd expected.

Her faith in Garren had been like a prayer, she thought, staring at a wave erupting onto the crag where the seagulls huddled. God's answer was cruel.

Splashing as high as she stood, the spray misted her lips with salt. On a jagged rock, a gray bird spread black-tipped wings. Lifted by the wind, he hovered above the rock, forced backwards, unable to rise. Finally, he folded his wings and fell back, clinging to the rock again.

Even birds could not fly against the wind.

Shaking, Dominica shut her eyes. Wind too sharp to breathe scrubbed her face. She didn't hear Innocent because the wind blew his bark away. He jumped up on her, ready to join her running game. She hugged the warm, wriggling body out of habit, without feeling comfort. Or pain or anger or joy. Only an overwhelming emptiness.

Barely aware of Gillian's arm on her shoulders or the Physician's voice, she let herself be led to the trees and lifted into the cart. Sister's arms encircled her, light as lost feathers. Dominica buried her face against the shoulder she had cried on so many times as a child. Now, the collarbone was fragile beneath skin transparent as oiled linen.

Garren's hand touched hers. She raised her head. His rugged face, sea-green eyes opaque, looked dear as one dead and remembered.

"Let the ass walk at his own pace," he said, draping the

reins into the cart. "We will be within sight. We should reach the shrine by sunset."

Kind, she thought, to let her alone. She watched him join the others, milling around Roucoud, looking back over their shoulders, each face clear and familiar, but no longer part of her world. Gillian stared as if she were an angel; Ralf as if she had seen God; Simon as if she were demented.

The ass, patient, clopped along the path without a hand on the reins.

"I tried to fly, Sister." Tears, or salt spray, seared her cheeks. "I was ready to prove my faith and God failed me."

Pale fingers strong as iron forced her face to Sister's, forced her to answer to the beloved, weary eyes. "Is your faith only as strong as answered prayers?"

The words stung. "I wanted to give my life to God, like you did."

"Any life can be given to God. I gave mine to the Church."

"God didn't give me the sign I needed." Her lip trembled and she swallowed the tears in her throat.

"Do you remember telling me about Gillian and her golden chain? You thought such a petition unworthy. 'God is not a dispenser of Twelfth Night gifts,' you said."

"But what I want is not like that! What I want is to serve God."

"You want what you want. What if God wants something else?" She shook her head. "To think you always know God's will is not faith. It is pride. You are trying to force God as you used to push the pen."

"But only as part of the Church can I spread His word."

"If you believed that, you would not want to write God's words so the people could understand without the Church."

The thought stunned her. "Then maybe God is punishing me for my heresy."

"Heresy is the Church's word, not God's."

And a meaningless one, she thought. If there was no reason for faith, there was no reason for heresy.

The plop of hooves on soft earth filled the silence. Sister stroked her hair. Lurching with the cart, she watched the world slide by, ordinary again. Just dirt and trees and sky. Nothing miraculous. "I thought God would let me fly." She whispered, in wonder now at her simple-mindedness.

"There's more than one way to fly," Sister said. "A sparrow flaps its wings until they blur. A seagull is lifted by the wind."

Not always, she thought. "Garren is right. God does what He likes despite our faith."

Sister's voice turned stern. "Your faith cannot depend on someone else. Garren may not understand his faith. He flies differently than the rest of us." Her voice sank to a whisper, as though she were no longer speaking to Dominica. "Maybe God works through him, even though he does not believe as you do."

"I no longer know what I believe."

Sister shook her head. "Maybe I forced my faith on you instead of giving you the freedom to find your own. But I wanted to make amends...."

Leaning back against the swaying cart's wooden slats, Dominica reached to squeeze Sister's hand. "You have done nothing but love me my entire life. There is no force in that."

"Tomorrow, my child," Sister sighed, a sound like dry leaves. "When we are at the shrine. Your sign may be there."

Dominica took the reins without answering. She would look for no more signs. She would jump off no more cliffs. No one would save Sister's life. Or hers.

Garren had emptied her universe of God.

* * *

With each steady step through the day, Garren's anger faded and his wonder grew. Reliving the moment he thought she was lost, he turned the words over in his mind.

Save her, God and I'll let you have her.

And she had been saved.

Too late to argue he could have reached her without that prayer. Too late to explain to God that he wanted her now to hold and protect and cherish. God knew. And because of that, God had taken Neeca from him, too. Not to simple death, but to a life where she would be as just as lost to him. And because he loved her so much, he wanted her to have what she wanted. If she were willing to die for it, he was willing for her to live for it.

He could offer her nothing to compete with God.

Only his heart.

Faced with God's will for Neeca, he knew the Prioress would still need her sign. What would convince her to allow Dominica into the order?

He laughed. Simon and the Physician stared, as if wondering if he were touched like Dominica. Garren shook his head and waved a hand to reassure them, but his lips twisted in an ironic smile.

He would create a sign that even the Prioress would believe. When he returned, he would tell her that God had appeared to him in a vision and told him not to touch the girl. Told him to keep her pure, for He had chosen her to be a bride of Christ. He would let the Prioress know that God himself had reached down and disrupted her petty schemes and transformed a sinning doubter's heart to do His will.

Oh, yes, he thought, stifling the pain of losing her, he would be God's instrument after all.

Chapter Twenty-Two

"Holy Mother of God!" The Widow's voice boomed into Dominica's left ear as pilgrims, horses, ass and cart clustered on the shore. Together, they stared across the water stretching between them and a rock barely large enough to call an island. "It isn't the Cathedral of Santiago, is it?"

Biting back her own disappointment, Dominica staggered as Sister sagged against her. Pleas from Dominica and Garren had not dissuaded her from stubbornly trudging the final mile barefoot. Now, her bleeding feet scarcely held her upright.

"Each time, I come to the Blessed Larina a humble sinner," she insisted.

No more humble than Larina's shrine, Dominica thought.

Scorched by the dying sun, the shrine of the Blessed Larina thrust indistinguishable from the stone that supported it, built by loving, untutored hands, sculpted by relentless wind and waves, splattered with the leavings of gulls who did not distinguish stone from shrine.

"Cathedral?" Lord Richard snarled. "It's a dung-covered rock."

Even Garren's shoulders slumped.

Dominica understood. Grateful he had not let her come

to this place wide-eyed with misplaced faith in heavenly miracles, she now wondered about the earthly ones. Where was the seat of the Church's power and authority that would clap Lord Richard in chains and take him to judgment?

"Welcome, pilgrims." A stiff-ankled lay brother, with a headful of untidy speckled hair, hobbled out of a rough, square hut. A childlike smile split his round face as he tottered toward them. "Sister Marian! Is that you?"

Sister lifted her head from Dominica's shoulder, groping for his hands as if too weary to open her eyes. "Brother Joseph? Are you still here?"

Dominica glanced at Garren and he shook his head. This simple man was not the one they needed.

Close enough to see Sister's pale face, Brother Joseph's smile drooped. "You are sick?" He patted her hands with his pudgy fingers. "Be not afraid. The Blessed Larina will cure you as she did before."

"I come with different needs today, Brother Joseph," she said.

"We need to see the brother responsible for the shrine," Garren interrupted, gently. "Where is he?"

The child's smile creased his round face again. "Why, at the shrine, of course."

Lord Richard snickered. "Ask a fool, get a witless answer."

Dominica winced at his cruelty, but Brother Joseph's sweet smile never wavered. Edging closer to Garren, she nodded toward three small boats hugging the beach. "We could take a boat and be there before the sunset."

Brother Joseph's ears were sharp, even if his brain was simple. He shook his head like a dog flinging off water, hair flying. "No, no, no. Boats carry supplies."

"What are we supposed to do?" Lord Richard sneered. "Swim?"

"Crawl," Brother Joseph replied, with a beatific smile, as Sister Marian nodded. "When the tide is out."

Dominica gritted her teeth, ignoring the gasps behind her. Then crawl she would to deliver the message.

"When will the tide be out?" Garren asked, patiently.

"Tomorrow at midday. But our shrine is small. Only three may go together. Let me count." Brother Joseph walked among them, touching each pilgrim's nose with a different finger. He ran out of fingers and started again, finally smiling with success. "It will take four days for all of you to visit."

Lord Richard nearly licked his lips as he smiled. Dominica shuddered. Four more days he might use to kill them. They could not wait.

Sister's frail voice quavered beside her. "Perhaps I might rest now."

Guilty she had forgotten Sister, even for a moment, Dominica turned back. Garren, quicker, scooped Sister into his arms and started toward the small hut. She lay limp in his arms.

"Put Sister Marian in my room," Brother Joseph said.

Dominica followed him into the hut, past a splintered wooden bench where a collection of badges lay spread for sale.

Lead feathers. Heavy as her heart.

The hut was no more than a stable for pilgrims; his room no more than an alcove without even the comfort of a fireplace. In the corner a fat, round candle, never lit, squatted on a footed iron spike. A mound of straw nestled on the dirt floor in perfect position for Brother Joseph to sleep in sight of the shrine.

"He signals me," Brother Joseph said, lighting the precious candle and nodding toward the rough, square hole set low in the wattle and daub wall, "if he needs something."

Dominica cushioned the straw with her own cloak before Garren gently laid Sister down in view of the rock she had come so far to reach.

"I will see to the others," Brother Joseph said, leaving them alone.

Beside her, Garren, warm and solid, had replaced The Savior. Yet he had saved her in a different way, she thought, saved her from foolish illusions and she had not even thanked him. Even as she prayed for Sister's life, she had no faith that God listened. All she believed in was what they could do: deliver the message that would bring a murderer to justice.

"You still have the message?" she whispered.

He nodded, his eyes lingering on hers. "Dominica, when we return to Readington, there's a way..."

"Fast? I'll not fast tonight!" Lord Richard exploded behind them. "My feet are bloody! Find me some food in this hovel."

Garren sighed, straightening his shoulders as he stood. "I must go."

She marveled as he assumed the burden of leadership again, wondering why an unbeliever had come at all.

Gillian crept to her side as he left. Grateful for her silent offer of help, Dominica turned to make Sister comfortable. She pulled off the black veil and unwrapped the white-edged wimple. Thin wisps of faded hair mingled with the stiff straw. Together, they took off her habit. Stripped of the black robes and covered with Gillian's blanket, her small body looked as if it were shrinking away.

Innocent hopped atop the blanket, nudging his cold nose under Sister's hand until she scratched behind his ear, cold fingers the only part of her that still seemed alive.

The Physician entered, empty-handed. There would be no warmed wine tonight. Gillian made room for him to touch

Sister's forehead and hold the narrow bones of her wrist where a little life still pulsed.

"After a night's rest, she'll be better," Dominica said, as if she still believed words could make it so.

"If God wills." His hooded eyes spoke the truth. Tomorrow would be no better than today.

Gillian hugged her, then left her alone with Sister's labored breathing and Innocent's melancholy eyes.

As a child, she had often spread her fingers atop Sister's hand, wishing her middle finger would grow a groove and a bump like Sister's where the quill could nestle. Now, in the flickering candlelight, she saw that her hand had overgrown the precise fingers and the little mountain at the side of her knuckle rivaled Sister's.

The hiss of the waves blurred the murmurs from the other room as the others dwindled into sleep. Through the hole in the wall, clouds dulled the darkening sky, blotting out the moon and stars. Only the feeble glow of a perpetual lantern above Larina's bones lit the outer darkness.

She didn't know she slept until Sister's words woke her. Throat stripped raw by days of coughing, the voice was barely recognizable, but the words were as familiar as the mass. "It was a summer morning. I was still a novitiate, sent to open the gate for travelers, but the sun awoke hours before I did that morning."

Dominica smiled. The words took her back to her childhood where nothing would ever change. "Hush, you are too tired to tell the story tonight."

She spoke as if never interrupted, soft words barely audible over the waves. "And I went to the gate and there was a basket covered with a cloth."

"Apples," Dominica finished, out of habit. "Like Moses."

"Covered with a cloth of Readington blue."

Dominica dragged her ears open. Surely she had misheard over the waves. "Blue like my eyes. That's the way the story goes."

"I've not told you the whole story, Neeca."

The skin prickled on the back of her neck. She pushed herself away from the wall, trying to read Sister's eyes. "What haven't you told me?"

Outside, waves rolled ashore, one upon the next before Sister answered. "I was that young, foolish woman."

She must be tired. Or not hearing Sister's frail voice over the sea. She leaned closer. "What do you mean?"

"I am your mother."

The waves kept coming, impossible, for surely the world must have stopped. Their sound made her dizzy, as if she had reached the end of the earth and could fall off.

"My mother?" She twittered like a brainless sparrow. "Oh, yes, you've always been like a mother to me...."

"Dominica. You are my daughter."

She laid her head on Sister's, no, her mother's shoulder. The woman who loved her most in the world. Now she knew why. "All the time. All the time I had you. You were there for me. And I didn't know."

A small hand touched her head. "You knew. In your own way. I never meant to tell you more."

Her life, Sister's life, nothing in the world was what she thought. She had a mother. That meant...

"Who was..." She swallowed. She couldn't say *my father*. "Who was the man?"

Three waves flowed and ebbed before Sister answered. "John. Earl of Readington." She brushed a hair off Dominica's forehead. "You have his eyes."

"Lord William's father?" Like his son, a large, blond lion of a man, admiring her childish letters spelling out The

Lord's Prayer. *Pater noster, qui es in cailis…* "But how…" she stammered, not knowing how to ask.

A tear as old as Dominica trickled from Sister's eye into her thinning hair. "He was so interested in our work. More than a patron. He wanted to learn to write. The Prioress selected me to teach him. We spent hours tracing the letters. Together."

Together. Close. Close enough to feel the spirit move between them. Close as she had been to Garren, Dominica thought.

"When I discovered I was carrying you, I hid beneath a pilgrim's cloak and came to the Blessed Larina for help. She told me to keep you."

"I was born here? Then how did I get to the Priory?"

Sister's fingers fluttered, too weary for details. "John sent a wet nurse with me. Left you at the gate. He was so proud that you could write. He wanted you to have a home at the Priory always. 'All who dwell there.' He wrote those words for you."

The Priory and all who dwell there. The home she had always wanted had always been hers. "Does Mother Julian know?"

She shook her head.

"Lord William?"

"No."

"His brother?"

"You were my sin alone."

Sin. She could not stretch the word to fit Sister, no matter what the Church might say.

Sister fumbled for Dominica's hand with cold fingers, squeezing with strength Dominica thought had left her. "You must keep the secret." She gasped for breath. "Dangerous…if they thought Sir John's daughter wanted…Readington."

"I will tell no one. I promise." The promise was for Sister's reputation, not for her own safety. A female foundling born on the wrong side of the Readington blanket posed no threat to Lord Richard. Besides, he wanted her dead already. No need to give him more reason. Enough that she knew Readington was truly home.

Sister swallowed. "I came…to thank her again. You come. When I am gone."

"That will be a long time from now."

"No time for lies," she croaked.

An incoherent jumble of words bounced through Dominica's head, trying to be a prayer. She knew Sister was right. There would be no miraculous cure. God had already answered No.

Dominica pushed herself off the hard dirt floor. If Death were here, at least she could smooth Sister's road to Heaven. "I will get Brother Joseph to perform last rites." Surely God would understand if a lay brother conducted the rites instead of a priest.

Sister clutched her skirt. "No."

She must be delirious, Dominica thought, kneeling beside her, gently loosening her fingers. After such a pious life, she must want the last rites. "If you die without confession, you cannot go to Heaven." Words she no longer believed. A residue of training over experience.

Sister gripped her skirt and shook it. "No confession."

"But every day, you went to confession."

"I never confessed this."

"He forgives you. He forgives all those with a repentant heart."

"I do not repent." Sister fell back against the cloak-covered straw and looked out toward the sky empty of stars. "God knows my secrets. He, not the Church, must judge my life."

"But you gave your life to the Church! It was the meaning of your life!"

"It was the purpose. You were the meaning. I wanted you to be the nun I couldn't be." She closed her eyes and let her fingers relax. "Maybe I tried to push God too hard." She whispered.

Dominica stuck the candle back on its spike. Let Brother Joseph sleep. "I shall tell them you made your last confession to me."

I wanted you to be the nun I couldn't be. Maybe I tried to push God too hard.

Dominica's life's pilgrimage had never been her own. Now, it had ended at an empty rock on the edge of the world. The one she had modeled her life on, the one with perfect faith, had lived a lie. How many times must she learn? Even perfect faith led nowhere. No reason to have faith in God. No reason to do anything but exist until the release of Death.

Sister's skin glowed transparent in the warm candlelight. Innocent nuzzled her pale hand, his brown eyes accusing Dominica, as if she should do something instead of let her go.

Sister scratched behind his good ear. "Take care of Innocent."

When I'm gone.

"Don't worry." She petted him and they were joined in a circle. With one hand holding Sister and the other on Innocent, she had no hand to wipe the tear that dripped off her chin.

Sister whispered with a voice like dry leaves. "We were only…together once. I have cherished that memory every night of my life."

"*Pater noster, qui es in caelis,*" Dominica began, "*sanctificetur nomen tuum.*"

She fell asleep holding Sister's hand and awakened to a cold, dark room, empty of Sister's immortal soul.

Chapter Twenty-Three

Outside, impossibly, hissing waves rolled one after the other, just as before. Dominica looked out the rough hole in the wall to be sure. Leftover clouds scowled on the horizon, masking the sunrise. Sleeping gulls blanketed Larina's rock.

How could the world look the same when everything she knew lay shattered?

She turned back to Sister. No, to the body Sister would reclaim upon resurrection. Maybe she was wrong. Maybe she was not dead.

She crept closer. No breath stirred Sister's chest. Deliberately, Dominica opened her own mouth and gulped air. Maybe if she breathed, Sister would breathe again.

Atop the lifeless form, Innocent blinked forlorn eyes.

Snores and wheezes intruded from the main room. Pilgrims were supposed to pray the night before going to the shrine, but they slept instead, thoughtlessly willing to leave the world for a few hours. Sure they would return.

With listless fingers, she pulled parchment, quill and knife from her sack. They lay like dead weight in her hands. She wanted to write words of praise and remembrance for Sister, but there were no words left.

She would not pick up a quill again.

Suddenly, she had to leave the room. Later, she would face the consequences of death, answer each pilgrim who came to politely say good morning and was Sister feeling better today? Now, she must howl, cry and sob where the sounds would wake no one.

She kissed Sister's cold forehead. Stretched on the blanket, Innocent did not lift his head.

''Guard her well,'' she whispered. As she tiptoed past the slumbering pilgrims, she did not even look to see if Garren slept.

Outside, she filled her lungs with salt air, free of the scent of death, and strode across the damp sand, clutching her parchment in one hand and the knife and quill in the other. The ebbing tide stranded Brother Joseph's little supply boats high on the rocky beach. *Pilgrims crawl when the tide is out,* he said. Today, at midday, after a night of fasting and a morning of confession, she would have crawled across wet stones to lay her prayer before the saint.

She no longer prayed for a sign to join the order. There was nothing to hold her to the world she knew. No God. No Sister. No writing.

A wall of jagged rocks marked the end of the beach. She stuffed parchment, quill and knife in her pouch and scrambled up, welcoming the scrape of ragged stone against her palm. Atop the rocks, the daybreak wind cooled her eyelids. Each breaking wave brought a whiff of seaweed.

The last time, God had cast her writing to the waters to drown. This time, she would kill her own words.

She opened her eyes, held out the parchment, and stabbed.

The stubborn hide fought back, allowing only a small gash. She slashed again, harder, tearing a larger hole.

Letting the knife skitter away down the rock, she grabbed

with both hands, wrestling with the reluctant parchment. Finally, she crushed one side against the rock beneath her leather sole and yanked. Half the parchment lay limp in her hand. She flung it into the dull, gray-green water.

"Neeca, what are you doing?"

She started at the sound of Garren's voice. He stood below her, frowning, on a sandy beach nestled on the other side of the rock.

"Don't," he said, not waiting for an answer before he hoisted himself up beside her. Before he could reach her, she sent the other piece sailing into the outgoing tide.

Too late, he grabbed her arm. "Neeca, why? Your writing is part of you."

"Forgive me. You paid good coin for it."

"The coin is nothing. The writing is you."

She looked toward the fuzzy line barely separating sea and sky where the parchment would fall off the edge of the earth. *The writing is gone. Everything I knew is gone.*

"Sister has gone to God." The words fluttered in her throat and her shoulders shook and he pulled her into his arms, sheltering her from the wind.

"My poor Neeca," he muttered, his moving lips warm against her hair.

His touch filled some of the aching emptiness. Garren permeated her being. Garren who had been at her side, in her breath, in her skin for the days and leagues they had walked together. Garren who had brought her joy and doubt.

She snuggled closer, reveling in his heat, the man smell of him, the melting, shaking feeling of being near him. The heavy weight in her chest eased.

"But even without Sister, you cannot give up writing. The writing is your life."

"My life is not what I thought."

"No one's is."

I thought I was a nameless foundling and longed to live for God's glory. Instead, I am a bastard of a nun and a lord. What do I long for now?

She searched his sea-green eyes, wanting to tell him, to share their mutual love for William, but she did not have the right to reveal Sister's secret.

Strands of her hair, loosened by the wind, tickled her nose and he tucked them behind her ear. "I would save you from God's disappointments if I could."

She smiled with a sense of peace and surety she had not felt in days and miles. She knew what was left to her. To be a woman. To live one day at a time. Here on earth. Just once. *Once to remember every night of my life.*

Wrapped snugly in his big arms, she tipped her head back to search his eyes. "Perhaps God means for us to save each other."

She wrapped her arms tighter and ran her hands up and down his back, loving every inch of life she felt as he arched beneath her fingers. Her lips found the hollow of his throat between the leather strap holding the empty relic case and tasted him there. His moan vibrated through her lips.

He pushed her away and jumped off the rock. "I cannot."

She followed him, clambering down onto wet sand. Without his shelter, chill salt air swirled beneath her skirt. She clutched his arm, wobbling on the uncertain sand. "*Carpe diem,* you said. Death may come tomorrow."

He shook free. "Your tomorrow is with the Priory."

"God gave me my sign. I am not to be a nun."

"Just because you could not fly? There is a way. I can make Mother Julian believe…"

"God doesn't always answer our prayers the way we expect. I understand that now. You are my answer."

His eyes caressed her, yearning, hopeless, full of pain from some place inside him, deeper than he had ever let her see. "And you are the answer to prayers I could never say. But the answer is too late."

"No, no. The spirit moves between us. I feel it."

He waved his arms wildly, as if he were trying to do anything but touch her. "You can't give up your dream because of...." He clenched his fists and held his arms stiffly to his side. "Because of this."

This. Such a small word for the link that split open her soul. She laid her hand on his chest, wanting to feel his heart throb beneath her palm. "No, not because of this."

He stood rigid as a statue. "You can't. I won't let you." Agony cracked his voice.

She grabbed his tunic. "I won't leave until you do."

"No." Sharp. "Not now. Not ever."

"Why?" Tears flowed into her eyes from the deep, sweet place inside her body that cried out for him.

"Because," he said, his voice sharper than her blade's edge, "it is not God's will."

She flung her arms to the sky. "Don't speak to me of God's will!" The words ripped through her throat. "I believed in God's will. I even thought I could shape it. Now I know. He has no will for me."

"But He does." Grimness, sadness, and joy warred in his face. "When you were about to jump, I promised God. If He saved you I would let Him have you."

All the heat drained from her cheeks. And she heard God's laughter in the scream of the waking gulls. She clenched her fists and threw her answer back. "I don't care what promises you made to God."

"I will tell the Prioress Larina gave you a sign. You can still have the life you want."

"There is nothing in that life that I want now." She smiled with the sadness of the old woman she had become in three weeks. "I want you."

More than my immortal soul.

* * *

Garren's heart pounded at her words. The wind, revived by the sunrise, cooled the sweat sheening his upper lip. The birds shrieked for their breakfast and the waves raced toward the beach fast as the blood through his veins.

Behind the pain of Sister's death, he had kindled a spark of life in her fierce, blue eyes. Some part of him had died with each death until he only thought he lived. He would not let that happen to her.

She stretched her fingers to touch his cheek. He did not pull away. "Please."

I saved her, God. She is mine.

She stepped toward him, stroking his beard, tracing his ears, tangling her fingers in his hair. When she pulled his mouth to hers, he tasted salt on her lips. All the wanting he had felt with every step at her side burst, and he squeezed her gently, gradually wrapping his arms more tightly, as if he could make them one person.

He took her sweet mouth, absorbed her tongue and her lips and felt the moan deep in her throat, devouring her as if he had been starving and wanted to savor the life-giving food.

The ebbing tide rolled over their shoes, sucking the sand from beneath their feet. She clutched his arms, uncertain.

"Come." He grabbed her hand, leading her to a sheltered crescent of dry sand, sheltered from the wind, out of sight of the hut and the island. He shrugged off his cloak and spread it over the sand.

When she fumbled with the laces of her dress he plucked her hands away, kissing each finger in turn. "Slow. Slow." He spoke to himself as well as to her.

Her lips curved in a smile more knowing than he expected. "Glide, don't push."

"What?"

"That's what Sister always told me when I practiced my letters. That I was trying too hard."

A wisp of satisfaction curled in his stomach. "Don't try at all."

He let his mouth linger on her fingers, teasing the sensitive V-shape between them with his tongue. He licked the little bump on the middle finger where the quill rested, then slipped each finger into his mouth, watching as her eyes widened with shock and half closed in ecstasy with each flick of his tongue. As he swelled, ready for her, he wondered whether her breasts ached beneath the coarse wool, whether she were wet with wanting, as she had been the night she confessed.

"Come," he said, surprised he could still speak. "Sit down."

She sat on the cloak, stretching her legs. He unlaced her wet leather shoes and cupped his warm hands around her cold toes. Slowly, he pushed up her skirt, uncovering her bit by bit. She bent one knee and the sight of her moon-pale legs, softly sculpted from days of walking, almost undid him. He rested his large square brown hand on her knee and stroked her inner thigh with his thumb.

She wiggled as he pressed his lips to the warm skin above her knee. Her fingers tangled in the stiff curls at the base of his neck. "Your hair is coarse as a thistle bush," she gasped, letting her fingers wander down the back of his neck and slip under his tunic. Eager as her lips, her fingers kissed his bare back. Heat seared his spine and pounded between his legs.

Answering, his hand drifted up her thigh and lingered in the untouched skin near her nest. She moved closer to his hand. He pushed her gently to her back and took her lips again, reveling in the feel of her body pressed the length of his.

She broke off the kiss, panting. "Turn over. Lie on your stomach."

"Why?" he whispered against her mouth, unwilling to let go.

"You'll see." Smiling, she pushed his shoulder.

Reluctant to turn away from her, he settled on the cloak. "What are you doing?"

She pushed his tunic up, baring his back to the prick of sea air, and scooped a handful of sand. "Shh. Keep your eyes closed."

He felt her rub the sand between his shoulder blades, down his spine, and across his shoulders, then brush it away. With a finger delicate as a feather, she traced rippling strokes left to right across his back. A warm buzz drifted down his arms and legs, comforting and exciting. He eased the weight away from his hips, giving his stiff member room, and peeked.

Through half-closed eyes, he watched her teeth tug at her lip in concentration. With the last stroke, he felt the punctuation of a warm, wet kiss, under his right shoulder blade.

"What was that?" he said, rising to his elbows to look at her.

She stretched beside him on the cloak. "I wrote on your back. 'My beloved is mine and I am his.'"

He scooped her against him, his arm tight around her waist, her soft breasts pushing against his chest. *Mine.* "Beautiful words," he murmured in her ear.

"God wrote them."

Startled, he pulled away to see her face. "What?"

"In the *Song of Solomon.* Didn't they make you read the Bible in the monastery?" she said, grinning.

He had never seen her so willing to tease and he gloried in it. "Reading was never easy for me."

Her smile turned solemn. "I wanted us to feel that way." Tightening her arms around his back, she squeezed, cutting off his air, her words smothered against his chest. "Just once."

"Not once," he murmured. "Always."

Regretting his rough calluses, regretting all that had slipped through his fingers, he let them flow down her back, into the curve of her waist, over her hips, up her arm, and over her breast, where the nipple felt hard through the rough wool. She gasped at his touch.

She pressed her lips to his and he lost himself in her, as lost as he had been in the mist, until he forgot where he was and who he was and what he had promised the Prioress and even what he had promised God.

And as he slipped inside her, coming home, he even silenced the voice inside that whispered *What if you lose her now?*

The keening cry of the gulls wakened Dominica from what seemed a wonderful dream. Neither her time with Garren nor the nightmare of Sister's death could be real. But Garren still lay beside her, tangible, comforting. Her skin still glowed with his touch.

She turned her head to face his smiling eyes. "Your eyes look different."

"Mine?" He raised his brows. "How?"

"They were darker before. Like moss over a tree trunk. Now, they look like the sun through green leaves."

He traced her eyebrow, then ran the tip of his finger down her cheekbone and up her nose. "And *yours* are no longer fierce enough to skewer a barbarian."

She lay back, gazing at the gray blue sky, murky as the

sea. Lapping waves comforted the silence. "I could fall asleep again right now."

He laughed and held her, covering her with his body, whispering into her ear. "Probably because you barely slept last night. You're too tired to notice the sand is gritty."

She stretched an arm above her head, where the waves hadn't reached, picked up a handful of dry sand, and let it flow down the neck of his tunic over his bare back. "I don't care if we're covered in sand."

He whooped, and grabbed her arms and rolled her over on her back again. She giggled and kissed him and he kissed her back and she explored his skin with her hands again, pleased to find that the sand had still not found its way into his most secret places.

Later, she listened for noises from the hut, surprised and grateful it was still quiet since it was after prime.

The tide still moved. Beyond the sheltering wall, the shrine still squatted on its rock nest. Strange to have come so far and not care if she set foot on the rock.

Sister had still cared.

She stood, abruptly, shaking gritty sand from her rumpled skirt, brushing it from between her toes, unraveling her braid and running her fingers through her hair to shake it out.

It was time to face Death again. And life. But now, life meant Garren.

"We must bury her where she can see the shrine," she said.

He rose and wrapped his arms around her shoulders. "She would like that. Neeca, I'm sorry about Sister. I will miss her, too."

Tears flowed, finally, blurring the line between sea and the sky. Sobs gripped her throat, pounded her chest, and twisted her stomach until she could not hold them back and she shook in his arms, turning and burying her head against his chest.

He rocked her without words of false comfort. No talk of an eternity with God. She would not have believed it now.

She cried until her throat was raw and her eyes hot and swollen and she had no more sobs left.

"She understood our frailties and loved us anyway," he said.

"Because she had frailties of her own." And now, she, like her mother, was humbled by the recognition of her own weakness for this man.

She inhaled the scent of his warm skin, mixed with the tang of the sea. There was still a dampness between her legs and on her thighs, and perhaps, even a child in her belly. She closed her eyes so she could remember later the warmth of his body pressed against her and the lapping of the lazy water against the morning sand.

And then she slipped out of his comforting arms.

At the tide's edge, kneeling in the damp sand, she dipped her fingers in the sea, then pressed them against her hot eyes. The salt stung, a chill baptism into a new world.

She brushed off the last bit of sand clinging stubbornly to her sleeve. Now she must do just one last thing. To get Lord William's message to the priest. To see that Richard was punished. "Today we bury Sister. Tomorrow, we bring Lord Richard to justice."

"It is too dangerous. I'll go alone."

"I must go because I was witness to his words." And because he was my brother, but she could not tell him that. "And afterwards…"

"I'll take care of you."

She nodded, unable to speak, and as she watched the wind swirl around him and a faint mist coat his hair, she knew with terrible certainty that just once for all her life would not be enough.

Chapter Twenty-Four

Shivering in the drizzle, Dominica sat on the wooden bench, empty of lead feathers. With the tide out, the sea floor stretched tantalizingly bare all the way to the shrine, but the priest did not return from the island, even to bury Sister.

Brother Joseph shrugged. "Oh, he never leaves the Blessed Larina. I take what he needs. Food, candles, wine." He smiled with childlike pride. "But I will take care of Sister Marian. I have since the first time she was here." He sighed. "Long ago."

She nodded, numb, deprived of even the consolation of Innocent, who refused to lift his head from his paws.

Stripped of shirts and rank, Garren and Jackin dug her grave side by side, the relentless rhythm of shovels and the thud of damp earth alternating with the waves. She took comfort in the curve of his shoulder, remembering how his muscles felt beneath her fingers. When he turned his back, she felt as if the words she had written must be emblazoned for everyone to see. "My beloved is mine and I am his."

They crept to her with consolations. The Miller brothers, speaking in harmony, the Widow, whispering her condolences. Even Ralf came, with red-rimmed eyes, wadding his tunic between gnarled fingers. "Would you write something for me to take to the Blessed Larina? I want her to know what Sister Marian did for me. To tell Larina she tried to come."

She shook her head. "I cannot write now." *I cannot write ever again.*

Too good to dirty his hands with digging, Lord Richard swaggered over to lie. "An inspiration to us all." She searched his squinty eyes, his narrow brow, his skinny fingers, for any resemblance to his father. Her father. "You will find comfort at the shrine."

"Garren and I will walk over when tomorrow's tide permits." *And return to make you stand trial.*

"I will join you." He patted her arm. "I am anxious to pray for my brother's recovery."

"But you can't!" They needed time alone to explain everything to the priest. "I mean, Sister was going to be the third and now..."

"Now I will be with you." He smirked. "Praying."

She looked frantically for Garren. "I believe Brother Joseph must approve any changes."

"Oh, don't worry. I've talked with him." He squeezed her arm as he left, hard enough to be a pinch.

Gillian and the Widow came out from the hut where they had prepared Sister for burial. "She is ready," Gillian said. "Do you want a time alone with her?"

Dominica nodded.

A precious new candle flickered in the damp gloom. Innocent watched her enter, never moving. Sister's tiny body, wrapped in the shroud of her pilgrim's cloak, was already smaller, as if her spirit had taken up physical space.

"I have come to say goodbye," she began to the barren room. "I am a different woman than I was last night. I will not choose the path you did, but I know you will understand.''

Speaking aloud to Sister comforted her. ''And I want to thank you. For everything. Even the life I do not know what to do with.''

She listened. For a sound or a sense of surety. She had been so sure in Garren's arms. She wanted Sister's blessing, even now. But if Sister had gone to God, she did not come back for Neeca.

She rose, sighing, to join the burial ceremony.

Muscles coiled, Garren lay with eyes closed and ears open, listening for the chorus of even breathing before he slipped out of the hut.

Opening one eye, he scanned the room.

He could not see Dominica, sleeping in Brother Joseph's alcove, but the rest slept sprawled across the hut's dirt floor, tired of the journey, tired of death, tired enough to sleep so that tomorrow would come as quickly as possible. Wave by wave, the sound of the sea smoothed over their coughs and snores.

Only Richard lay on his back, hands behind his head, blinking at the ceiling.

Through the long day of grave-digging and filling, Garren watched Richard maneuver himself into the first group that would crawl to the shrine the next day. Garren let him. Time had run out. If William were to have his feather and his justice, Garren must go to the shrine tonight.

Alone.

He peered at Richard again. His slack face quivering in a snore.

Now.

Garren crept outside, clutching his lead shell in his hand,

and slipped it over his head before he pushed one of Brother Joseph's little boats into the water.

The journey took longer than he hoped. Wind shuddering from the west swept away the day's drizzle and fought him for control of the boat. Sore from digging, his shoulders ached as he wrestled the oars against the waves rolling to shore, relentless as the arrows of English archers who crashed against the rocks of the French king's men at Poitiers.

Remembering the morning, guilt swamped him as the waves threatened to swamp the boat.

I want you.

Everything had changed.

They had never had another moment alone. He barely spoke to her during the day, afraid he could not fool her, afraid he could fool none of them. Afraid if he got close enough to touch her he would sweep her into his arms and claim her as his own, regardless of who was watching.

Tomorrow. After he made her safe from Richard.

She would be angry when she found he had gone alone, but surely she would understand when William had his justice. And she would not, even now, understand why he had to desecrate a shrine.

He was no longer sure he understood himself.

I will take care of you. He promised. He would, although he did not know how.

The boat hit the rock-filled beach with a sound like crunching bones. He pulled it into the lopsided moon shadows and sneaked up to the small wooden door, waiting to open it until the next wave drowned the creak of the hinges.

The rough shelter, built with stones from the rock it sat on, was barely larger than her grave. The rock of the island formed the floor. Stone walls of stacked boulders towered higher than he could stretch, as if trying to imitate a cathedral ceiling. East and west, a hole in each wall let in the sound of the waves and the faint light of the waning moon.

In a dark corner, a bird squeaked.

A polished slab piled with stones marked her resting place. Unlike some saints, her countenance was not displayed for the masses. Not even a stray bone. No doubt because there was nothing worth saving after she had smashed on the rocks below.

A small door opposite led to the priest's cell. Garren took a step. Tensed. Listened.

Snores. Louder than the Widow's.

The feathers first. An uncertain light wavered in a lantern above the pile of stones where the saint lay. A small, faceted brass box hung beneath it. He peered through the little piece of glass on the door.

Something fluffy lay inside.

Just a small one, he had promised William.

Salt air cooled a trickle of sweat welling up on his scalp. Just a small feather he had promised a man who was probably dead. Why didn't he just pick up more goose feathers? William, if he still drew breath, would never know the truth.

But as the reliquary swayed in time to the endless waves, he had the strangest feeling that God was watching and expected him to fulfill his promise.

Awakened by an unknown noise, Dominica lifted her head to see the moon, like a half-eaten biscuit, through the rough square hole in the wall. It must be compline by now.

Sister, no, *Mother,* was buried today.

Brother Joseph said the burial words. After, as the dirt covered her shroud, Innocent curled into a ball by the grave and refused to move. So now, Dominica slept alone, with neither Sister nor Innocent for comfort.

Without even Garren.

I will take care of you.

There had been no way to talk today, to be alone again after the magical morning. But his eyes met hers when he realized what Lord Richard was trying. *Don't worry,* they said.

But she would worry until they had delivered the missive to the priest tomorrow. Then they could plan their lives.

She tried to pray, for Sister's soul, for Lord William's soul. Strange to think of praying for her mother, her brother. But she was as empty of words to pray as to write.

Tired of lying awake, she rose, leaning on the rough stones to look at the star-filled sky framing Larina's rock. The waning moon flickered on the moving black waves like stars twinkling in the water. A small black shape seemed to bob on the water but it might have been a trick of the moonlight and the waves.

She blinked.

It was still there. It was a boat.

Squinting, she recognized the familiar curve of broad shoulders. Garren. Relief left her limp. That was why he didn't want her to worry. Garren was taking the message to the priest tonight.

A twinge of disappointment tweaked her. She should be there, too, to avenge her brother. Now wide awake, she watched the bobbing boat until it disappeared in the shadows beneath the shrine. She thought his shadow moved, but shadow and moonlight and moving waves confused her eyes.

Behind her, a noise, like the skittering of rat's feet, startled her. She stiffened. Creeping out of the hut, Richard scurried across the cove and wrestled the second boat into the water.

She ducked, not wanting him to see her. The splash of the oars faded.

She peeked over the ledge.

His boat was headed toward the shrine.

She grabbed her cloak, not stopping to wonder how she would handle a boat or how she could stop Lord Richard. God had saved her from the waters once. Surely He would help her for William's sake.

And for Garren's.

She shoved the boat into the water and waded in. Seawater sucked at her cloak, soaking her skirt. She struggled to hoist herself into the boat. Salt stung the palm she had scraped on the rocks. The boat rocked wildly. Splashing, she tried to hold on. It slipped and drifted away, caught by the changing tide.

She waded into deeper water, dragged into the waves by her soggy cloak.

She fought the memory of the horrible moments in the river. This time, she had no Savior. This time, she must save herself. And Garren. She gritted chattering teeth and pulled the boat back to water no deeper than her waist. Finally, she heaved herself over the side and flopped, facedown in the puddle, her nose pressed against the salt-wet wood.

When she lifted her head, she saw that the ebbing tide was taking her toward the shrine.

She sat up, watching the shore recede, and fumbled for the oars. She pushed one, then the other, trying to keep the boat in line with the hut. The oars slid along the edge of the boat and pierced her palms with splinters. She looked with longing at the boulder hiding the little cove where she and Garren had lain. No time to dream. Too far to her left, she would hit the rocks; too far to her right and she would be carried out to sea.

She looked over her shoulder to see if she was rowing straight.

Lord Richard's thin shadow waited.

She could not turn back now, she thought, heaving both oars. God, or fate, had given her this opportunity. She must be brave enough to take it.

Her shoulders ached and a blister burned her right palm. Purgatory would be no worse than this jagged movement toward disaster with nothing to cling to but hope.

With a thud, her boat hit the beach. She jerked forward as he hauled it up from the water.

His chittering laugh jarred her ear. "How nice of you to come. You saved me the effort of finding another way to kill you."

She opened her mouth to scream a warning, but he stuffed a gag around her mouth before she could shout.

"When I'm finished with him, I'll just push you off the top. They'll find you dead on the rocks. Everyone saw you try to fly. They'll just think you tried again. And this time, there was no one to save you."

She slapped his face, but he grabbed her hands and wrestled her to the bottom of the boat, tying her hands together and then her ankles. She had winded him, at least, she thought, watching his chest heave. Maybe she had bought Garren a few minutes.

Lord Richard drew his dagger and dipped it carefully into a small pouch. "Stay," he muttered, as if to a dog.

The rocks crunched with his footsteps as he slipped into the small building where a swaying light flickered.

She started picking at the rope around her ankles with numb fingers.

Even perched precariously on the rocks piled on Larina's grave, Garren could barely reach the swinging reliquary.

A gull, head cocked, watched him from the hole in the

east wall. Odd, he thought, frowning. Birds usually have the sense to sleep at this hour.

He wiped a palm, slick with sweat, on his tunic and turned back to the feathers.

He grasped the little latch. Jiggled it. Flake-encrusted from years in salt air, it creaked reluctantly as he opened it. Tipping it down, he peered into the hanging box.

Inside were three feathers.

One was gray as a gull's wing. The second, longer, was stripped for use as a writing quill. Finally, he saw a small, fluffy wisp of down.

He reached for the down with shaking fingers.

A breeze snatched it away.

He slapped the little door closed. It clattered on its hinges and spilled the other feathers into the darkness. He chased them across the floor, falling to his knees, pressing damp palms on the gritty floor, trying to feel a feather amidst dirt tracked in by years of pilgrim feet.

Behind him, the large wooden door creaked.

Senses sharp as in battle, Garren slipped his dagger from his sheath and rose, assessing the tiny room as a fighting field.

Richard, dagger drawn, stepped inside.

Even in this, God handed him the worst.

Richard bared his teeth, more a snarl than a smile, and waved his dagger at the open door sagging from the swaying brass box. The lantern cast crazy yellow candlelight around the walls. "Tsk, tsk. Stealing relics. The Savior is not as holy as he pretends."

"What brings you to the shrine in the dead of night, Richard? Private worship?" He raised his voice. "I'll wake the priest."

Richard snickered. "Don't bother to shout. He's passed out from drink as he is every night."

"Then you must have come to kill me like you killed your brother."

"What an accusation!" Richard grinned, fairly dancing on his toes. "I am here to recover a certain letter." He held out his hand. "Now give it to me."

"I don't know what you are talking about."

"Of course you do. It's the one that purports to be from my brother accusing me of poisoning him. The one that leaves everything to you. It's such a tragic story. A man everyone called The Savior was actually scheming to take over the land of the man he claimed to have saved."

"You and I both know who killed William for the land."

"Yes, so tragic, you even seduced Dominica to forge it for you. You didn't know I knew, did you?"

"Knew what?" He stepped carefully to his right, keeping the small pile of rocks between him and Richard. He had to keep control.

"Never knew that the money you were promised for bedding her came from me, did you? The Prioress hasn't two farthings to rub together."

"From you?" Garren clamped a mask of surprise over his hate. Let him think he is clever. Keep him talking. Play along. He held out his hand in a mockery of Richard's gesture. "Then give me my money. I earned it."

"You won't live to enjoy it." Richard's grin collapsed into a pout. "Now give me the letter or I'll take it off your dead body. No one will blame me for killing a murderer. And the little scribe will be smashed on the rocks after trying her wings again."

Neeca. She slept safely in the hut. "What do you mean?"

"She followed me here." He laughed. "I guess she thought she'd be *your* savior this time."

The grit from the floor burned against the palm that

gripped the dagger. He held back the urge to lunge for Richard's throat. The man's tongue defiled her. "Where is she?"

"Ah, so you enjoyed your taste of her?"

He cursed himself for exposing his vulnerability. "Envy me, Richard?"

"I left it to a sinner like you to take a virgin. Once she's fallen…" he shrugged, "well, a man might be tempted."

Let Richard wear himself out with talking, Garren thought. He stepped to his right. Richard mirrored him. The lantern, steady now, cast shadows around the grave. Walking in and out of them, Richard's face turned white, then black as death.

"Don't gird yourself for a long battle, Savior." Moonlight polished Richard's feral teeth. "Niccolo is quite adept with poisons." A glint of candlelight sparked the tip of the dagger. "It will only take a scratch."

Poison. He shivered. Not even an honorable death. He shrugged his shoulders to loosen his muscles for battle. "Then I'll take you with me."

Richard hopped, humming, waving his dagger in little circles. He didn't need to wait for an opening for a good thrust. All he needed was a touch to break the skin.

Garren held back, fingers aching with the effort. He would have only one chance, for Neeca, as well as himself.

Back where they started, with Richard at the door, neither had made a move. Richard snickered. "I hope you fought more bravely when you were paid, mercenary."

Between them, the door opened and Neeca stumbled into the room. Hands tied in front of her, a gag tied around her face, she looked at Garren, eyes wide, trying to talk. And his heart stopped because he knew Richard would reach her before he could.

"Neeca! Behind you!"

Richard grabbed her around the throat, his elbow like the

ferocious jaws of a weasel. "Didn't I tell you to stay in the boat?" His dagger hovered just below her ear.

"Don't move, Neeca. It's poisoned."

Richard laughed, his victim secure in his grip. "This will be perfect. They will find you together, struck dead by God for desecrating Larina's shrine." He put his lips against Dominica's ear, whispering loudly enough for Garren to hear. "Pity. I was hoping for a taste of you first." Richard pulled off the gag and put his lips in its place.

Garren lunged, but Richard pulled back, shaking his head in warning and pressed the dagger against her neck.

She stuck out her tongue as if trying to rid her mouth of his taste. "Where is the priest? Why haven't you shown him the letter?"

"I was fulfilling a vow."

She leaned away from Richard's dagger, her eyes never leaving Garren. "You don't believe in vows. And you don't keep the ones you make."

The creaking reliquary swayed above his head, the little door flapping, empty as his excuses.

Richard laughed. "She's right, mercenary. Your vows are only as good as the gold you are paid for them." He tightened his grip around her neck, bending to whisper a secret in her ear. "I caught him stealing Larina's feathers."

Helpless, Garren watched comprehension chase disbelief from her face. She looked at the empty silver vial around his neck.

"So that's what the feathers were for," she murmured. "Who paid you to switch them with the real ones?"

"No one."

"Why should I believe that?"

"But that wasn't the most important thing he was paid to do," Richard sneered. "You still think Garren is some saint? I'll tell you how holy he is."

The world slowed and he could see every precious eye-lash around Neeca's big blue eyes, and he knew, helpless, what Richard would say next.

"You knew William paid me to be his palmer," Garren said, desperate. The churning fear in his stomach was stronger then he had ever felt for himself in battle. Even if he saved her life now, could he save her trust? He clenched the dagger more tightly.

Dominica watched Garren tighten his grip on his dagger. Richard's body pressed against her back. The swaying candle made it hard to see. She felt disoriented, as if the world were moving around her.

Where is the priest? Think. Richard is just trying to confuse me.

Maybe she could confuse him and save Garren. She turned toward Sir Richard, hating the feel of her body pressing his. She swallowed, dagger cold against her throat. "Garren is innocent. He knows nothing of Lord William's message."

"Innocent!" Richard laughed, thrusting his twitching nose so close to her face she could smell his sour breath. "Innocent is a dog."

A shudder rippled through her. She did not want to hear, but her tied hands could not cover her ears. His lips brushed her temple. She bent away, but she could not block his words. "Your precious Garren who touched and kissed and caressed you did it for money."

Shame seared her cheeks. "You lie." She did not think to deny Garren's touch. "Who would pay him to do that?"

The stink of Richard's laughter filled her pores. "I would."

"Why would he do anything for you?"

"Oh, he didn't know it was me. He thought it was the Prioress."

If there is a hint of trouble, she had threatened. So even the Prioress pushed her will on God.

She watched Garren, silent, as Lord Richard continued, glibly. "Garren wanted the money. He never wanted you."

And she felt cold and hot and sick at her stomach as if she had taken some of the poison Richard had fed William and she wished she really had. Through her tears, Garren blurred into something unrecognizable.

"Neeca, please, let me explain…"

He never wanted you.

She asked him, begged him to take her. Because she believed in him, even when she knew he was not the man she thought. Even believed that to seize today was a way to live.

"Is it true? Did you do it for money?" She swallowed and her throat pressed dangerously close to the blade.

"Neeca, I'll take care of you. I didn't know you then."

"You knew me yesterday." *You knew me when you took me.*

She closed her eyes against him and when she opened them, she was a different woman and the world was infinitely old and everything she had clung to was gone and she knew she was going to die in this dirty little stone hovel that covered a dead woman's bones. "It seems I was as naive about you as I was about God."

Chapter Twenty-Five

Garren's tongue was dust and his chest was tight and he wished she had never met him. He had destroyed everything that sustained her and given her nothing. She had no reason to believe in him at all. God must be laughing now, for he had taken the perfect revenge. "Neeca, you must believe me." Why? He didn't believe himself. "When we—when I—I wasn't thinking of—"

"Enough." Richard jerked her to his chest. Hands tied before her, she looked ready to die as a martyr tied to the stake. "The pilgrimage is over," he snarled. "Give me the message."

Garren slipped his hand into his tunic and drew out the precious, folded parchment, stained with the sweat of the journey. He held it up, turning it in the moonlight, drawing Richard's eyes. "Here." He watched the knife sag away from her throat. "Let her go and it's yours."

Richard licked his lips. His blade left Neeca's throat and pointed to the floor. "Put it down."

Garren tightened his shoulders against the relief. The distraction was working. "But if I put it on the floor, it could blow away." Garren took a step. Richard was still more than arm's length away. "Come get it."

"No! You promised William." Neeca twisted against Richard's grip. He pulled back, and jabbed the point of the dagger under her jaw again. Garren's heart wobbled like the candle flame.

He fanned the air with the folded message, tempting Richard to reach for it again instead of holding Dominica. "What are you waiting for? Her hands are tied."

"She walks with her feet, not her hands."

"I'll avenge him if you won't," she said.

Be still, Neeca. Let me save you. "Here, Richard. Come get it."

Still clinging to her with his left hand, Richard shifted his balance, stretching his dagger hand toward Garren. Poised between the two, unbalanced, he could thrust at neither.

Now.

Garren lunged for Richard's exposed ribs.

And missed.

Dominica whirled away and slammed her still-tied hands into Richard's belly like a battering ram. Richard slashed back, gashing her right arm. Stumbling away from him, she hit the wall and slumped onto the floor.

"Don't move, Neeca." Neither of them would survive if he missed again. "The poison will spread."

Silhouetted in the moonlight, Richard danced from one foot to another, slashing empty air with the bloody dagger. "Watch her die. Then I'll kill you."

Garren forced himself to look at Richard instead of Neeca. He must get close enough for a fatal thrust.

Laughing, Richard swung his dagger arm in a huge circle, sweeping the blade within a breath of the gray gull perched on the east window. Screeching, the bird flapped its wings and swooped.

Startled, Richard swatted her away from his head with both hands.

Garren grabbed his chance. He thrust at Richard's left side.

Flailing, Richard lost his grip and his dagger clattered into the shadows. "Damn you," he screamed, snatching it up before Garren could strike again. A small, terrible smile blessed his face. "That was your only chance, mercenary."

All his self-preservation could not keep him from glancing at Neeca. Instead of sitting still, she struggled to stand, using her legs instead of her bound hands.

Richard's shout drew him.

The gull had attacked again.

Claws snagged in his hair, her wings flapped around his ears. Waving one hand wildly to bat her away, he jabbed blindly at her sleek, feathered body. She flew out of reach, then swooped, dived, pecked at his ears and cheeks and clawed at his hand until he was bloody with the tiny jabs, frantic, as if trapped with only his fear and the bird.

Then, as if he were a tree branch on a May morning, she perched on his left forearm, quiet. In a moment, he realized where she was. Then he raised his dagger, letting it hover above her. The gull, seemingly fearless, stayed motionless.

Until he hurtled the blade toward her.

The bird fluttered away, and he cut his arm to the bone.

He screamed at the poison dagger, embedded in his arm. Falling to his knees, he clamped his teeth against pain that was only beginning. Mad eyes looked at Garren. "I don't want to die like her." His lips trembled. "Please, finish me."

Garren's dagger lay slack in his hand. *I should let him die. Surely that would be God's vengeance.*

Behind him, Neeca moaned.

Yes, a swift death would be too good for the man who killed William and destroyed Neeca's life. What work could a Savior do for this man?

But as tears of pain and pleading washed his face, Garren found he had some mercy left. Compassion crowded out vengeance. "You will only arrive in Hell more quickly."

"Do it. Now."

And as Garren dealt the blow, he realized Hell would be all too familiar for Richard.

He did not stop to wonder at his luck. Dropping his dagger, he knelt beside her. Blood muddied the frayed cut in her sleeve below her right elbow. "Keep your hands down, Neeca." He steadied his voice, but he could not calm his shivering heart that lifted the lead shell with every beat. "Let me look."

He peeled back the blood soaked gray wool and stared at the wound. Helpless. If Richard preferred swift death, even a shallow cut would mean a slow, painful end. Death had been the kindest thing for Richard.

She hugged her arms to her chest. "Is it true? About why you…why we…you touched me?"

Her eyes accused him of all his failings, but this was the biggest. This time, he wanted to be her Savior. He wanted her to live, even if he lost her to God later. But this time, he didn't know how.

His thoughts shrieked louder than Richard's scream. *God, I am in your hands. Thy will be done.*

Instead of an answer, he heard the slosh of the waves and the coo of a bird.

His racing heart slowed, beating with the waves. Calm, tangible as a cloak, settled over him. It silenced Richard's death rattle, blocked Dominica's hurt look, and quieted his fears.

He looked at her wound and knew what he could do.

Ripping the sleeve away from her cut, he wiped off the blood. It welled up again, black in the shadows.

He put his lips on the cut and sucked, filling his mouth with the sharp, sweet taste. Then he spit it out.

Again.

Again. Sucking and spitting, pulling blood and poison away and never wondering what would happen if he swallowed the poison himself.

"You are right, you know." He could barely hear her. "There is no reason…to believe…in anything you cannot see." Her fingers slipped. She blinked, slowly. Her eyes, still open, took on a vacant look.

For a moment, he saw William's blue eyes instead of Neeca's. Smelled William's blood again, mixed with French dirt. And knew she must want to live, as William had, if he were to save her from Purgatory or Heaven or wherever God wanted to take her.

He wanted to shake her, but squeezed her shoulder instead, afraid that anything more would only spread the poison. "Neeca, look at me."

She squinted, with puzzled eyes, as if she didn't know where she was.

"You once called me The Savior. Well, I'm going to save you." His voice cracked. He cleared his throat. "But you have to help."

She shook her head. "Why should I believe in you?"

He looked at her, slumped against the wall, and knew he believed in her more than anything else he ever had in his life. "You had faith in me when you didn't even know my name. Believe in me now that you know everything I am."

She closed her eyes. Silent.

He forced himself to wait. He wanted to keep sucking out the poison, but he knew she must be with him. She and God both.

Eternity passed.

"Neeca?"

She did not answer. He held his finger beneath her nose, reassured by the feel of her hot breath. But he was losing her. The spirit he had felt on the moor was slipping away. He had to reach her, grab her, bring her back.

He raised her hand to his lips and tickled the sensitive spot between her fingers with his tongue.

The edge of her mouth lifted.

He slipped her middle finger between his lips. Inside of him. One. As joined as this morning when they rolled in the sand.

Her smile broadened.

Hope rushed to his tingling fingertips as he kissed hers. "Now I'm going to suck out the poison and you are going to lie still and pray to the Blessed Larina."

A faint smile blushed her lips. "Sometimes, God needs a little help."

"Give it to Him," he barked, as he put his lips back in place to suck death away.

Richard's moans faded. He heard the sea again, steady as his heart. Behind him, the empty reliquary creaked in time with the waves.

When her breathing was steady and strong, he lifted his head to take his first full breath. Poised on the window's edge against the pale gold morning sky, the gull tilted her head. Outside, her fellows screamed, greeting the new day. She answered, then raised her wings and flew away.

Leaving three feathers in the dust.

He stared at them for a moment, unable to move. One was a long, gray, black-tipped wing feather. The second, a wisp of white down. The shaft of the third was bare, with just a fringe of feather at the top.

He reached for them, just as the wind swirled, blowing them across the little pile of stones that was Larina's grave.

He chased them.

On the other side of the grave, six feathers clustered in the dust.

A shuffling scrape wafted from the priest's cell.

I hear you, God. She belongs to you. I'll make sure this time.

"Who's there?" he heard, from the priest's cell.

Fingers shaking, he twisted the top off the empty reliquary around his neck and scooped up the three closest feathers.

"What," said the blinking, red-eyed priest, emerging from his cell just as Garren tightened the case, "is going on here?"

The sun was high before Garren made the priest understand why the blood of a dead man and a wounded woman soaked the stones of his shrine. Cradling Dominica, impatient to take her back to the relative comfort of the shore, he explained and re-explained the Battle of Poitiers, William's request, Richard, the midnight visit and the poison dagger.

Blinking watery eyes against the light, the old man unfolded the creased parchment. Three times he read the message. Finally, he said God had selected his own punishment for a Cain who would kill his brother. Then, with trembling, reverent fingers, he picked up three feathers from the floor, put them back in the reliquary, and turned the latch.

Garren did not mention the gull.

Chapter Twenty-Six

Dominica did not return to the shrine.

Brother Joseph clucked over her wound and the Physician tied a bandage tightly around her arm and she resisted Gillian's insistence that she heal lying down. Garren explained something about Richard going to the shrine for private penance where God, hearing his prayer, took him immediately.

The Widow remarked loudly that she did not think God took him to Heaven.

It was clear, however, that the Blessed Larina had worked another mysterious miracle. Renewed faith, or fear, drove even Simon to crawl humbly across the damp sea bottom on hands and knees.

She didn't ask how Garren explained her injury.

For three days, as the rest completed the pilgrimage, she rose with the sun to sit on the little beach she and Garren had shared. Innocent trailed her steps, refusing to leave her side, afraid she might vanish, too. Matching her breath to the waves, she scratched his good ear with newly-grown fingernails long enough to make Sister proud.

She spoke to Sister sometimes, explaining why she would not return to the Priory.

"It is as if I am a bird." Innocent listened with one ear.

"A bird who has outgrown the nest and discovered the entire sky."

He wagged his tail, encouraging, but the wide blue sky stretched empty of landmarks.

Garren's touch had pulled her back to this world, soul and body. He cradled that wounded body all the way back in the boat, murmuring words meant to be soothing. That he would take her home. That he would make it right with the Prioress. That she would have the life she wanted.

And she wanted to say *I want a life with you,* but she was a foundling and he was a knight and he had done it all for money even if he regretted it now. He clearly wanted her in the convent. Out of his way.

They were not alone again.

And on a dreary morning of the Feast of Saints Peter and Paul, Dominica, swinging her throbbing arm beside her, joined the weary silent group that turned for home.

They returned to Tavistock on market day. Dominica could not bear to face the booths with the others. After supper, the heat of high summer drove her to the courtyard where vespers hymns echoed off the pillars. She had fled him down this cloister. Fled all he made her feel. Fled to the scriptorium where she renewed her vow.

The vow she broke, just as he broke his.

Suddenly, he stood framed under the arch, broad shoulders filling the space between the columns. Her body saw him now, as well as her eyes. The rough texture of his curls. The feel of his lips gently spreading hers. The skin of his back warm against her palm.

She closed her eyes to stop the memories, trying to thank God for what she had without asking for anything more.

He started abruptly, as if they had just spoken. "I asked you to have faith in me."

She nodded.

"Despite what Richard said."

She smiled, ruefully. "I did, didn't I?"

"You deserve to know what I did. And why."

She patted the bench beside her, skin longing for him. "Would you sit?"

He shook his head, shrinking from her as if she were flame. "You know I promised to carry William's message. And that he wanted to pay me."

"I knew that long ago."

"I owed him so much. You know why."

She closed her eyes and saw the sun-dappled deer park again.

"I wanted to make the journey a gift."

She folded her hands, silent, as he strode the stones beside the thyme plants.

"William's faith was as strong as yours. I told him I would bring him a feather. From the saint."

"So Lord Richard was right." She wondered why she felt no disappointment. What was the difference, after all, between a gull feather or a saint's wing? "You were there to steal the relics."

"For William. I thought the hope might…," he drew a breath. "Might keep him alive."

"But you have no faith."

He smiled. "I had faith in his."

The last note of the vesper chant died away. "And the rest of your confession? Lord Richard did not lie, did he? About…," She swallowed, the words ashes in her mouth. "Why you touched me?"

"I wanted to make William a gift." His words came like stones he had to lift. "The Prioress offered me money. She said you did not have a vocation."

He sat next to her now, now when she no longer could bear it, and took her hand in both of his, not letting her pull her fingers away, nor letting her turn her eyes away from the pleading in his own. "I wanted to take someone back from God." He whispered. "God had taken everyone from me."

"And the money might have been enough—"

"But then, when I knew you—" He stopped.

"I came to you."

"You were distraught. I never should have." He dropped her hands and buried his face in his. "I'm sorry, Dominica. I will not tell the Prioress the truth. You will have what you want."

"What I want is…" *You. No. What I want is for you to want me, too.*

"Sole fide."

"What?" A foreign language, echoing.

"Faith alone, Dominica. Your faith brought you your dream."

Never had faith brought so hollow a victory. "I flung that dream to the waves with my parchment and quill."

He covered her clasped hand with his, a gesture as brotherly as his words. "You will write again."

Longing, fierce as her regret, tugged at her chest. "I have neither parchment nor quill."

From under his tunic, he pulled out the dented silver reliquary and opened it. Three feathers filled the slender case. He held one out to her. "This is for you. From the Blessed Larina."

Speechless, she took it. The smooth, yellowed shaft, stripped of feathers long ago, had been dry of ink for a long, long time. Smaller than a goose quill, it fit snugly in her hand. Openmouthed with wonder, she stared first at the quill and then at him. "What do you mean from the Blessed Larina?"

Instead of answering, he rummaged in his sack, then

pulled out a small piece of used parchment, a knife and an inkhorn, laying them on the bench. "And these are from me."

She picked up each one and weighted it in her cupped hand like precious metal.

"Write, Dominica." He rose and slung the sack over his shoulder. "God did not intend for you to abandon your dreams."

Fingers tight on the quill, happiness warred with the sorrow of losing him. She smiled, sadly. "So God speaks to you now?"

He answered without turning. "About you, He does."

He was gone before she could say more.

She clutched the inkhorn and the quill. Then put them down and picked up the parchment and the knife, wanting to hold them all tightly at the same time, afraid they would vanish as Garren had. She sat on the ground, spreading the sheet on the courtyard bench, anxious to write a word before sunset. The used parchment was already striped with neat lines, old ink carefully scraped away by a meticulous former owner.

I don't know how to imagine a life outside the Priory, God. I just know that's where I must go. I can no longer tell you what to do. You tell me.

She dipped the quill in the ink and wrote. For Sister. For Garren. For God.

Thank yeu.

The Prioress spent the first Monday of July on her knees in penance, as she had spent every Monday since Lord Richard's departure. Outside her chamber, bees droned lazily over a garden gone to seed without Dominica.

She eased her weight off her numb left knee. Three more

Hail Marys and God might forgive her. She was not sure she would ever forgive herself.

"Mother Julian, the pilgrims have returned."

Odd, she thought, pushing herself up from the wooden prayer bench. No elation stirred Sister Agnes's voice. She thought she was the only one who dreaded this day. "What a joyful day, Sister Agnes. Bring Sister Marian to me." She would talk to Dominica later.

"I cannot."

"What do you mean you cannot?"

Sister Agnes sniveled. Tears spilled onto her cheeks. "Sister Marian is dead."

Mother Julian crossed herself with shaking fingers. "How did this happen?"

"I am not sure, Mother Julian. Dominica was with her."

She sighed. Time to face her sins. "Bring the girl to me."

Uninvited, the mercenary came with her. Came to collect his fee, no doubt, for he had earned it. She knew that the minute she saw them together, standing so close that both fit in the doorway, but she would have known anyway. Lushness smoothed the restless energy that used to enliven the girl's every move.

No longer a virgin. Lord Richard will be pleased, the Prioress thought, shuddering, but the sin is mine. The girl shall not bear the punishment. "Welcome home, Dominica." She hugged her like the child she used to be. "I'm so sorry about Sister Marian."

"Prioress," the mercenary began, "I must tell you—"

"Not now," she said, shaking her head over the girl's shoulder. "My lamb is back."

"But God gave me a sign—"

"I'm sure it was a sign that Dominica was to join the order."

His mouth hung open for a moment. Then he smiled. "Exactly, Mother Julian."

"He sent me a similar sign." She would deal with Lord Richard somehow. The mercenary seemed relieved. Good. Perhaps he would not ask for the money.

She held Dominica at arm's length. Had the girl grown taller? Sister Marian's good habit wouldn't reach halfway to her ankles, even if they let it down, and they scarcely had time or money for a new one. "Sister Marian will watch from Heaven when you take your vows next week."

The girl stepped away. "I shall not join the order."

"You fulfilled your vow, my dear." She crossed her arms and tucked her hands in her sleeves. "I have no objection." She recognized newfound humility, like her own, softening those defiant blue eyes. She thought she recognized something else, too. Or maybe someone else, but she couldn't think who.

"Neeca," the mercenary started. "This is what you always wanted—"

"God gave me a sign, Mother Julian. It was not the one I expected."

God works in mysterious ways, the Prioress thought, feeling just a little guilty at her relief. She sank into her chair and waved a hand. "Sit, my child. Tell me."

Dominica glanced at the mercenary. "Later. Perhaps."

Tight-lipped, he gazed at the girl as if she were the Holy Grail.

So. That's the way it is. Does she even know?

"What will you do, my child? How can you live?" Surely she would not expect to come back to work as a servant. It would be a pity for Lord Richard to have her after all, although it was certainly not her problem now. Maybe the mercenary would want her. Not as a wife, of course.

Dominica clasped her hands. "First, I shall pray for Lord William's soul. And for forgiveness for the responsibility I bear for his death."

"His death? But Lord William is alive."

The girl's mask of maturity slipped.

A grin split the mercenary's face. "Another miracle."

He gripped her hand and kissed her knuckles. She squeezed his fingers, smiling, then pulled away.

Well. They would have to work that out between them. She'd be lucky to catch him, although he didn't have a farthing that wasn't on his back. "He began improving shortly after you left," she said. Or after Lord Richard left.

"We must see him." The girl turned to leave without asking permission, grasping the mercenary's hand to pull him with her.

She called a warning to their backs. "The Earl is not the man he was."

Dominica ran ahead, but the mercenary turned. "Neither, Mother Julian, am I."

And she thought a great many miracles had happened on this pilgrimage. "Is Lord Richard already at the castle?" She would have to answer to him now. "I'm sure he will be pleased at his brother's recovery."

"Lord Richard is dead." Grim satisfaction sat on his lips. "God's will be done."

She crossed herself. Yet another result of her sin. Dear Father, forgive me for my joy at his death. She looked at the mercenary. How could she pay him with the coin of a dead man?

A smile twitched at the edge of his mouth. "His debts died with him."

Oh Lord, she thought, as she made the sign of the cross, forgive my lack of faith in the working out of your great plan.

* * *

No black mourning banners fluttered above the Reading-tons' ramparts. Held tightly by Garren's arms on a galloping Roucoud, Dominica had no breath left to ask whether he believed her now. She would leave the Priory behind. In Exeter, God had shown her another way.

But Garren had taken her hand. Right in front of Mother Julian.

"Garren! Welcome home!" A tall, gaunt, fair-haired man strode onto the bridge, impatient, arms flung wide.

Her brother.

Garren handed her down from Roucoud's back and slipped off. William enfolded him in a fast hug. They beat each other's backs, stood back gawking as if both were raised from the dead, and hugged again.

Dominica blinked, amazed. William lived. Perhaps God had a plan after all.

Garren stood back to look at him, still holding William's arm. "How is it that you live?"

William smiled, still weak, a faded copy of his father now, hair less blond, eyes not quite so blue. "As soon as Richard left, Niccolo stopped the poison." Behind him, the large-lipped Italian stood patiently as Innocent sniffed his soft leather boots. It was the first time she had seen the man in sunlight. He showed his teeth to her in a strangely sweet smile.

Garren glared. "He tried to kill you! Why does he stand at your side?"

"He gave me enough poison to fool Richard. Not enough to kill me."

"Only by God's grace," he answered, angrily.

William clasped Garren's shoulder. "He had reasons. He nursed me to health. He asked for forgiveness."

Garren flushed. "Which of us does not need forgiveness?"

She waited for him to look at her, to beg her forgiveness again. Yes, she would tell him. Yes and more.

William turned to the empty road. "Where is my brother?"

Garren shook his head. "Dead."

A flicker of what might have been regret crossed William's face. "The Church took vengeance swiftly."

"Not as swiftly as God."

William frowned. "I see God gave us both long stories to tell, my friend."

"God gave you something more." Garren opened the dented reliquary and pinched the smallest feather between his thumb and forefinger. "A bird left this at the shrine." He placed the fluff in William's callused palm and curled the still spotted fingers over it.

William paled. "Is it…?"

Garren nodded, twisting the top carefully over the one remaining feather in the reliquary and dropping it back under his tunic. It clinked cheerfully next to his lead shell. "Let it remind you miracles still happen."

Gripping the feather, William looked at Dominica for the first time. "Well, Dominica, forgive me for not greeting you properly. Where is Sister Marian? Still at the Priory?"

Sudden tears nearly overflowed. Perhaps they would hide her secrets. "Sister Marian died in sight of the shrine."

William touched his fist to forehead, chest and shoulders. Pain creased his face. "She will be remembered by the Readingtons. I know you will miss her presence at the Priory more than anyone." He looked at her expectantly.

"I do miss her, my lord," she began, slowly. Garren's eyes never left her face, as if her words were meant for him instead of William. "But I will not return to the Priory."

Garren's voice stumbled in his throat. "What will you do?"

"You saved my gift as well as my life." And my soul, she thought. "I met a scribe in Exeter who needs help." A kindly man, eyes weak with age so that the letters blurred on the page. She would write, though few of the words would be God's.

"That's absurd," Garren snapped. "I won't let you live alone in the city."

"I won't be alone. I will live with his family. You said God wanted me to write."

"I meant you should copy scripture at Readington Priory."

"'I meant?' So it wasn't what God wanted. *You* wanted me out of your life."

"That's not true!"

"I told you, just once. And you wanted to make sure."

"I ruined your life, your faith, everything!"

"You did not ruin my life. You gave it to me. Just as you gave William his."

"I want to make it right."

"I don't want your guilt. I want your love!"

Her words echoed in the silence. Mortified, she bit her lip. William and Niccolo turned away, pretending to be deaf.

Garren did not take his eyes from hers. "I am not the same man who left this castle. I know now we need faith to give us courage to act. Faith is as strong as God Himself."

Her blood warmed at his words, but they did not change her future.

The man who had no faith took her hand and did not let go. "You must understand. About what Richard said. It is true they offered me money. But once I knew you, I wanted you…'' he floundered. ''For yourself. When God saved you again, I vowed to go to Compostela.''

''You believe so much?''

He nodded. ''Come with me as my wife, Neeca. Write a new guide for pilgrims.''

Her cheeks ached with smiling. ''We could be God's instrument, spreading word of His works in the world.''

He winced and squeezed her hand. ''I have nothing to promise you once our pilgrimage is over.''

William cleared his throat. ''Yes, you do.''

They turned together, surprised not to be alone. Garren's arm lay warm around her shoulder.

''Garren, when I thought I was going to die, I wanted you to have my land. Since I live because of you, I want you to have tenure of the castle and lands of White Wood.''

His hand tightened on her shoulder, but he shook his head. ''I already am too much in your debt. Even for this journey.''

''You gave me my life. Nothing you owe compares to that.''

The blessed joy on his face nearly made her cry. Finally, he had the home he had always wanted.

But it meant she would not. A castle needed a lady, not a foundling. She stepped away, missing him already. ''Congratulations, Sir Garren of White Wood. I'm sure Lord William will help you find a suitable lady.''

''When I offered the land, I assumed you would be the lady, Dominica.'' And her brother's smile made her wonder whether someone else knew Sister's secret.

''Say yes, Neeca, and our pilgrimage together will never be over.'' He took her hand. ''Do you have faith enough in me?''

She put her hand in his, said yes with her eyes and her heart. *''Credo quia absurdum est.''*

He laughed. "Tell me. What does it mean?"

"'I believe it because it is impossible.' I have faith in you. Faith enough to fly."

* * * * *

From Regency romps
to mesmerizing Medievals,
savor these stirring tales from
Harlequin Historicals®

On sale January 2004

THE KNAVE AND THE MAIDEN by Blythe Gifford

A cynical knight's life is forever changed when he falls
in love with a naive young woman while journeying
to a holy shrine.

MARRYING THE MAJOR by Joanna Maitland

Can a war hero wounded in body and spirit find
happiness with his childhood sweetheart, now that she
has become the toast of London society?

On sale February 2004

THE CHAPERON BRIDE by Nicola Cornick

When England's most notorious rake is attracted to
a proper ladies' chaperon, could it be true love?

THE WEDDING KNIGHT by Joanne Rock

A dashing knight abducts a young woman to marry his
brother, but soon falls in love with her instead!

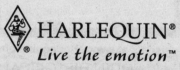

PICK UP THESE HARLEQUIN HISTORICALS AND IMMERSE YOURSELF IN THRILLING AND EMOTIONAL LOVE STORIES SET IN THE AMERICAN FRONTIER

On sale January 2004

CHEYENNE WIFE by Judith Stacy
(Colorado, 1844)

Will opposites attract when a handsome
half-Cheyenne horse trader comes to the rescue
of a proper young lady from back east?

WHIRLWIND BRIDE by Debra Cowan
(Texas, 1883)

A widowed rancher unexpectedly falls in love with
a beautiful and pregnant young woman.

On sale February 2004

COLORADO COURTSHIP by Carolyn Davidson
(Colorado, 1862)

A young widow finds a father for her unborn child—
and a man for her heart—in a loving wagon train scout.

THE LIGHTKEEPER'S WOMAN by Mary Burton
(North Carolina, 1879)

When an heiress reunites with her former fiancée,
will they rekindle their romance or say goodbye
once and for all?

Visit us at www.eHarlequin.com

HARLEQUIN HISTORICALS®

HHWEST29

COMING NEXT MONTH FROM

HARLEQUIN HISTORICALS®

- ### COLORADO COURTSHIP
  by **Carolyn Davidson,** the second of three historicals in the *Colorado Confidential* series
  Jessica Beaumont's husband had cheated Finley Carson's brother out of a land claim and killed him. Now a pregnant widow, Jessica needed to marry…and her only choice was Finn!
  HH #691 ISBN 29291-0 $5.25 U.S./$6.25 CAN.

- ### THE CHAPERON BRIDE
  by **Nicola Cornick,** author of THE EARL'S PRIZE
  Lady Annis Wycherley might have been feisty, but she was a chaperon and her reputation was first-class. Rakes and romance were strictly off-limits…especially the likes of Lord Adam Ashwick, who seemed all too intent on seducing her….
  HH #692 ISBN# 29292-9 $5.25 U.S./$6.25 CAN.

- ### THE LIGHTKEEPER'S WOMAN
  by **Mary Burton,** author of RAFFERTY'S BRIDE
  After her father's death, heiress Alanna Patterson sought out Caleb Pitt, her former fiancé, to determine if their love was still alive. What she found instead was a broken man who had never forgiven her. Would they find their way back to each other or say goodbye once and for all?
  HH #693 ISBN# 29293-7 $5.25 U.S./$6.25 CAN.

- ### THE WEDDING KNIGHT
  by **Joanne Rock,** Harlequin Historical debut
  When knight Lucian Barret abducted Melissande Deverell from a convent, he never expected the sizzling attraction he felt for the woman he intended to be his younger brother's bride. But would a secret from Barret's past be an insurmountable obstacle to their love…?
  HH #694 ISBN# 29294-5 $5.25 U.S./$6.25 CAN.

KEEP AN EYE OUT FOR ALL FOUR OF THESE TERRIFIC NEW TITLES